the UPSIDE of UNREQUITED

by
Becky Albertalli

BALZER + BRAY
An Imprint of HarperCollins*Publishers*

Balzer + Bray is an imprint of HarperCollins Publishers.

The Upside of Unrequited
 For information address HarperCollins Children's Books, a division of HarperCollins Publishers, 195 Broadway, New York, NY 10007.
www.epicreads.com

Library of Congress Control Number: 2016938957
ISBN 978-0-06-234871-5

Typography by Torborg Davern

19 20 21 PC/LSCH 10 9 8 7

❖

First paperback edition, 2018

Praise for *The Upside of Unrequited*

"*The Upside of Unrequited* is heart-achingly adorable. Albertalli has a talent for writing a love story so beautiful, you can't help but wish it would never end."
—Hypable

"While first kisses, first loves, and even first sexual experiences have all been dealt with in some form or another, Albertalli tackles these big milestones head-on and with aplomb. This, coupled with her exploration of Molly's worries about her own weight, results in a character that is not only immensely relatable but also feels real—whether you've had 26 crushes or not."
—*Entertainment Weekly*

"If you're in the mood for a snappy romance to vicariously bathe you in the pain and elation of first love, Becky Albertalli's *The Upside of Unrequited* provides. . . . An ideal mix of fresh, snarky, and poignant."
—NPR.org

"In her second, relationship-rich novel, Albertalli's take on the agonies and ecstasies of adolescent love are spot-on."
—ALA *Booklist*

"A perceptive dramedy that tackles substantial themes with warmth and subtlety."
—*The Horn Book*

Seventeen Magazine Best Book

Also by Becky Albertalli

Simon vs. the Homo Sapiens Agenda

Leah on the Offbeat

For the women who know me way too well:
Caroline Goldstein, Eileen Thomas, Adele Thomas,
Gini Albertalli, and Donna Bray.
And in loving, wistful memory of Molly Goldstein.
This one's for you.

the UP SIDE of UN REQUITED

1

I'M ON THE TOILET AT the 9:30 Club, and I'm wondering how mermaids pee.

This isn't random. There's a mermaid Barbie attached to the door of the bathroom here. Which is a pretty odd choice for a bathroom mascot. If that's even a thing. Bathroom mascots.

But the door opens, letting in a burst of music from the club. This is not a bathroom you can enter discreetly. A stall door clicks shut just as I'm opening mine. I step out.

There are mirrors above all the sinks. I suck in my cheeks so it looks like I have cheekbones. And it's quite a transformation. Sometimes I have the idea that I could maintain this. I could spend the rest of my life gently biting the insides of my cheeks. Except for the fact that it makes my lips look weird. Also, biting your cheeks definitely gets in the way of talking, and that's a little hardcore, even for me. Even for cheekbones.

"Shit." There's a voice from the stall, low and sort of husky. "Hey, can you hand me some toilet paper?"

She's talking to me. It takes me a moment to realize that. "Oh! Sure."

I grab a wad of it to pass under the girl's door, and her hand brushes mine as she takes it. "Okay, you just saved my life."

I saved a life. Right here in the bathroom of the 9:30 Club.

She flushes, and steps out of the stall, and the first thing I notice is her shirt: red cotton, with an awesomely artistic rendering of the letters *G* and *J*. I actually don't think most people would recognize them as letters.

But I do. "That's a Georgie James shirt."

The girl raises her eyebrows, smiling. "You know Georgie James?"

"Yeah." I smile back.

Georgie James. They were a local DC band, but they broke up years ago. You never really expect to meet anyone our age who's heard of them, but my sister used to be obsessed.

The girl shakes her head. "That is awesome."

"It is the awesomest," I say, and the girl laughs—one of those quiet laughs that bubbles up from your throat. Then I really look at her. And oh.

She's beautiful.

This girl.

She's short and slender and East Asian, and her hair is such a dark shade of purple, it's almost not purple. Thick-framed glasses. And there's something about the shape of her lips. She has very well-defined lips.

Cassie would definitely be into her. The glasses, especially. And the Georgie James shirt.

"Anyway, thanks for saving my butt. Literally." She shakes her head. "Okay, not my butt."

I giggle. "It's okay."

"Thanks for saving my labia."

I shrug and smile back at her. There's just something about this kind of moment—this tiny thread connecting me to a total stranger. It's the kind of thing that makes the universe feel smaller. I really love that.

I drift back into the club, letting the music settle around me. It's a local band I've never heard of, but the floor is packed. People seem to like how loud the drums are. I'm surrounded by dancing, moving bodies and dimly lit faces, heads tilted up at the stage. Suddenly, everything starts to feel huge and impossible again. I think it's because there are so many couples, laughing and leaning and earnestly making out.

There's this feeling I get when I watch people kiss. I become a different form of matter. Like they're water, and I'm an ice cube. Like I'm the most alone person in the entire world.

"Molly!" shouts Cassie, waving her hands. She and Olivia are near the speakers, and Olivia is actually wincing. She's not exactly a 9:30 Club kind of girl. I'm not sure I am, either, but Cassie can be pretty persuasive.

I should put this out there: my twin sister and I are nothing alike.

We don't even look alike. We're both white, and we're both sort of medium height. But in every other way, we're opposites. Cassie's blond, green-eyed, and willowy. I'm not any of those things. I'm brown-haired and brown-eyed and nowhere close to willowy.

"I met your dream girl," I tell Cassie immediately.

"What?"

"I made a friend in the bathroom, and she's really cute, and I think you guys should fall in love and get married and have babies."

Cassie does her raise and wrinkle eyebrow thing. She's one of those blond girls with brown eyebrows, and it's hard to explain how perfectly it works on her. "How does that happen?"

"How does love happen?"

"No, how do you make friends in a bathroom?"

"Cass. You're missing the point. This is the dream girl."

"Wait a minute." Cassie flicks my arm. "Is this a Molly crush? Is this crush number twenty-seven?"

"What? No." I blush.

"Oh my God. Your first girl crush. I'm so proud."

"We're at twenty-seven already?" Olivia asks. Which I'm choosing to interpret as her being impressed with me. So, I'm a prolific crusher. That's not a bad thing. *Not* that this is a Molly crush.

I shake my head and cover my eyes. I feel a little helium-brained. Maybe this is what it's like to be drunk. My cousin Abby told me being drunk feels like you're floating. I wonder if it's possible to get drunk without drinking.

"Hey." Cassie peels my hands away from my face. "You know it's my job to mess with you."

But before I can reply, Olivia holds up her phone. "Hey, it's eleven forty-five," she says. "Should we be heading to the Metro?"

"Oh!" I say.

The Metro closes at midnight. Also, I'm starting work tomorrow. I have an actual summer job. Which means I should probably get at least a little bit of sleep, so I don't pass out at the register. I hear that's not professional.

We weave toward the exit, and it's honestly a relief to step outside. It's cool for June, and the air feels nice against my legs. I'm wearing this cotton dress that was plain black when I got it, but I sewed on a doily lace Peter Pan collar and some lace around the bottom. It's completely improved.

Cassie and Olivia both text as they walk, and they don't even trip over the curb. I admire that. I hang back a little, just watching them. They fit here, on U Street. Cassie's got this perfect messy ponytail, and she's dressed like she threw on the first thing to fall out of her closet. Which is probably accurate, but it works on her. More than works. She has this way of making everyone else look overdressed. And Olivia is tall, with this fresh-scrubbed kind of prettiness—except she has a nose stud and blue-streaked hair that make you look at her twice. And I guess she's considered chubby, but not as much as I am.

I do wonder, sometimes, what people think when they see me.

It's strange how you can sometimes still feel self-conscious around people you've known your whole life. Literally. We've known Olivia since our moms were in La Leche League together. And for seventeen years, it's been the four of us: Cassie, Olivia, me, and my cousin Abby. Except Abby moved to Georgia last summer. And ever since, Cassie's been dragging Olivia and me to the stuff she used to do with Abby—open mic nights and concerts and wandering down H Street.

A year ago, Olivia and I would have been tucked up on her living room couch, watching *Steven Universe* with Titania, her schnauzer-beagle mix. Instead, I'm surrounded by people who are infinitely cooler than me. Everyone on U Street is doing one of three things right now: laughing, smoking, or making out.

I turn toward the Metro pole, and right away, I see the dream girl.

"Cass, it's her!" I pull on Cassie's tank top. "In the red. Look."

The girl leans forward, digging through her purse. There are these two hipster white guys hovering near her, both absorbed in their phones: a redhead wearing skinny jeans, and a dark-haired one with dramatic bangs.

"But you never explained why she's Cassie's dream girl," Olivia says. The girl looks up from her purse, and Olivia turns away quickly.

But she sees me. The dream girl waves, and I wave back.

"Oh. She's cute," Cassie whispers.

"I told you." I grin.

"She's walking over here."

And she is. The dream girl is walking toward us, smiling. So now, Cassie's smiling. She's staring at the ground, but I can tell from her cheeks.

"Hi again," says the girl.

I smile. "Hi."

"My savior."

This girl must seriously hate drip-drying.

"I don't think I even introduced myself," she says. "I'm Mina."

"I'm Molly."

"Your shirt," Cassie says, "is the most perfect thing I have ever seen in my entire life. I'm just." She shakes her head.

Mina laughs. "Thank you."

"I'm Cassie, by the way. And I've never met anyone who's heard of Georgie James."

Okay, that's bullshit. I'm standing right here.

"You know what's funny," Mina starts to say—but then the dramatic bangs boy pokes her arm.

"Eenie Meenie, let's go." He looks up, catching my eye over

Cassie's shoulder. "Hi. Nice to meet you guys, but we have to catch this train."

"Oh shit," says Mina. "Okay. Well—"

"So do we," Cassie says quickly. And somehow it happens: our groups merge. Cassie and Mina fall into step beside each other, and Olivia's right behind them, in her own world, texting. I step onto the escalator and lean into the handrail, trying not to look like a sheep that lost its herd. Molly Peskin-Suso: disoriented introvert, alone in the wild.

Until I look up and realize: I'm not actually alone. The hipster boys are a step below me on the escalator. I accidentally lock eyes with the redhead, who asks, "Why do you look familiar?"

"I don't know."

"Well, I'm Will."

"I'm Molly."

"Like the drug," says Bangs.

Like the drug. Like I'm a person you would associate with drugs.

The train pulls into the station almost as soon as we step off the escalator, and we have to sprint to catch it. I slide into a seat, leaving room for Cassie, but she plops down next to Mina.

Olivia settles into the seat beside me instead. And then moments later, Mina's hipster boys drift toward us. Bangs is reading something on his phone, but the red-haired guy grips the pole and smiles down at us.

I look up at him. "Will, right?"

Okay. So he's cute. He's a tiny bit really extremely cute.

"Good memory!" he says. And then Olivia introduces herself, and there's this weird, hanging pause. I wish I were the kind of person who knows how to fill a silence.

I'm not. Olivia's definitely not.

"Oh, and this is Max," Will says after a moment.

Bangs glances up from his phone with a tiny smile. "What's up?"

And ugh—he's cute, too. Except no: I'd actually describe him as hot. He's one of those guys who's so hot, he's not even cute. But he should rein in the bangs.

"So, who does Molly look like?" Will asks, staring me down. "Sorry, but it's driving me crazy."

Max appraises me, pressing his lips together. "No idea."

"She seriously looks like someone."

Actually, I get this a lot. I think I must have one of those stupidly generic faces. Weirdly, three entirely unrelated people have told me I look like this particular teen actress from the seventies, though I'm sort of a fat version of her. And strangers are always telling me I look like their cousin or someone from their summer camp. It freaks me out just a little bit. Like, there's this part of me that wonders whether I actually am related to all these cousins and camp friends.

Here's the part where I should probably mention that Cassie and I are sperm donor babies. So that's a thing in my life:

that tiny niggling idea that everyone I meet might actually be my half sibling.

"I'm just going to gawk at you until I figure it out," Will says.

Across the aisle, Cassie snorts—and I suddenly realize she and Mina are watching us. They look extremely entertained.

Heat rises in my cheeks. "Um, okay," I say, blinking.

The train slows to a stop, and Olivia stands. "Well, here's Chinatown."

"That's us, too," Will says. I guess that's not surprising—half the world gets off here to transfer. The doors spring open, and Cassie and Mina trail behind us as we step onto the platform. Cassie's typing something into her phone.

"Where are you guys headed?" Will asks, still staring a little too hard at my face.

"Takoma Park. Red Line."

"Oh, okay. Opposite direction. We're Bethesda," he says. "So, I guess this is good-bye."

I never really know the protocol for this kind of situation. It's like when you're in line at a store, and a grandma starts telling you all about her grandchildren or her arthritis, and you smile and nod along. But then it's your turn to check out, so you're just like *okay, well, good-bye forever.*

Which is kind of tragic, if you really think about it.

There's a little computer sign that says how long you have until each train gets in. Red Line to Glenmont arrives in ten minutes. That's us. But the Red Line train to Shady Grove is basically pulling in now. Will and Max and Mina leap up the escalator to catch it.

By the time we reach our platform, their train has already left the station.

So, that's it.

2

EXCEPT CASSIE HAS MINA'S NUMBER. It shouldn't surprise me, since Cassie's great at getting girls' numbers. Sometimes she gets a number and immediately forgets about it. Or she hooks up with a girl once and then loses the number on purpose. Cassie can be kind of ruthless.

Olivia nudges me. "That Will guy likes you."

"*What?*"

"That's a thing. You pretend to recognize someone as an excuse to talk to them."

"According to who?"

"The internet." She gives a very serious nod. Olivia is a very serious person in general. I honestly think there are two kinds of quiet people. There's the kind like me, who are secretly full of storms and spinning gears. And then there's the kind like Olivia, who is the actual personification of an ocean on a sunny day. I don't mean that she's simple. There's just something peaceful about her. There always has been. She likes dragons and stargazing and those calendars with paintings of faeries on them. And she's been dating the same guy since we were thirteen. Evan Schulmeister. She met him at summer camp.

"Hey, guess what." Cassie pops up over the back of the seat in front of me. "Your boy is single."

"What are you talking about?"

"Your ginger. Mr. Peach Butt Hipster Pants. He's single and ready to mingle." She waves her phone at me. "Mina confirmed it."

"Cassie!"

She grins. "You're welcome. Mina's going to get the ball rolling."

I freeze. "What?"

"You think he's cute, right?"

I don't respond. I just gape at her, and Olivia giggles.

"Because you looked pretty happy to be talking to him." Cassie pokes my arm. "Look. I know your crush face."

"I don't have a crush face!"

Holy shit. Do I have a crush face? Does the entire world know every time I think a guy is cute?

My phone buzzes in my pocket, startling me. A text from Abby. Molly!!! Tell me about the hot redhead guy!

"Are you kidding me?" I show Cassie the phone. "You told Abby?"

"Possibly."

I feel sick. I might actually throw up. Preferably all over Cassie, who's now texting *again*. Probably about me. And my supposed giant crush on some guy I talked to for five minutes. Cassie always thinks she knows me better than I know myself.

I mean, yes. Will is pretty fucking cute.

Olivia gives me this tiny smile. "You look so horrified right now, Molly."

I shrug wordlessly.

"I thought you wanted a boyfriend."

"Exactly," Cassie interjects, turning back to us suddenly. "Like, this whole Molly thing with the secret crushes that go nowhere. I'm over it."

"Oh, you're over it?" My throat tightens. "Uh, I'm sorry boys don't like me."

"That is such bullshit, Molly. You don't even talk to them."

Here we go.

Cassie's soapbox: the fact that I've had twenty-six crushes and exactly zero kisses. Apparently, it's because I need to woman up. If I like a guy, I'm supposed to tell him. Maybe in Cassie's world, you can do that and have it end in making out. But I'm not so sure it works that way for fat girls.

I don't know. I just like to be careful about this stuff.

Cassie leans over the seat, toward me, and her expression softens. "Look. I'm not going to embarrass you. You trust me, right?"

I shrug.

"Then let's do this. I'm going to get you a boyfriend."

I push my bangs out of my face. "Um. I don't think it's that easy." I hit her with this particular facial expression of mine, known to my moms as the Molly Face. It involves eyebrows and a certain twist of the mouth, and it conveys infinite, everlasting skepticism.

"I'm telling you. It is."

But it's not. I don't think she gets it. There's a reason I've had twenty-six crushes and no boyfriends. I don't entirely understand how *anyone* gets a boyfriend. Or a girlfriend. It just seems like the most impossible odds. You have to have a crush on the exact right person at the exact right moment. And they have to like you back. A perfect alignment of feelings and circumstances. It's almost unfathomable that it happens as often as it does.

I don't know why my heart is beating so quickly.

The train pulls into Takoma, and Cassie stands abruptly. "And I need to know if Mina's queer."

"Aww," I say. "Look who has a crush face now."

"Why don't you just ask her?" Olivia says.

"Yeah, no." Cassie shakes her head. "Okay, let's see if she's on Facebook." She types while she walks. "How do you even search for someone?"

"Are you kidding?" I ask.

This is a fundamental difference between us. I was basically born knowing how to casually stalk people on social media.

But I guess Cassie's more the kind of person who gets casually stalked.

"Want me to ask Will, since he's apparently my future boyfriend?"

"Hush." She's still staring at her phone.

I mean, I'm sure it's a *total* coincidence that Cassie wants to turn this particular boy into my boyfriend. I bet it has *nothing* to do with him being friends with the dream girl.

Cassie gets off the escalator with a little hop, and Olivia and I follow her through the turnstiles. There's a couple making out against a SmarTrip machine. Which is definitely not how you're supposed to use SmarTrip machines. I look away quickly.

"Are you still texting Mina?" I ask.

She smiles. "I'm not telling you."

But she will. No question. Because once you've shared a uterus, there's no such thing as a secret.

Of course, I sleep terribly. I'm up for hours, staring at the ceiling.

I keep remembering little moments from tonight. It's like my brain won't stop spinning. Will squinting at my face, trying to place it. Olivia's blue-streaked hair, extra bright beneath the fluorescent lights of the Metro. And the tiny, secret smile on Cassie's face every time her phone buzzed.

Certain nights have this kind of electricity. Certain nights carry you to a different place from where you started. I think tonight was one of the special ones—but I can't pinpoint why.

Which is strange.

I drift off to sleep, finally—and it feels like only seconds have passed when my phone buzzes with a text.

Are you up? Smiley face. It's Cassie.

There's this horrible taste in my mouth, and my eyes feel sore and crusty. I guess it's fitting. I managed to get drunk last night on absolutely no alcohol. Now I have a nonalcoholic hangover.

I stare at the screen.

My phone buzzes again. MOLLY, WAKE UP!!! IT'S YOUR FIRST DAY OF WORK!!!!

I write back: I'm coming!

I add a sleepy-face emoji.

She sends back this horrible wide-awake emoji with giant eyes.

I send a frowny face back. My head feels heavy on my pillow, and I think I weigh a million pounds. But I force myself out of bed and pull on this ruffled dress from ModCloth, with leggings. And I take my pill. I've been on Zoloft for four years. I used to get panic attacks in the middle school cafeteria.

Long story.

Anyway, when I step into the hallway, the air smells like butter and bacon. We are definitely the kind of Jews who eat bacon.

"Is that the young professional?" asks Patty.

Patty is one of my moms. She pops out from the kitchen, wearing an oversized batik tunic. "Here, bring these to the table." She hands me a plate stacked high with pancakes.

"Okay . . ."

"You look kind of out of it, sweetie. You all right?"

"Yeah, I'm . . ." I look at the pancakes. "What are these supposed to be?"

"Hearts?" she says. There's flour on her chin.

"Ohhhh."

"I guess they kind of look like penises."

"Yup."

"And scrotums," she adds.

"Mom, that's so appetizing."

Honestly, it's not the first time Patty has thrown down the word *scrotum* in reference to a meal. She's a midwife, so I may be a little too used to her talking about this stuff. Once she spent an entire drive to the mall explaining to Cassie and me that the so-called "doggie lipstick" was really the dog's penis coming out of the shaft. She seemed to know a lot of the anatomical details.

I don't think either Cassie or I will ask about the lipstick again.

"You should let your brother try one," she says.

I nod. "Xav loves scrotums."

Patty raises her eyebrows.

She takes the plate back, and I peek into the dining room. Of course everyone's already awake. Nadine is a teacher, so even in the summer her body is used to waking up "butt-early," as she calls it. Sometimes she calls it the ass-crack of dawn. And Xavier wakes up butt-early because he's a butt-early kind of baby.

"Don't drop that," Nadine says, giving him the evil eye. Xavier gives me a giant grin from his high chair and says, "Momo," which means "Molly."

So, here's us in a nutshell: Patty used a sperm donor to conceive Cassie and me. Nadine used the same donor two years ago for Xavier. Strangers have a really hard time wrapping their minds around that. There's this subset of people who like to inform me that Xavier's my half brother, not my real brother. They're the same people who tell me Abby's not really my cousin. Nadine's not really my mother. I'm pretty sure people wouldn't question any of this if Nadine, Abby, and Xavier were white.

Needless to say, I hate these people.

Xavier flings a chunk of banana to the floor and starts whimpering.

"Dude, no," Nadine tells him. "Banana's gone. You're SOL."

"Do you even know what that means?" Cassie asks from across the table.

"I know so much more than you think I do." Nadine grins. Then Xavier lets out another goat wail, and she leans over to kiss his head. "Hey. Xavor Xav, be cool."

Xavor Xav, like Flavor Flav. Nadine is just like this.

Patty walks in with a plate of bacon, pressed between paper towels. "Hope you're ready," she says to Cassie.

Cassie's love of bacon is well documented and notorious.

But she leans back, smiling. "I'm actually not hungry."

"Who are you, and what have you done with Cassie?" Nadine asks, eyes narrowing.

Cassie laughs and shrugs, and I notice she hasn't touched her food. Not a bite. And it's a little surprising. Normally, Cassie's one of those skinny girls who eats like she's about to go into hibernation.

"I'm serious, Kitty Cat. What's going on?"

"Nothing. I'm not . . ." She trails off, hands disappearing under the table. She glances downward, quickly.

She's reading a text.

From Mina. I'm sure of it. Probably scheming about how to get Will to date me. My whole face heats up just thinking about it.

"So, Molly, how are you feeling?" Nadine asks. "Are you nervous? Are you freaking out?"

"About what?"

"About your big day. About entering the world of the working."

I wrinkle my brow. "You realize this isn't like a brain surgery residency, right? I'm working in a store."

"Momomomo!" Xav interjects. "Cacacacaca!"

Cassie gives him the side-eye. "Hey. Stop calling me that."

"Never stop calling her that," says Nadine.

Cassie makes a face, and then she slides her foot against mine under the table, lengthwise—toe to heel. Our feet have always been the same size, almost to the millimeter. I guess we grow at the exact same rate.

"Hey, when are you leaving?" Cassie leans forward on her fists, smiling.

"In a few minutes . . . ," I start to say, but she gives this very meaningful stare. I try again. "Right now?"

"Great! I'll walk you to work," she says, standing abruptly, slipping her phone in her back pocket. "Let's go."

"I texted with Mina for four hours last night," she says as soon as we step outside. It tumbles out of her mouth like she's been bursting to tell me.

"Wow."

"I know."

I feel Cassie looking at me, and I can tell she wants me to say something. Or ask something. Maybe it's twin telepathy—I can just feel her excitement. It's like it has a pulse.

Somehow, I don't think this is about finding me a boyfriend.

"What did you talk about?" I ask.

"Just, you know . . ." She laughs. "I honestly don't even know what we talked about. Music. Photography—she does photography. We just talked about everything, really."

"For four hours."

"Yup." She smiles.

"That's awesome." I pause. "Did you find out if she likes girls?"

"Molly. I don't know."

There's this edge to her tone, and it throws me. "Okay," I say softly.

And for a minute, we're both so quiet I can actually hear tweeting birds.

I should mention that Takoma Park is beautiful. You kind of don't notice it most of the time, but then it hits you all at once. Like, when it's eight fifteen on a summer morning, and the sun is soft and filtered through tree branches. And the houses are brightly painted, with porch swings and wind chimes and front steps lined with flowers.

I think I just want to stare at the flowers. I want to walk up Tulip Avenue, and be hungry and sleepy, and I want Cassie not to be annoyed at me. I guess asking her about Mina was a mistake. Though if she's going to be prickly about her own love life, it's pretty messed up that she's got her hands all over mine.

Except a minute later, she says, "So, we're meeting Mina at FroZenYo this afternoon to talk strategy."

"Strategy?"

"For seducing the ginger. Operation Boyfriend. Operation Molly Makeouts."

Oh my God. Seriously.

I shake my head. "Okay, well, I have to—"

"Molly, I know you have work. But you get off at three, and we're meeting her at three thirty. Okay?"

"I don't want to intrude. I don't want to vag-block you."

"Molly." Cassie laughs. "You can't vag-block someone in a frozen yogurt shop. A frozen yogurt shop vag-blocks itself."

"That is true."

"And seriously." She looks at me. "I need you there."

She looks so sincere. "Okay," I say finally.

"Hell yeah." Cassie high-fives me. "Oh man. It's on."

3

SO, THIS IS PROBABLY MY own fault for being a smartass, but I'm actually a little nervous about starting work. Even though this isn't a brain surgery residency. I'm very glad this isn't a brain surgery residency. I don't think anyone wants me operating on their brain right now, or ever. Especially because my hands are shaking—just a little—on the door handle.

The store looks the same as it always does—which is to say, it looks like Zooey Deschanel exploded into five thousand tablecloths and painted plates and letterpress notecards. It's called Bissel. Not like the vacuum. Like the Yiddish word, meaning "a little bit." As in, good luck only spending a bissel of money when you walk into Bissel. Good luck not spending your entire paycheck on a bissel of handcrafted artisan jewelry.

I can't believe I'm walking into Bissel as an employee.

I'm an *employee.*

Deborah and Ari Wertheim, the owners, are behind the counter, and I feel this wave of shyness. "Hi," I say, and my voice comes out comically high. Squeaky Molly. Super professional.

Deborah looks up from the register. "Molly—hi! Oh great, you're here." She presses both palms against the counter, beaming. "We are so, so glad you're joining us."

She's intensely nice. They both are. That's the main thing I remember about the Wertheims from my interview. They're nice in the way therapists are—like, you get the impression they'd be up for hearing your thoughts about life and humanity. They're married, and they're a perfect matched set: tall and big-boned, with thick-framed glasses. Ari's bald, and Deborah has this kind of wild black hair she wears knotted into a messy bun. Or sometimes two meatball Sailor Moon buns, even though she's probably in her forties. I really love that. Also, they both have these brightly colored, amazingly intricate tattoos all up and down their arms. Literally, they are the two coolest adult humans on the planet, or at least in Maryland.

"Hmm, so I guess we probably went over most of this stuff at the interview. You remember how to use the register?"

I nod, even though I definitely don't remember how to use the register.

"Cool. Though the register is being an asshole today, so I'll probably stick you in the back room with Reid. And he can kind of show you around. You've met Reid?"

"I don't think so."

"Oh, I'll introduce you." Deborah gives me a little shoulder squeeze. "One sec."

She walks toward the back of the store, through the baby section, and I try to act casual. There's music playing—something soft and indie. Cassie would know the band. And right beside me, there's a display of ceramic mugs shaped like whales. Of course Bissel sells ceramic mugs shaped like whales. Of course those exist. I literally don't understand how anyone could walk into this store and not fall in love.

Deborah comes back a minute later with a guy I've actually seen here before. He's tall and kind of big, in that way people describe as *husky*. His shirt has a map of Middle Earth on it. And his sneakers are so electric white, they're either brand-new, or he puts them in the laundry.

"Molly, this is Reid. Reid, Molly."

"Hi," he says, smiling shyly.

"Hi." I smile back.

Deborah turns to me. "Molly, you're going to be a senior, right?"

I nod.

"Perfect! You guys are the same age. I bet you have a lot in common."

Classic adult logic. Reid and I are vaguely the same age, so of course we're basically soul mates. It's like horoscopes. Somehow

I'm supposed to believe that I'm similar in some meaningful way to every single person born on my birthday. Or every single Sagittarius. I mean, I barely have anything in common with Cassie, and we were born six minutes apart.

Sorry, but this guy is literally choosing to advertise Lord of the Rings on his body. I don't think there's going to be a whole lot of common ground.

We walk through the baby section, and the whole time, I get the impression that he's trying to think of things to say. It reminds me a lot of those meaningless syllables people spew, like "Um, yeah, so . . ."

Reid doesn't actually spew the syllables. He's like the personification of those syllables. I wish there were a secret signal you could use to communicate: HELLO. I AM OFFICIALLY COOL WITH SILENCE.

Not that I actually am cool with silence, but maybe it would help him relax.

For a moment, we just stand there in the entryway to the back room, surrounded by cardboard boxes and rustic wooden furniture. I bite my lip, feeling awkward and unsettled.

"Welcome to your first day," he says finally.

"Thanks." I smile, looking up at him. He's so tall, I actually have to tilt my head back. He's not awful looking. He definitely has good hair. It's this perfect, tousled boy hair—brown and soft and sort of curly. And he wears glasses. And there's this sweetness to his mouth. I always notice people's mouths.

"You've been working here for years, right?" I say. "I've seen you before."

As soon as I say it, I blush. I don't want him to think I've NOTICED him. I mean, I have noticed him. But not in that way. I've noticed him because he sticks out here. He doesn't quite fit. I think of Bissel as a place for people who care about tiny details—like the texture of a woven place mat or the painted pattern on the handle of a serving spoon.

I would say Reid gives a pretty strong impression that he doesn't notice patterns on serving spoons.

"Yeah, I'm here all the time. Kind of unavoidable." He shrugs. "My parents."

"Your parents?"

"Ari and Deborah."

I clap a hand over my mouth. "Ari and Deborah are your parents?"

"You didn't know that?" He looks amused.

I shake my head slowly. "Okay. You just blew my mind."

"Really?" He laughs. "Why?"

"Because! I don't know. Deborah and Ari just seem so . . ." Punk rock and badass and not into Lord of the Rings. "They have tattoos," I say finally.

He nods. "They do."

I just gape for a minute.

He laughs again. "You seem so surprised."

"No, I'm just . . ." I shake my head. "I don't know."

There's this silence.

"Um. So, do you want to unpack some baby stuff?" Reid asks, nudging a cardboard box with the toe of his sneaker. We settle onto the floor next to it, cross-legged. I'm suddenly glad to be wearing leggings under my dress.

Reid lifts a stack of onesies out of the box. "So these need price stickers," he says. "Do you know how to do that?"

"Do I know how to use stickers?"

"It's pretty complicated," he says. We grin at each other.

I pick up a onesie. "This is very Takoma Park."

It's undyed cotton, gender neutral, printed with a picture of vegetables. Seriously. Babies here are forced to declare their allegiance to vegetables before they're old enough to say, "Suck it, Mom, I want ice cream."

"This is actually a reorder. We sold out of them last week," Reid says.

"Of course it's a reorder."

"Vegetables are just really popular right now." He looks down and smiles.

We work in silence, putting price stickers on the tags and folding the onesies up neatly again. When we finish, Reid says, "I think there are some swaddling blankets, too."

I pick one up, reading the label. "Organic hemp."

"Yes."

"Really?" I look at him.

He laughs. "Really."

So, I guess there are parents who like to roll their babies up like blunts.

It's funny watching Middle Earth Reid while he works. All this delicate baby stuff, and he's the least delicate-looking person I've ever met. He's struggling to roll up the swaddling blankets. I think his hands are too big.

Maybe this is why they hired me: for my smallish hands and my blunt-rolling abilities.

He looks up at me suddenly. "So, can I ask you a question?"

"Sure."

"Just curious. Why are you so surprised about my parents' tattoos?"

Um. Because these people are related to you.

"Is it because they're Jewish?" he adds.

"Oh no! It's not that. I knew they were Jewish. I mean, the store is called Bissel. Their last name is Wertheim."

He laughs. "Me too. I'm Reid Wertheim." He leans forward and offers his hand for me to shake. He has a surprisingly confident handshake.

"Molly Peskin-Suso," I say.

"Peskin!" he says. "Are you Jewish, too?"

"I am."

"Really?" His eyes light up, and I know exactly what he's thinking. I don't think of myself as super Jewish or anything, and I basically never go to synagogue. But there's this thing I feel when I meet another Jewish person in the wild. It's like a secret invisible high five.

And it's funny. Normally, I go totally blank and silent when I meet a boy for the first time—which is how a person can end up having twenty-six crushes and zero kisses. But around Middle Earth Reid, I feel exactly as nervous as I'd feel around any new person. No more, no less.

It's actually kind of wonderful.

By three o'clock, Reid and I have unpacked, priced, and set out six boxes of baby stuff. And we've talked. There has been ample time for talking. So far, I've learned that he really likes Cadbury Mini Eggs. When I asked if this was relevant in June, he said Cadbury Mini Eggs are always relevant. Apparently he buys them in bulk after Easter and hoards them.

Honestly, I respect that.

I leave work exactly at three, and the Metro's on time, so I'm early to Silver Spring. I walk down Ellsworth Drive and lurk near the entrance of FroZenYo. There are fifty billion restaurants here, and even on a weekday afternoon, it's packed with people: dads pushing strollers and girls who look like they're my age but dress like they work in a bank. My moms talk a lot about how Silver Spring was better before it got gentrified. It's sad to think about. I guess it just sucks when change makes things worse.

I lean against the side of the building so I can play on my phone. Social media is the actual worst today. It's one of those days where both Facebook and Instagram have been taken over by selfies, and they're not even the kind that own their selfie-ness. It's more the kind where the person is looking off in the distance, trying to seem candid. I need an anti-favorite button. Not that I'd actually use it, but still.

I'm sort of wondering where Cassie and Mina are. Cassie's not usually late, but it's already ten minutes past the time we're supposed to meet. I don't know whether to be grumpy or concerned. But at 3:45, I finally see them: walking together, giggling about something and carrying bags from H&M. They're not even rushing.

Anti-favorite. *Dis*like.

"Hey," Cassie says. She smiles when she sees me. "You remember Mina."

"From the bathroom. With the labia," Mina says.

I can't help but giggle.

Here's a frustrating thing about me: if everyone else is happy, I usually can't stay pissed off. My moods are conformists. It sucks, because sometimes you really want to be angry.

"Oh my God, I love your necklace," Mina adds.

I blush. "Oh. I made it."

"Are you serious?"

"Yeah, it's easy. See, it's an old zipper." I lean forward to show her. "You just cut off the end and unzip it, and curve it into a heart. And then you sew the bottom together."

"Molly makes shit like that all the time," Cassie explains, but she says it sort of proudly.

They set their bags on top of a table next to each other. I

guess they spent the afternoon together shopping. Which is a horrifying group activity, if you ask me—though maybe it's different for people with single-digit sizes. They probably modeled for each other. Maybe they got matching outfits.

I pick up an empty yogurt cup. This is one of those places where you serve everything yourself. You can pick whatever yogurt flavors you want, and once you do that, there are fifty million toppings to choose from. There are people who can't handle this kind of freedom. But I can, and I rule at it. You just have to know your own tastes.

I pay and sit down, and Mina settles in beside me. She peers into my cup. "What'd you get?"

"Chocolate with cookie dough."

Like I said.

I rule at this.

Mina tilts her cup toward me, and of course she's one of those fundamentally confused people who mixes gummies with chocolate.

"So, Cassie said you go to Georgetown Day?" I feel tongue-tied.

"Yup. I'll be a senior."

"Us too. And you do photography?"

"You know everything!" she says.

Which makes me blush. I don't know. I feel like a creeper. I always seem to know more about people than they know about me.

I feel an awkward silence blooming. I have to head it off at the pass. "Our friend Olivia does photography," I say quickly.

"Oh, cool!" Mina says. "I mean, I'm really new at it. Will—you met him—the redhead. He's actually super talented, but he's teaching me the basics. He has this software where you can tweak the lighting and color on the images after you upload them. And he's going to teach me how to do sun flares." Mina pauses. "I'm talking too much, aren't I?"

"No, you're—"

"I talk a lot when I'm nervous."

"You're nervous?" I ask.

She shrugs, smiling. "I don't know. This feels so formal, right? Like, isn't this weird? To put actual effort into becoming friends?"

"I guess so," I say.

"My friends and I were never like, 'Hey, let's be friends.' It's more like, 'Yeah, okay. You're there and you're cool.'"

"That's literally what I said to Cassie in the womb," I say.

She laughs, scratching an invisible spot on her arm. Which makes the sleeve of her shirt ride up, revealing the edge of a tattoo. I can't quite make out what it's a picture of. But seriously. This girl has a tattoo. And she's in high school. I feel slightly inadequate.

Cassie slides in across from me.

"You take forever," Mina says.

"Yes, but. *Decisions.*"

That's Cassie. Every time we come here, she takes her flavor profile deadly seriously, but she always gets the exact same thing. Vanilla yogurt. And some type of gummy. MEMO TO CASSIE: all gummies taste the same. They honestly do.

"Okay, I have to finish telling you about my theory," Cassie says. She shovels a spoonful of yogurt into her mouth. "So, Molly, you missed this, but we were talking about ancestors."

"Um, what?" I ask.

"Like, ancestors. Like, all your relatives who died before you were born."

"Why were you talking about this?"

Cassie pauses, her spoon midair. "Oh. I don't remember."

"Well, first we were talking about sperm donation," Mina says, "and whether or not your sperm donor's relatives count as your relatives."

"Right," Cassie says. "But, okay, here's my theory. You've got your ancestors, and they're just hanging out in heaven or hell—FYI, this is not like a rabbi-endorsed, official tenet of Judaism."

"I gathered that." I smile a little.

"Right. So, here's what I think. They're sitting around, drinking ambrosia and everything."

"This is definitely not rabbi-endorsed."

She ignores me. "And then one of their descendants has a baby. And it's you! And as soon as you're born, for your whole life, your ancestors get to watch everything. And they're rooting for you and discussing among themselves, but they're not allowed to intervene. They just watch. It's like a reality show."

"A really, really boring reality show," I say.

"Yeah, but it's not boring to them, you know? Because you're their descendant." Cassie clasps her hands together. "So they're invested."

Mina purses her lips around her spoon and nods.

"And then when you eventually get old and die," Cassie continues, "you show up in heaven, where you're basically a fucking celebrity. And your ancestors are like, *yeah, I was shipping you with that other girl, but it's cool.* And *sorry you got old and died, though.* And you're like, *yeah, that sucked, but you know.*" Cassie shrugs. "And so then you actually *become* one of the ancestors, and the next time a baby is born, you get to watch everything. And the cycle continues."

"That's horrifying," says Mina.

Cassie tilts her head. "How so?"

"Um, having a bunch of dead people watching you all the time? Watching you pee and have sex and masturbate. And, like, discussing it with each other?"

"Eww. No." Cassie shakes her head quickly. "They're not creepers. They're not watching *that* stuff. And anyway, they have like a million descendants to keep up with, so it's not like they can watch anyone that closely. It's more like flipping through the channels."

"But, see, that's not what you said," Mina argues, poking

the air with her spoon. And I like this. I like watching Cassie get challenged. I think Cassie likes it, too.

"Well, I'm still tweaking the theory," Cassie says, smiling.

"Good. Make sure no dead people are watching me pee," Mina says. Then she glances at me and groans, covering her face. "God. Molly, you must think I only talk about peeing and labia."

"That is true," I say.

She sticks her tongue out at me.

And in that moment, I realize I might actually be becoming friends with this girl. That's two legit new friends today, and it's not even four thirty. Mina of the Labia and Middle Earth Reid. A pretty good day's work. I feel myself smiling.

Cassie nods. "Okay, so let's say certain things are censored. They're not allowed to watch you in the bathroom or having sex or anything like that."

"But you can't just decide that," Mina says. "This isn't a reality show pitch. It's a metaphysical theory."

"But it's *my* metaphysical theory." Cassie sniffs.

I roll the idea around in my head for a moment. It's funny—I think I actually like it. I find it strangely comforting. I guess it's nice to imagine a roomful of people caring about what happens to you. Rooting for your happiness. They'd be pissed off when someone was a jerk to you. They'd want your crush to like you back. They'd want all twenty-six of them to like you back.

You would *matter.* That's the thing. I get into this weird place sometimes where I worry about that. I've never told anyone this—not my moms, not even Cassie—but that's the thing I'm most afraid of. Not mattering. Existing in a world that doesn't care who I am.

It's this whole other level of aloneness.

And maybe it's a twin thing. I have never truly been alone in the world. I think that's why I fear it.

"They're watching us right now," Cassie says. She tilts her face to the ceiling. "Hey, ancestors. You guys should try fro yo. It's the best." She gives them a thumbs-up.

Mina buries her face in her arms and just laughs.

4

OF COURSE, MINA IS THE only thing Cassie wants to talk about for the rest of the week—anytime we're alone together, anytime our moms aren't around. She slides onto the couch beside me on Friday, just as I'm settling in to watch *Teen Mom.*

"Did you know Mina's Korean?" she asks. "Korean American, actually."

"Yup, you mentioned that."

"So, like, her parents were born here, but she has relatives in South Korea, and she's taking a trip there in August. I think she's going to do a photography project."

I mean, I'm not one of those people who can't handle commentary during TV shows—but it should be commentary *about* the TV show. For example: I am completely cool with Nadine ranting about the *rat-faced, why-are-they-so-virile, why-do-you-even-watch-this* baby dads.

Cassie leans back, legs in a pretzel. "And she really likes penguins."

Penguins. No respect for the baby dads.

"I'm glad she likes penguins."

This actually reminds me of Abby, when she started dating her first real boyfriend. We were fifteen, and he was in her math class. And it was one of those things where every word out of Abby's mouth was *Darrell.* Darrell hates applesauce. Darrell's a really good dancer. Darrell went to Florida once. Like Abby got some kind of thrill from saying his name.

"Also," Cassie says casually, "Mina's pansexual."

I pause the TiVo and sit up ramrod straight. "Wait. What?" I ask.

Cassie buries her face in a throw pillow.

"How do you know?"

"I asked her. And she told me."

"Cassie!" I gasp into my hand. "Are you kidding me? This is so awesome!"

"Yeah, well. It doesn't mean she likes me."

I twist all the way around to look at her.

"Not that it matters," she adds, smiling faintly. She hugs the pillow and sighs.

"Cass."

I don't think I've ever seen her like this. Cassie flirts with girls all the time—and she's usually charming and sometimes careless and sometimes focused, but never, ever vulnerable. I've never seen her look nervous.

"It matters," I say softly.

"I mean, yes, she's fucking adorable. Yes, I want to make out with her." Cassie groans into her pillow.

"Oh my gosh. You have a crush. This is a real crush."

"Whatever," she says.

But her cheeks tell the story, and they're basically radioactive.

It's usually me who does this. I blush and swoon and am essentially the heroine of a romance novel. Except with 100 percent less kissing. But Cassie? Not so much.

Until now. And it's fascinating.

"Why are you looking at me like that?" she asks.

My mouth twitches. "I'm not."

"I hate you."

She's grinning, and I grin back at her. Cassie has kissed a fair number of girls—and believe me, I've heard about every molecule of saliva involved in these transactions—and yet.

Something's different with Mina.

I wake up Saturday to a text from Abby.

Not that this is unusual, because Abby isn't just my cousin. Other than Cassie, she's my best friend. Even more than Olivia. It's funny, because Cassie and Abby are the bold ones, and Olivia and I are the quiet ones, but when we pair off, it's usually

Cassie and me, Abby and Olivia. Or Abby and me, Cassie and Olivia. Friendship is like that. I guess it's not always about common ground.

Anyway, Abby used to live two blocks away from us, but she moved to Georgia a year ago. It sucks, but we talk every week, and we text so much, it's like a single ongoing conversation.

When I tap into the text window, there are actually two messages. The first says: We need to talk ASAP. The second is a winky-face emoji.

In certain contexts, a winky face is a clear code for sex.

So, I guess this means Abby had sex with her boyfriend last night. I should mention this: Abby has a boyfriend in Georgia. Named Nick. And he's pretty cute in pictures. Boyfriends don't seem to be a particularly complicated thing for Abby. Honestly, nothing seems really complicated for Abby. But Abby is my cousin, and she's amazing, and I'm happy for her, and I'm not jealous. Because that would be shitty.

I don't want to be shitty.

I yawn and rub my eyes, and then I tap out a reply: Why, hello, winky face. What's up?

Moments later, her reply: a blushing smiley emoji.

Definitely sex.

I call her.

"Congratulations," I say as soon as she picks up.

She laughs. "Excuse me. How do you even know what I'm about to say?"

"Because you're really obvious." I roll onto my side, cupping the phone to my ear. "But I want you to tell me anyway."

"Now I'm embarrassed!"

"What? Why?"

"I don't know!" She giggles softly. "Ugh. Okay, let me make sure my dad's not creeping in the hallway."

"Good idea," I say. My uncle Albert is insane when it comes to dating. Once, he caught Abby holding hands with a guy, and she was grounded for a week.

"Okay," she says, after a moment.

"All clear?"

"Yeah." I hear her take a deep breath. "So . . ."

And the weird thing is, I get this tense, almost nauseated feeling. I can't figure out why. I don't have a crush on Abby's boyfriend—I've never even met him. And it's not like I'm in any kind of suspense here. I know what she's about to tell me.

She's about to tell me she had sex with Nick.

"I had sex with Nick," she says, her voice hushed.

"I knew it!"

She laughs. "Oh my God. I feel weird talking about this."

I can just picture her flopped back on her bed, hand covering her face. Abby doesn't blush—kind of like Cassie—though Abby has dark-brown skin, so it's hard to tell. But her mouth does this tiny upward quirk in the corner when she's embarrassed or awkward or pleased with herself.

I can actually hear it. I can hear that little mouth quirk in her voice.

"How was it?" I ask.

"It was . . . you know. It was good."

But I don't know. I'm bad at this. I never know what to ask.

"Better than Darrell?"

She pauses. "Yeah," she says finally. "Definitely."

"Well, awesome!"

"You don't think I'm a slut, right?"

"What? No!"

"We've only been together five months. It's kind of slutty."

"No it's not," I say. "Not at all."

"I know. But ugh. So, there's this girl I know here, and she's the actual worst. Like, you need to hear her talk about her metabolism, which is apparently superfast, and apparently we all need to know this, and I don't even know why I listen to her—but anyway. She made this comment the other day that couples in high school shouldn't have sex until they've been dating for a year. And I can't get it out of my head. You know?"

"Oh, Abby. I'm sorry."

"No, it's fine. Like, she didn't actually use the word *slut*, but I felt like it was implied, and now I'm just like, great. I'm a slut."

There's this catch in her voice, and I don't know what to say. I'm not really the expert on this.

Here's what I would never, ever admit out loud: a part of me always thought it was some kind of a secret compliment when someone got called a slut. It meant you were having sex. Which meant people wanted to have sex with you. Being a slut just meant you were normal.

But I think maybe I'm wrong about that. Maybe I'm so wrong.

"Abby, you are not a slut," I say firmly. "Who is this girl? She's full of shit."

"I know, I know. I'm being ridiculous."

"Olivia's had sex. Cassie's had all kinds of sex. You're fine. And it's not anyone else's business."

"No, you're right."

"So, tell me how it happened," I say. "Like, tell me the whole story leading up to it."

"Okay." I hear rustling, and I picture her sitting up straighter. "So we were actually at a concert. We saw the Weepies—tell Cassie that. But anyway, afterward, we were hanging out at Simon's house, and we're watching TV, and then Nick gets a text from his mom."

"Uh, I'm not seeing how this story ends in sex."

"Ha. She was letting him know she was called in to the hospital for work."

"Ohhhh."

I can hear Abby grinning. "Yup. So then we left . . ."

"So, you and Nick were home alone . . . ," I say. "And?"

"And yeah!"

"Hey, well done."

"Why, thank you." She yawns happily. "So what about you?"

"Did I have sex last night?"

"No!" she says. "Unless, I mean—did you?"

If Abby were physically present right now, she'd be feeling the wrath of my side-eye. She would so be feeling it.

"Oh, totally," I say. "You know me."

"Molly! I want to know what's going on with you. Hey, whatever happened with the sideburns guy?"

"From my SAT class?"

"Yes!"

Crush number twenty-five: Quinn of Test Prep. I never exchanged actual words with him, but I'm 80 percent sure that was his first name. Once, we shared a potentially significant moment of eye contact after finishing a math practice test.

"I have no idea. I hope he did well."

"What do you mean?"

"On the SAT."

"You are ridiculous."

I shrug, and even though she can't see me, it's like she can sense it through the cellular radio waves.

"How come you never tell me about boys anymore?"

"There's literally nothing to tell."

We hang up, and I scoot backward against my pillows, feeling off-kilter. So, Abby had sex with Nick. That means she's had sex with two guys. I haven't even kissed two guys. Actually, I haven't even kissed one guy. I know it's not a competition, but I can't help but feel like I'm falling further and further behind.

Of the four of us—Cassie, Abby, Olivia, and me—I'm the last virgin standing. Which has been the case for a while now, and I don't know why it suddenly bothers me. But it's not about the sex, exactly.

It's the other stuff. I can picture it: Abby and Nick hanging out after the concert, sleepy and content and surrounded by friends. Her feet in his lap. This text coming in. And the way all their friends must have teased them when they left so abruptly. I bet they looked sheepish. I bet they held hands the minute they stepped outside.

I think that's what I'm jealous of. I'm jealous of the moment Nick slid his key into the lock. And I do not mean that as a euphemism. Just a key in the lock of an empty house. Just that sweet, anticipatory moment. I wonder what Abby was thinking and feeling at that exact second. I'd be wrecked with butterflies, if it were me.

Here's the truth: I want this so badly. To the point where it's almost physically painful sometimes.

I want Olivia's soft-voiced conversations with Evan Schulmeister, where she takes five steps away from us before she even answers the phone. Just to be alone with him. And I want the palpable waves of electric crush energy that radiate off Cassie these days. I want to know what it feels like to have crushes that *could conceivably maybe one day* turn into boyfriends.

All this wanting.

I pull out my phone. My mind is spinning. I need to zone out on BuzzFeed or something. I know this doesn't exactly make me unique, but I love the internet. I love it. I think the way I feel about the internet is the way some people feel about the ocean. It's so huge and unknowable, but also totally predictable. You type a line of symbols and click enter, and everything you want to happen, happens.

Not like real life, where all the wanting in the world can't make something exist. I don't even think Cassie has the ability to make this come true for me. It's just hard to believe in the concept of Molly-With-a-Boyfriend.

Especially a cute hipster boyfriend. Especially Will.

But I want it. The wanting is almost too big to hold.

5

THINGS FEEL MORE MANAGEABLE IN the morning. I don't know if it's the sunshine or the Zoloft or just the fact that I'm working today, but I feel completely energized. I'm even a little amped up.

As soon as I get to Bissel, Deborah starts me off setting a tableau of baskets and things around a raw cedar coffee table. Here's a fact about me: I'm excellent at arranging vintage stuff into rustic, artful displays. Abby calls me a Pinterest Queen, which is a compliment. I think. I guess it's my one skill set.

The storage room door nudges open, and Reid slips through, carrying a cardboard box. He sets it down on the counter and talks to Ari for a minute.

And then he looks up at me and smiles and walks over. "Hey, Molly."

"Oh hey! I was wondering where you were."

God, I don't know why I do this. Ninety-nine percent of the time, I'm amazing at shutting up, but every so often, it's like I lose my filter. And it comes without warning.

I was wondering where you were. Way to sound like a happy little stalker on your second day of work, Molly. But Reid just smiles again and picks up a basket. "What are you working on?"

"Oh, Deborah wanted me to update this display."

"Cool."

He ruffles his own hair, which is a pretty cute thing for a boy to do. And then he stands there for a minute, like he doesn't know what to say.

Poor, awkward Middle Earth Reid.

Though he's wearing what appears to be a *Game of Thrones* T-shirt today. So, I guess he's House Lannister Reid now.

The silence is a little painful. It's funny, because you always think the hard part is meeting someone the first time. It's not. It's the second time, because you've already used up all the obvious topics of conversation. And even if you haven't, it's strange and heavy-handed to introduce random conversational topics at this stage in the game. *Hi, Reid. Let's converse about topics. HOW MANY SIBLINGS DO YOU HAVE? WHAT BOOKS DO YOU LIKE?*

I mean, I could probably answer the book one.

"So, what's your favorite thing for sale here?" I blurt.

Excellent conversational topic, Molly.

"Oh, I'll show you," Reid says. He starts walking toward the stationery corner, peeking over his shoulder to see if I'm following. So I follow. He goes straight for the greeting cards, and pulls one off the display.

A greeting card. This store is essentially Anthropologie's cooler, hotter big sister, and Reid's most cherished item is a greeting card.

He hands it to me, and I hold it gently in both hands. And I have to admit: this is a pretty fancy greeting card. It's on heavy card stock, intricately painted with a portrait of—I'm almost positive—Queen Elizabeth I. She's wearing this outfit with epic puffed sleeves and a collar that basically looks like the sun, and she has the world's greatest Don't Fuck With Me expression on her face. Underneath the portrait, in old-fashioned script, is the quote "I observe and remain silent." I read it aloud.

"That's Elizabeth the First," Reid says.

"Oh, I thought so." I look up at him. "That's a quote from her?"

He nods seriously. "As far as I know."

"That's a really ominous card to send someone."

"What?" He laughs.

"It's like, *I'm watching your every move, and I choose not to say anything . . . yet.* Look at her expression." I hold up the card.

"Noooooo!" The faintest dimple appears in his cheek. "No. Don't ruin Elizabeth for me. She is perfect."

"Is she, Reid? Is she really?" I flash him the Molly Face. Everlasting skepticism.

"Yes. She is. She is perfect."

Now he's looking at me, and I have to admit: his eyes are a cool shade of hazel. I don't know if his glasses kept me from noticing before. But now I'm noticing.

"Okay," I say, because I need to say something. "So, is this like a romantic thing, or . . . ?"

His head whips toward me. "What?"

I hold up the card. "You and Elizabeth?"

"Very funny." He plucks it out of my hand, smiling.

"So, that's a yes?"

It's the strangest thing. I am *not* like this. I mean, I am around my family, but not around boys. I've never really joked around with a boy like this before. Not where I was the one making the jokes. I think I like it.

"We should look busy," Reid says suddenly, glancing over his shoulder. I follow his gaze, catching Deborah's eye.

She smiles and waves, and I feel my cheeks go warm.

Crap. Yeah. Job. Work.

"We can rearrange stuff in the baby section again," Reid says.

"Okay."

"It's kind of like . . ." He lowers his voice, glancing briefly at Deborah again. "There's not always a lot to do here? I guess it depends on the day."

"Ah."

I fall into step beside him, walking toward the baby section—which is essentially Pinterest come to life. The ceiling is draped with softly patterned pastel bunting, and there are hanging hot air balloon decorations (not for sale) and impossibly soft stuffed animals (for sale) and everything is organic.

Reid turns to me suddenly. "You're not going to quit though, right?"

"What?"

"I shouldn't have said anything."

"About there not being a lot of work to do here?"

He bites his lip.

"I love not doing work," I assure him. And it's true. Not doing much work is my favorite thing. And my other favorite things include: being around a lot of mason jars, rearranging table displays, and teasing geeky boys about their fondness for historical queens.

"Well, good."

I smile.

"Otherwise, I was going to have to bribe you with Mini Eggs," he adds.

"Wait, really?"

"Absolutely. Too late, though. That's a shame."

I give him a glare, and his dimple flickers, and hey. Looks like House Lannister Reid knows about jokes, after all.

• • •

Here's the funny part: all the way home, I replay this conversation with Reid in my head. I don't even realize I'm doing it until I arrive at my own doorstep.

Admittedly, this is the kind of thing a person might do while establishing her twenty-seventh crush. Hypothetically speaking.

But Reid isn't a crush. I don't know how to explain it, but a crush is a very particular thing for me. Like crush number eight: Sean of the Eyelashes. It was the second-to-last night of camp, the summer after eighth grade, and it was raining, so we were all watching *Wet Hot American Summer* in the Lodge. By coincidence (or fate. It felt like fate), Sean was sitting next to me. I found him massively cute: kind of short, with spiky dark hair and bright-blue eyes. And the eyelashes. At least 75 percent of Sean's body weight was eyelashes. He was sitting in one of those folding nylon camp chairs, and at one point, he leaned toward me out of nowhere to say, "This movie rules."

I agreed with this statement. And at the time, that felt cosmically significant.

I could barely catch my breath for the rest of the movie, and my heartbeat was probably making those giant zigzags. Literally all my mental energy was devoted to trying to come up with something clever and nonchalant to say to this boy—this perfect boy, whom I'd noticed around camp for weeks, who was now miraculously sitting beside me, and who had—even more miraculously—spoken to me first. But I was suddenly frozen and electrically self-conscious. My thighs felt enormous, and I was acutely aware of the waistband of my shorts digging into the fat on my stomach. It occurred to me that Sean—of course I already knew his name—wouldn't be talking to me if he knew about the shorts and the fat and the waistband.

So, I just stared at the movie screen, not really watching it.

But when the movie was over, Sean nudged me and said, "That was really cool, right?" I smiled and nodded really fast.

I never talked to him again. I haven't even thought about him in years. But as I climb the stairs to my bedroom, his face is vividly clear to me. And the mental image of him still makes my heart race.

Molly Peskin-Suso: crushing on the memory of eighth-grade boys. Am I the biggest creeper in the universe? (Check yes or hell yes.)

I sink onto my bed. So, there was Sean. And Julian Portillo, my friend Elena's older brother. Crush number eleven: Julian of the Experimental Breakfasts. That's the main thing I remember: the way he used to make these very complicated gourmet breakfasts for us in the mornings after our sleepovers. I guess I found that really charming for some reason. Even though I'm *not* a person who experiments with breakfast.

Anyway, Julian was a senior when Elena and I were freshmen, and their parents were from El Salvador, and they both had giant dimples in both cheeks. Julian had a really loud laugh, too. I kept a diary back then, and I took note of every single time he spoke to me, which was rare. Mostly because I lost the ability to speak when he was around, and I guess cute senior boys don't like speaking to walls of awkward freshman silence. Anyway, Julian ended up at Georgetown, and Elena got a scholarship to private school, and neither of them is on Facebook, so I have no idea what they're up to now. Not a clue.

But the point is, I can't talk to guys I like. Not really. My body completely betrays me. And it's a little different with every guy, so it's kind of hard to generalize—but if I had to describe the feeling of a crush, I'd say this: you just finished running a mile, and you have to throw up, and you're starving, but no food seems appealing, and your brain becomes fog, and you also have to pee. It's *this* close to intolerable. But I like it.

More than like it. I crave it.

Because there's nausea and fog, but there's also this: an unshakable feeling that something wonderful is about to happen. That's the part I can't explain. No matter how unlikely, I always have a secret shred of hope. And as feelings go, that's a pretty addictive one.

6

CASSIE BUSTS INTO MY ROOM at six in the morning, without knocking. "Yo, sleepyhead. Where's your stringy-ding? Olivia needs bead therapy."

I blink up at her. "Now?"

"She's on her way over. Some kind of Evan douchery."

Right. So here's a confession: I've never entirely understood the appeal of Evan Schulmeister. This is not just me being jealous that Olivia has a boyfriend. I think Evan's an acquired taste, but without the part where I actually acquire the taste.

"Should I get dressed?"

Cassie laughs. "For Olivia?"

Pajamas it is.

Twenty minutes later, we're cross-legged on the front porch, surrounded by magazines and scraps and scissors. I'm bleary-eyed, but it's cool and breezy and actually kind of nice. I think the whole neighborhood is still sleeping.

"So what did that dumbfuck do this time?" asks Cassie.

"He's not a dumbfuck." Olivia fidgets with a bead, tugging it up and along the string. This is a thing she and I have been working on for years: our bead strings. Mine is over ten feet long now—maybe thousands of beads. And every single bead is homemade, cut from magazine pages. All you do is cut triangles out of paper and roll them tightly around a coffee straw, starting with the wide point. Seal it with glue and maybe a layer of clear nail polish. Then you slide them onto your string and repeat. Mine's kind of an ombré rainbow pattern, starting with red, but I've worked my way up through the indigo section. Almost ready for violet. When it's done, I'm going to line it along the top edge of my bedroom wall so it drapes down like lace.

"So, okay. This isn't even a big deal," Olivia says. "It's just something he said that's kind of been bugging me."

"Not a big deal?" Cassie asks.

Olivia shrugs, smoothing glue over the end of a bead.

Cassie grins. "You texted me at five thirty in the morning."

"Ugh. I'm sorry. I'm being ridiculous."

"Livvy, you're not being ridiculous." Cassie scoots closer and hooks her arm around her. "I just don't like seeing you sad."

"I'm not sad. I'm just . . ." Olivia looks down at the finished bead nestled in the palm of her hand.

"That's really pretty," I say.

"Thanks. Yeah. Anyway, it was just Evan being weird. He was asking me a bunch of questions about waxing . . ."

"What?"

"Like Brazilian bikini waxing."

"Um. Okay." Cassie raises her eyebrows.

"Yeah. It was out of nowhere, and he kept saying he was just curious about it, and I was finally like, 'Are you trying to tell me something?'" She pauses to slide her bead onto her string. "And he says, 'No, of course not, why do you think that?'"

Cassie sighs. "Jesus Christ."

"I don't know." Olivia smiles tightly. "I really think he was just curious."

"Pretty sure he's trying to police your vagina."

"I mean, he didn't ask me to, like, get waxed."

Cassie laughs. "Uh, I'd say he hinted pretty strongly. Fuck that, though. That is so not his call."

It occurs to me, suddenly, that I've been staring at the same magazine page for the last five minutes. And it's not even the right color scheme. I feel slightly on edge.

I just honestly hate this kind of conversation. It's not that bikini waxing is a foreign concept to me, but . . . I mean, I guess it kind of is. Like, it's one of those girl habits that's so far beyond me, it makes me feel like a different species. Do boys require hairless vaginas? Is this a known thing?

Of course, the magazine I'm holding makes me think so.

Not that there's a big hairless vagina in my face. But it's one of those models with perfect shadowy cleavage. How do they get their cleavage to do that? I'm pretty sure I could drive a boat through my boobs, they're so far apart. I guess it's just this feeling that my body is secretly all wrong. Which means any guy who assumes I'm normal is going to flip his shit if we get to the point of nakedness. *Whoa. Nope. Not what I signed up for.*

It makes me never want to be naked. And it's not like I could be a Never Nude. I don't even like jean shorts.

". . . am I right?" Cassie asks.

I look up and realize they're both looking at me.

"Yes," I say. Which is probably a safe answer. Cassie usually is right.

"Ugh. I don't know." Olivia shakes her head. "Like I don't even mind the idea of it or whatever. I just don't want it to be a thing. I hate confrontation."

"Uh, clearly."

Olivia smiles shyly. "What do you mean?"

"Well, you just confirmed that you would literally rather get the hair ripped off of your vagina than deal with confrontation."

"Oh," she says. "I guess so."

"That is—nope. Just. Give me your phone." Cassie makes a grab for it.

"Cassie!"

"Are you texting him?" I ask.

"I'm just letting him know"—she starts typing—"that Olivia would be happy to get waxed if he's willing to wax his tiny, microscopic little peen at the same time. . . ."

"WHAT?" Olivia makes a violent grab for the phone. "Don't you dare hit send."

Cassie leans back on her elbows, laughing. "There's that fighting spirit."

"Fuck you," Olivia says, grinning down at her phone.

Immediately, my phone buzzes in my pocket.

Text from Olivia: luv my hairy vag!! Vag FTW!!! go wax ur butthole pls schulmeister.

I snicker, tilting my phone toward Olivia. "Oops! I think this text was meant for Evan. Should I forward it to him?"

"I hate you both," Olivia says, halfway between a laugh and a scowl.

We burn out on beads after an hour or so—and by that, I mean Cassie burns out and starts dumping the magazines back into their reusable grocery bags. But I really think the bead therapy helped. By the time Olivia leaves, she's her unruffled self, even if the situation still has Cassie amped up.

"What was that about?" Nadine asks when we walk into the living room. She's nursing Xav on the couch.

Cassie sinks down beside her. "You don't want to know."

"Is Olivia okay? I was just talking to her mama. Sounds like she's looking at art programs."

"That's definitely not what we were talking about," says Cassie.

"Evan's being a shitbag again," I say, and Cassie beams down at me like a proud parent. Must be the word *shitbag*. Cassie loves compound curse words.

"Schulmeister?" Nadine says. "What did that little fuckwipe do now?"

Come to think of it, Nadine loves compound curse words, too.

Cassie tells her the whole thing, and you can tell Nadine loves every moment of this. I don't think there's a single thing on earth that brings more joy to Nadine than throwing shade at Evan Schulmeister. She's never liked him, ever since he asked if Cassie was actually queer, or if she was trying to emulate our moms. He actually used the word *emulate*. I don't even want to remember that particular stretch of awkward silence.

Actually, I do. It was kind of amazing.

But my mind keeps drifting back to the way I felt this morning on the porch. There's so much I don't know about. And everyone else seems like they were born knowing. Things like waxing. And birth control. I know the mechanics, obviously, but how does it play out in real life? Who brings the condom? Can anyone buy condoms? Can you use the self-checkout U-Scan so there's no eye contact involved? Except—oh God—what if the machine announces it?

CONDOMS! Twelve ninety-nine! Please place your GIANT

BOX OF CONDOMS IN THE BAG. Oh, but your VALUE PACK OF CONDOMS is too big for our sensors. Please wait, and someone will assist you shortly.

"Why are you so red, Momo?" Nadine asks.

Whoa. Molly. Hey. Get your shit together.

I guess I shouldn't worry about this until I've actually, you know, kissed a guy.

7

ON WEDNESDAY, I SOMEHOW END up in the backseat of Mina's ancient but immaculate Lexus.

"I can't believe this is your car," Cassie says. "I mean, it's so cool that you even have a car."

"It was my grandma's," says Mina.

"Our grandma's not supposed to drive anymore," Cassie says. "Because she hit someone."

Mina gasps. "Are you serious?"

"Dead serious. I was with her. I mean, she was going really slowly, and the guy was totally okay. But she cursed him out and called him a bitch."

Mina laughs. "I have to meet this woman."

"She's visiting next week," I say. "You should come over."

"Okay, no," Cassie says. "Mina does not need to meet

Grandma. That is a solid nope." She grins, and I look at her, curled up in the passenger seat, her whole body turned toward Mina. She's like a flower tilting toward the sun.

"So, Molly, can I ask you something?" Mina says, after a moment, eyes flicking up to meet mine in the rearview mirror.

"Sure."

"Cass says you've had crushes on twenty-five guys."

"Twenty-six," Cassie corrects immediately.

"But you haven't dated any of them?" Mina asks.

"No," I say. I feel the usual prickle of self-consciousness.

But when Mina glances at me again, her expression is sweetly curious. "Is there a story behind that?"

"There's no story. It just never . . ." I lean back against the seat, squeezing my eyes shut.

I have this sudden memory of middle school. There was this table of boys in the cafeteria who would yell *boi-oi-oing* when hot girls walked by. Except when I walked by, they made a *womp womp womp* sound, like a boner going limp.

I remember feeling frozen. Cassie was screaming at them, and I couldn't catch my breath. I thought I was dying.

My first panic attack.

I mean, here's the thing I don't get. How do people come to expect that their crushes will be reciprocated? Like, how does that get to be your default assumption?

"Well, she doesn't put herself out there," Cassie says. "Like, at all. So, Molly's never actually been rejected, either."

"And I'm okay with that," I say. Cassie snorts.

I stare out the window. Bethesda looks so different from Takoma Park. Everything's a little quieter and fancier, and there are definitely fewer mixed-media art installations in people's front yards. But it's nice here. Some of the houses are really, really big.

"Well, what kind of guys do you like?" Mina says, slowing for a stop sign. "Other than Will."

Jesus Christ. Hipster Will. I never actually said I liked him. I don't even know if I do. I've met him *once*.

"Oh, she likes all kinds of guys. Molly's a crush machine," Cassie says. "Let's see. Noah Bates. Jacob Schneider. Jorge Gutierrez. That guy Brent from Hebrew school. The eyelash kid from camp. Josh Barker. Julian Portillo. The short guy from pre-calc. The student teacher. Vihaan Gupta. And Olivia's little cousin."

"Okay, I did *not* know he was thirteen."

Cassie grins. "Oh, and Lin-Manuel Miranda. That's a major one."

"Aww, really?" Mina says, beaming at me in the mirror. "Me too!"

"Yeah, well. Just so you know, he's Molly's currently reigning crush number twenty-six, so this may end in a fight."

I stretch forward to smack Cassie, maybe harder than I need to.

"Or a duel," she adds, under her breath, and Mina bursts out laughing.

I close my eyes again. Mina and Cassie are murmuring softly now. About something unrelated to my wasteland of a love life. So, that's good. I let my mind wander—but it keeps snagging on a single point.

Molly's never actually been rejected.

I just hadn't really thought about it like that before. But it's true. I've never been rejected. Not directly. I've never given anyone the opportunity.

I've never rejected anyone either.

And maybe that's even weirder than the fact that I haven't kissed anyone. At the very least, I'm pretty sure these things are all related. Somehow.

Cassie nudges me suddenly. "Hey, we're here."

I let my eyes slide open.

Mina's house is brick and medium-sized, with a super-gorgeous front yard. You can tell they planned in advance where the bushes would go. Mina parks in the driveway, and Cassie and I follow her down this little path to the front door. Her parents are at work. She slides a key into the lock.

Immediate first impression: everything in Mina's house looks like it's there on purpose. The walls are white, with framed family pictures placed almost symmetrically. The windows are huge and clean, so everything feels really sunny. Also, everywhere I look, there's art: paintings and sculptures and even the light fixtures. Lots of animals, especially tigers—some realistic, but mostly stylized, and it's the perfect mix of cute and badass.

I kind of want to pin this whole house to my design board.

A painting in the hallway catches my eye—maybe my favorite one yet. "Your parents must really love tigers," I say.

"Oh, that's like a Korean thing," Mina says.

"Oh geez, I'm sorry."

"Why are you sorry?"

"Okay, this is really cute," Cassie interjects. She taps the edge of a canvas-wrapped photo of Mina hugging the life force out of some goat in a petting zoo.

"Oh God," says Mina.

"I love it." Cassie steps closer. And then their fingertips almost touch. Not quite.

Makes me wonder.

Mina clears her throat. "Um. So, the boys are on their way, but we can head down to the basement. I'll leave the door open for them."

"The boys?"

She gives me this painfully knowing smile. "Will and Max."

"Oh." I blush.

We follow Mina downstairs. The basement is enormous. I don't think Takoma Park has basements like this. She walks us through it, and it's a whole other floor of the house. There's a bedroom with its own bathroom, a little mini-kitchen, and an actual sauna. But the main room of the basement is a TV room with a giant flat screen and the mushiest denim couches I've ever encountered. As soon as I sit down, I can actually feel my butt leaving an imprint. I never want to stand up.

"Can I get you guys something to drink?" Mina tucks back a strand of hair and adjusts her glasses, and she honestly seems kind of jittery. Maybe it's weird for her, having us here.

We both say no, so Mina ends up perching on the armrest of the love seat, next to Cassie. And there's this extra-drawn-out pause.

I take one of those deep cleansing yoga breaths Patty is so obsessed with: slow inhale through the nose, controlled exhale through the mouth. I think it's supposed to help with childbirth, but it actually helps me now.

Goal: don't be weird and awkward.

"So, how do you know Will and Max?" Cassie asks. "Are they exes, or . . . ?"

"Oh, God, no. Not like that. I've known them both forever."

"That's like us and Olivia," I say.

"Oh yeah! She's the tall girl with the blue hair, right? Cute, kind of curvy?"

"Yup," Cassie says, but I can't help but wince. Like, yes, Olivia is kind of curvy, and Mina didn't say it like an insult. I know it's not an insult. But I just hate when people talk about bodies. Because if Mina thinks Olivia's body is noticeably curvy, I'd like to know what she thinks about mine.

No. Actually, I would not like to know.

"Oh!" Cassie says. "Olivia wanted me to tell you she's really sorry she can't make it. She's working."

"Aww. Where does she work?"

"One of those pottery-painting places. Super Olivia-ish," Cassie says, and Mina nods.

Distantly, I hear the front door open, and someone yells, "Hello?"

"We're in the basement!" Mina calls.

The door thuds shut, and there are footsteps on the stairs. I'm definitely nervous to see the guys again. *Not* because I have a crush on Will. It's just that they're both so inaccessibly cool. And when they step into the room, it's immediately confirmed. There's just something about them that looks completely *right*. Like they're in the right bodies. Max is vaguely muscular, in an understated way, and his anime-boy bangs are actually kind of nice today. Maybe. And Will basically looks like he was born inside an American Apparel. He's wearing an old Ben's Chili Bowl T-shirt and jeans, and he still manages to look stupidly perfect. I think that's what I want. To look stupidly perfect in a T-shirt.

Also, Will is holding a beer.

There's a throw pillow beside me. I pick it up and hug it tightly.

"You guys all remember each other, right? Will Haley, Max McCone—and this is Cassie and Molly Peskin-Suso."

"What the what?" asks Will.

"It's hyphenated," Cassie says. She looks up at them. "You brought beer?"

"We stole it," Will says. And I guess I must look scandalized, because he turns to me and winks. "Just from upstairs. Mina's dad has a beer fridge in the garage."

"I can't believe your parents just let you take beer whenever you want it."

"Uh, no. But my dad is really unobservant, so . . ."

"I want unobservant parents with a beer fridge." Cassie sighs.

Mina grins. "It's actually a kimchee fridge."

"And all the normal food goes in the kitchen," adds Max.

"Oh, really?" asks Mina. "Care to explain why kimchee isn't normal food?"

"Max is like the verbal equivalent of a bull in a china shop," Will explains, settling in beside me on the couch. I can't resist sneaking a peek at him: his rumpled mess of red hair and sleepy blue eyes. He leans back and stretches, and his shirt rides all the way up, exposing his stomach—pale and flat, and dusted with light hair. I need to stop blushing. Especially because Max and Will are now exchanging what appears to be a very meaningful glance.

If it is a glance about me, I will die. *We are amused by the sad chubby girl who is clearly enchanted by our hipster beauty.*

Seriously, I will die.

I'm probably paranoid, but now I can't stop thinking about this. I get locked into this cycle sometimes. I develop counterarguments in my head. *Actually, gentlemen, I'm intrigued, not enchanted. And I'm anxious, not sad. And if you call yourself a hipster, guess what? You're not a hipster.*

Of course, it's possible the meaningful glance was about beer.

Cassie sits up straight. "Will, I hear you're an artist."

"Uh, I do photography."

"That counts." Cassie smiles. "Molly's really artistic, too."

Oh God.

"Hey, that's awesome. What do you do?" Will slides off the couch and settles onto the carpet, cross-legged, smiling up at me. I feel like a kindergarten teacher. If kindergartners drank beer.

"What do you mean?" I ask.

"What kind of art?"

I shake my head quickly. "I'm not artistic. I just like crafts."

"She makes jewelry," Mina says.

Okay, they need to fucking stop. This is so mortifyingly transparent. HEY, WILL, LOOK AT ALL THE STUFF MOLLY HAS IN COMMON WITH YOU. EXCEPT SHE ACTUALLY DOESN'T HAVE ANYTHING IN COMMON WITH YOU. SHE JUST THINKS YOU'RE HOT.

"That's not art," I mutter, burying my face in the throw pillow.

"She did all this Pinterest shit for our brother's first birthday party last month," Cassie says. "It was so cute. And she does all the decorations for our birthday parties. She did the centerpieces for our b'not mitzvah."

"Is that like a bat mitzvah?" Mina asks.

"Yeah, like a double bat mitzvah. Or, in our case, a barf mitzvah."

Mina laughs. "What?"

"Ooh. I'd like to hear this," Will says.

Cassie's eyes flick to me, and she looks suddenly sheepish. Like it just occurred to her that sharing the details of my vomitous past might not help the cause. Something tells me Will won't consider it a turn-on.

But it's too late. He's staring up at her, rapt.

"Molly, do you want to tell it?"

"I'm not telling it." I hug my knees.

Cassie shrugs. "Okay, so we're up at the bima, and the rabbi's holding the Torah. And Molly and I are supposed to undress it."

"Whoa," Will says, and he and Max smile at each other.

"What?"

"That's what they call it? Undressing the Torah?"

"Oh my God, guys, please stop." Mina shakes her head. "You're being offensive."

"I'm just asking!"

"Anyway," Cassie says, "the rabbi starts taking off the breastplate and the top thingies, and Molly's just standing there, looking, like, dead white. Like what's his name. The vampire."

"Edward Cullen," I say.

"Yes. Edward Cullen. And I'm whispering, like, 'Molly,

we're supposed to be undressing the Torah.' And she's like, 'I don't feel good.'"

"Oh no," Mina says, hand over her heart.

"But I'm like *okay, well, this is literally our bat mitzvah, so you're gonna have to suck it up.* And then I hand her the pointer . . ."

I remember this perfectly. The way the tip of the yad looked like a hand, with a tiny little metallic pointer finger. I used to think the yad was adorable. But when Cassie extended it toward me in that moment, it felt like an accusation. YOU, MOLLY, YOU. I remember the sudden sensation of bile burning the back of my throat, the tidal wave in my stomach.

"And she's like—" Cassie clutches her stomach, making gagging noises. "And she jets out of there. She runs down the stairs and out the side door, and everyone's like *oh holy shit.* It's totally silent. And then you could just hear these insane puking sounds going on for like twenty minutes."

"Okay, it was not twenty minutes."

Seriously. This. This is how Cassie's going to convince Will to make out with me.

"It was twenty minutes. And at first, we're all like, oh shit, she barfed in the lobby of the synagogue. Because, you know, we can hear it."

"Oh God," Mina says.

"But then . . ." Cassie raises a finger. "I remember." She taps her collarbone. "We're wearing microphones."

"No. Oh, Molly." Mina looks at me. "Oh my God. That is just. I'm sorry, but, can I hug you?"

I nod, and she actually slides down from her perch on the love seat. She actually hugs me. "That sucks," she says. "I'm so sorry."

"And then I chanted my entire Torah portion without missing a single syllable," Cassie announces smugly.

"Yeah, well." I wrinkle my nose at her.

"You know what I love about Jewish people?" Max says. He looks so different when he smiles. His face lights up entirely.

Mina side-eyes him. "What?"

"I love that you have your bar mitzvah in front of your parents and grandparents and everyone, and like, that's the Jewish version of 'becoming a woman.'" He leans forward, grinning. "But in *my* religion—"

"You are not religious," Mina says.

"*In my religion*," he repeats emphatically, "you become a woman by . . ." He forms an *O* with his left hand and pokes through it with his right pointer finger, again and again and again.

"Jesus Christ, Max. Stop it. I'm serious." Mina stands up.

"Yeah, that's pretty fucking problematic," Cassie says calmly.

"What?" Max looks wounded. "How is that problematic? The Jewish thing?"

"Um, let's start with the implication that becoming a woman has anything to do with whether or not you've had sex."

I have to admit, my sister is a badass. She just doesn't get intimidated by people. I don't know how to be like that.

"Ohhh, geez. Okay. I was kidding." Max sighs.

"And you know what? I'm pretty much done with this construct of 'virginity.'" Cassie does air quotes. "Which I'm sure you think applies to hetero, vaginal sex."

"You think a person can lose their virginity from oral sex?"

"Yes," Cassie says.

"Max, seriously." Mina glares down at him.

"Okay, but don't you think it depends on the couple?" Will chimes in. "It's like a case-by-case thing. Like, if oral is the endgame for a particular couple, then yeah. But if it's like a hetero guy and girl, I think there would have to be penetration."

"But why?" Cassie leans forward. "Why would that be considered more intimate than oral? Like, why do you get to decide what makes something intimate?"

I lean back against the cushions and tuck my feet up under my thighs. It's even worse than the bikini wax conversation. I feel so out of my league. I don't know. This is not the kind of sex talk I'm used to having. I'm not saying the concepts are new to me. I mean, Patty's a midwife, and she can get very specific about these things. But that's strictly informational mom stuff. And when Abby talks about sex, it's about the feelings, not the orifices. But I feel like we're jumping straight into orifices.

Will nudges me. "What do you think?"

And the whole room goes silent. At least that's how it feels.

I mean, he has to know I'm the last person he should be consulting about this. I'm pretty much the latest-blooming icon of teen purity to ever exist outside a Judd Apatow movie. Literally, the only penetration in my life involves monofilament cord and paper beads.

To be honest, I am Queen Elizabeth. I'm the Virgin Queen. And I think I know how she'd handle this conversation.

She would observe. And remain silent.

Of course, Elizabeth probably didn't have a roomful of hipster sex gods staring her down.

"I mean, I think people have this mentality that sex is only real if it involves a penis," Cassie says finally.

"Oh my God." Mina sighs. "Thank you. This is like my soapbox." She and Cassie beam at each other.

"And on that note," Will announces loudly, "I'm getting another beer."

He springs up from the carpet, and Mina murmurs something to Cassie under her breath. Then, Cassie laughs and whispers something back to Mina. And for a minute, I'm just sitting there, across from Max—who glances up at me for a moment, before deciding his phone is more interesting than I am. So maybe Max is one of those guys who only wants to befriend girls he thinks are hot (see also: guys who wear fedoras) (see also: guys who say "NO FATTIEZ").

Though maybe I'm being too sensitive. Cassie tells me this a lot.

Anyway, I feel a little better when Will slides back onto the couch beside me, lips pressed against the rim of his beer bottle like he's kissing it. He takes a quick sip, tilts his head toward me. "So, have you ever thought about doing photography?"

"Oh. Um. Not really."

"Molly, you totally should!" Cassie says. "You know, you guys should hang out and work on a project together or something."

Oh my God.

I feel sick. I actually feel sick. My sister is the least subtle person on the planet. This is so much worse than the barf mitzvah story. I don't care about the barf mitzvah story. But this.

He's going to think I want to hook up with him. That I'm in love with him. That I'm obsessed with him.

And I'm sorry, but there's a reason I'm so careful. Boys like Will don't like girls like me. And if they find out we like them, they are always cruel. Always.

I need to breathe. In through the nose. Out through the mouth.

"So, you have to hear the new Florence and the Machine album," Mina says. "I have it upstairs on my laptop. It's so great."

Max looks up, suddenly, turning to Will. "Dude, we gotta go. Come on."

"Wait, what? I want to hear Florence."

"I'm sure it's on YouTube," Max says. "And I'm your ride, so . . ."

"You're a dickhole, McCone."

Max shakes his keys—and then, to my utter surprise, he turns to me with one of those face-lighting smiles. "Need a ride to the Metro, Molly?"

So maybe I was wrong about the fedora and the no-fattiez.

"Um. Yeah. Thank you. That would be really great." I look at Cassie. "Cass, you ready?"

There's this pause.

"Um. I'm gonna stay and hear that album. Is that okay?"

I feel a tiny twinge, low in my chest. "Yeah! Yeah, totally." I pause. "So. Do you want me to stay, or . . . ?"

"Oh, no, it's fine," Cassie says quickly. "You should go."

Mina nods. "I can drop Cassie off after."

Oh.

I think this is how it happens.

"Okay, yeah!" I say again, trying to sound casual.

Suddenly, there's this pressure building behind my eyes. But it's probably just excitement or adrenaline, because I'm not a shitty person. If my sister wants to make out with this girl, I would like this makeout to proceed as planned. And if it means I have to ride to the Metro with two cute boys, so be it.

I should be excited about this, right? Not one. TWO. Two cute hipster boys.

Max leads the way upstairs, and already I know what this ride will be like. The boys will be jokey and knowing and familiar. And I will lose myself to shyness. I will be the ice cube.

Will isn't drunk, exactly, but he's sort of loose and happy. He curses Max out for making him leave, but you can tell he's not actually mad at all. Whereas Max just looks amused all the way to his car.

"So, where do you have to be so fucking urgently?" Will asks, sliding into the passenger seat. I tuck into the backseat, shutting the door quietly behind me. A part of me wonders if they remember I'm here.

"Seat belt," Max says. Will clicks his seat belt on. "If you're not buckled, we're not moving," Max explains, twisting around to check my status.

I'm buckled. I show him. Kind of funny and endearing, actually. Max is the last person I'd expect to care about seat belts. I'm not sure I understand him. I definitely don't understand these two as a unit. At first, I thought Will was essentially the alpha guy, since he talks more, but now I don't know. Because Max has this intensity. It makes me kind of nervous.

"You didn't answer my question," Will says, poking Max's arm.

"I don't have to be anywhere. I'm just following orders." He passes Will his phone.

"Oh shit," Will says.

Max laughs. And I feel like I'm missing something.

"Are they . . . hooking up?" I ask slowly.

"Well. Mina asked us to clear out, so . . . ," Max says. He starts the car and glances at me in the mirror. "Red Line okay?"

"That's great. Thanks." My head is kind of spinning.

So Mina planned this. I guess she texted Max when we were all in the room together. And now the boys and I have been exiled.

She and Cassie are probably making out right now. Literally right now.

And because I'm not a shitty person, I'm 100 percent thrilled.

8

AND NOW CASSIE'S BEING MYSTERIOUS, and it's really fucking weird.

Normally, when she hooks up with someone, she's bursting with the details. She's a kiss-and-teller. Maybe that's awful, but it's just a part of the hookup process for her. She told me once that a kiss isn't a kiss until she tells me about it. Me, specifically.

I loved hearing that.

And I guess I'm the same way with my crushes. Talking about them with Cassie makes them real.

But there's something happening, and I swear I'm not imagining it. Ever since Wednesday she's been so twinkly—smiling out of nowhere, and listening to that Florence album constantly. But she hasn't mentioned Mina. At all. And it feels wrong asking for details. I've never had to ask before.

Then I wake up on Friday to Cassie's face staring down at me.

"Oh my God," I say, sitting up abruptly.

"Wake up. Let's make breakfast."

I rub my eyelids and sweep my bangs off my face. "Give me one second."

She counts to one. If she wasn't my twin, I'd swear she was nine years old.

I have literally never seen her so bright-eyed. Her hair's pulled up high on her head, and she's wearing pink pajama pants, and I'd expect this level of bubbliness from Abby. From Cassie, it's just weird.

I follow her to the kitchen, trying to be quiet on the stairs. Our house is this one-hundred-and-two-year-old bungalow, and when you're trying not to wake your moms, it's essentially a giant booby trap. Creaky doors, creaky stairs, creaky everything—and a sleep-averse little brother with supernaturally good hearing.

Cassie's an awful cook, so I take the lead. I have to admit: I like being needed. She hooks her phone up to our little speaker, and there's that Florence + the Machine album again.

But she won't say Mina's name.

She just keeps opening and shutting cabinets, moving between the kitchen and dining room, setting out plates and folding napkins, all in this happy kind of daze. And yes, it's butt-early, and maybe she's just zoned out, but still. She should not leave me hanging. This is a flagrant violation of every code of twinship.

I'm just about to swallow my pride and become, as Abby calls it, "Mademoiselle Nosy AF"—except then Xavier ruins everything by waking up in a burst of full-volume babble. Our moms' room is above the dining room, so we can hear thudding footsteps and murmuring and the bathroom door shutting. Nadine always starts the day by nursing Xav, so Patty's the first to come down.

And it's funny: Patty's as wild-eyed as Cassie. For a moment, I wonder if Cassie talked to her first. But she wouldn't. She would never. I'm the person Cassie talks to about girls. I mean, I'm the one Cassie talks to about everything.

I think.

"That smells amazing," Patty says, smoothing my hair.

Nadine walks in with Xavier a moment later. "Holy mother of deliciousness. What is this?"

"Proof that we have the best kids in the universe."

Nadine hands Xavier off to Patty, beaming. "So you guys saw the news!"

Cassie and I look at each other. "No . . . ," I say finally.

"What?" Nadine yelps. "You people are supposed to be teenagers. Go look at the internet *right now*."

She's smiling so widely, I can't help but smile back. Something's happening. Cassie's already scrolling through her phone, and she gasps.

My phone's charging in the wall outlet. I tug the cord out and unlock my screen. "Where should I look?"

"Anywhere." Patty smiles.

"Go to Facebook!" Cassie says.

I tap into my Facebook app, and my heart skips. Scrolling through, it's all rainbows. Literally every single person on my feed is talking about the same thing.

"Is this for real?" I say softly.

"Yes!" Nadine grins up at me from across the table. "*Amazing*, right?"

I mean, I knew the Supreme Court would be voting about same-sex marriage, but I managed to put it out of my mind. I guess I didn't expect it to go well.

But—holy shit. It went well.

"It's legal everywhere. I can't believe this."

"I know!" Patty says. She glances at Nadine. "So, actually, we have some news."

"Oh my God." Cassie claps her hands together.

Patty and Nadine look at each other again, and when they smile at each other, it's like they're our age. Suddenly, I can almost picture how they must have looked when they first met. Which was years and years ago, when Patty was a grad student at Maryland, and Nadine was an undergrad. It's bizarre to think about this. I mean, there's literally nothing weirder than imagining your parents falling in love. But Patty and Nadine just keep smiling at each other.

"So, we're getting married," Nadine says.

"SHUT UP." Cassie jumps out of her seat, grinning so hard, I think her face might split apart.

"You're getting married?" I ask. There's a lump in my throat. I look over at Patty, and her face is almost completely buried in Xavier's hair. I think she might be about to cry.

"And we want you to be our maids of honor," Nadine adds.

"Holy shit," Cassie says. "Oh my God, this is so awesome. There's going to be a wedding?"

"Like the most epic, awesome wedding of all time," Nadine says. "Momo, you're our DIY girl, right?"

"Did you pick a date?" Cassie asks. "Where are we doing this?"

"This summer. Our backyard. Whatever—we're doing this." Nadine clasps her hands together. "*Finally.*"

"Finally," I agree.

It's funny. I didn't think they ever would—I guess because they could have two years ago in Maryland. But Nadine was pregnant at the time, and Patty was switching jobs, and they didn't even bring it up.

"Are you guys up for this maid of honor gig? It's a big responsibility," Nadine says. "Because I'm warning you now, we're gonna be bridezillas."

"Big-time 'zillas," says Patty.

"Oh man. I'm so excited," Cassie says. "Your bastard children are very happy for you."

"Oh my God! We won't be bastards anymore," I say.

"Aww, you guys will always be our bastards."

"Now I don't want to go to work!" I say. "We should celebrate."

"Nah, go do your thing. You gotta bring home the dough. And we'll have family dinner tonight," Nadine says.

"I'll walk with you," says Cassie.

I can't help but grin. Maybe she's about to tell me everything. Maybe things are normal after all.

Maybe they're better than normal.

It's beautiful outside. The summer heat hasn't set in yet—it's just sunny with a few cotton ball clouds. It's early, but lots of people are awake. I see our across-the-street neighbor out pinning up a giant rainbow flag, and farther down the street, someone's playing "Uptown Funk." It feels like a holiday.

"Okay, how excited are you?" Cassie asks, bouncing on the balls of her feet. "Because I'm, like, really fucking excited."

"I know!"

"Like, I didn't think I'd care this much, because it's not like they were less of a couple two days ago. But I'm just happy, you know?"

I giggle and nod.

"It's just been a really amazing week," she says, sighing.

Which feels like a door nudging open.

"Yeah, about that," I say. I feel my lips curving upward.

"Hmm." She's grinning.

"I'm just saying. I'd love to know more about some of the other amazing things that happened this week."

She laughs. "Yeah . . ."

But she doesn't say more.

I give her an elbow nudge and finally say it. "Are you seriously not going to tell me what happened with Mina?"

"With Mina?" she asks calmly.

Totally, perfectly, utterly calmly.

And now I'm confused. Maybe I misinterpreted. Maybe Cassie and Mina didn't hook up at all. Maybe I'm an asshole for assuming they did. As if girls who like girls can't be friends without falling for each other.

It's just that it seemed like they were falling for each other.

"If you were in love, you'd tell me, right?"

"In love?" She laughs again. "Uh, maybe we're getting a little ahead of ourselves?"

I stare her down. She wrinkles her nose and grins at me, and I can't help but grin back.

"I just like to live vicariously through you," I say.

"But it's the beginning of a new era," she says. "Now we live vicariously through Nadine and Patty."

"That is weird and sad."

"But they're getting *married*." Cassie sighs again. "This is the awesomest thing that's ever happened to us."

When I get to work, there's this charge in the air, even though the store isn't open to customers yet. Deborah and Ari are completely amped up.

"Molly!" Deborah calls over the music, which is maybe three times as loud as usual. "Get over here! You heard the news, right?" She's leaning next to the register, arms draped over the counter, beaming.

I get this hot chocolate feeling in my stomach—cozy and content. I love this day and I love this job. And Reid should be here any minute, too.

"Exciting stuff, right?" Ari says when I get to the register.

"Yeah!" I smile up at them. "My moms got engaged."

"Oh, sweetie, that's wonderful! I didn't even know—geez. You should take the day off and celebrate." Deborah squeezes my hand.

"No, it's fine. I like being here!"

"You are such a gem, kiddo. Are you sure?"

"Definitely," I say, nodding quickly.

Deborah smiles. "Well, that would actually be great. Reid has an eye doctor appointment, so we can definitely use you."

I feel strangely deflated. But Deborah and Ari put me in charge of a rainbow display at the front of the store, which is literally the most satisfying task I could ever be assigned. I get to pull stuff from other displays and place them in an entirely new context: a vintage red-painted teakettle, an orange ceramic owl, a yellow tablecloth, green mason jars, a blue repurposed picture frame, and (of course) an eggplant onesie from the baby section.

"Seriously, Molly. You have such an eye for this. Are your moms recruiting you for wedding décor?"

I laugh. "Yup."

"Smart women," she says. "Let me know if there's anything

from the store they can use. Or you can come over if you want and I can help you make stuff. As long as you're not allergic to cats."

"I love cats!"

Deborah laughs. "Well, we have five of them."

Which means Reid has five cats. Somehow, I'm not surprised to hear this.

Okay, so maybe this is random, but I once developed a crush on a guy for cat-related reasons. Crush number twenty: Vihaan of the Cutest Contraband. He was a trans guy from the Spectrum Club I went to with Cassie, and he always wore this hoodie with a kangaroo pouch in front. I never really thought about why. But then one day there was a kitten in the pouch. Vihaan literally carried a kitten in the pouch of his hoodie for an entire school day, and his teachers never noticed.

But when he saw me staring, he lifted the kitty out of his pouch and placed her in my arms. And our hands touched. And he looked at me with these twinkly brown eyes, like we were both in on a joke.

He had really, really, unforgettably gorgeous eyes.

ANYWAY. Have I mentioned I love cats?

I spend the rest of the morning stacking and arranging ceramic dishes and scented candles and thinking about weddings. There really is a dreaminess about today. Even our customers seem unusually coupled up. They're all holding hands. It's like a Valencia-filtered Noah's ark.

And it's nice.

Except . . . sometimes I feel like I'm the last alone person. Like maybe there aren't seven and a half billion people in the world. Maybe there are seven and a half billion and one.

I'm the one.

Though I have a theory. Kind of a fucked-up theory. But it's been poking around my brain since the day Mina and Cassie hooked up. Or didn't hook up.

This is going to sound weird, but I think I need to be rejected.

I think I need it like I need a flu shot. Or like those therapists who make you hold snakes until you're not afraid of snakes anymore.

I don't even know if that makes sense.

But I spend a lot of time thinking about love and kissing and boyfriends and all the other stuff feminists aren't supposed to care about. And I *am* a feminist. But I don't know. I'm seventeen, and I just want to know what it feels like to kiss someone.

I don't think I'm unlovable. But I keep wondering: *what is my glitch?*

My moms are getting married. My sister might be secretly hooking up with someone. Abby moved to Georgia and got a cute, guitar-playing boyfriend within months. Even Olivia and Evan Schulmeister made it happen. They actually met in the camp infirmary. The girl had pinkeye, and she *still* had more game than me.

And all these couples wandering through the store right now—the guys holding hands while they flip through cookbooks. The pair of grandparents asking Ari for recommendations in the baby section. It's not like they're all epic hotties with six packs. They're just normal people.

But I can't seem to get there.

And I can't shake this thought: I've had crushes on twenty-six people, twenty-five of whom are not Lin-Manuel Miranda. Twenty-three of whom are age-appropriate, real-life, viable crush-objects. Eighteen of whom were definitely single and interested in girls at the time of my crush.

And I never even tried. Not even with the ones who talked to me first.

So, maybe I should let my heart break, just to prove that my heart can take it. Or at the very least, I need to stop being so fucking careful.

9

ALL THE WAY HOME, I'M breathless just thinking about it.

Operation be less careful

Operation stop worrying about rejection

Operation it's good for me

I can't decide if I should tell Cassie about my revelation or not. It's not like it changes anything. She's still going to try to push me together with Hipster Will. And she's still going to be mortifyingly unsubtle about it.

I guess the only difference is I'm going along with it.

I hear Nadine and Cassie clanging around the kitchen, laughing and murmuring and opening drawers. I guess Nadine's pretty serious about tonight being a family dinner. I mean, we usually eat dinner together, but every so often it's a Family Dinner, which basically means cloth napkins and the meal being planned out ahead of time. Probably most people go to restaurants for this kind of thing, but we haven't done that much since Xavier was born.

I head down to help. Nadine's in the kitchen, squirting juice all over a chicken, and Cassie's stirring a bowl of something. So, I set the table, and we all settle in, and Nadine lifts a glass of champagne. "All right. Here's a toast: To us. To marriage. To a totally awesome Peskin-Suso wedding in the very near future."

We all toast. With champagne, because our moms are cool like that. Except for Xavier, because our moms are not that cool. Xavier toasts with milk.

"So, we're thinking mid-to-late July."

"Of this year?" I ask.

"Yup." Patty smiles up at me. She's cutting chicken into tiny pieces for Xav.

"You can't plan a wedding that fast."

They are nuts. I'm sorry, but it's true. You need to sample cakes and order your dress and plan your décor. Which takes time. I'm serious. And then you have to talk to caterers, photographers, florists, seamstresses, deejays, and a million other people.

I may know a little too much about this. I may be a little more familiar with wedding blogs than your average single seventeen-year-old girl.

"Why not?" Patty asks.

"Because." I shake my head. "You just can't. You have a lot to get ready. You need at least a year."

"Momo, I think you're thinking of the royal wedding."

"Okay, first of all, Will and Kate weren't even engaged that long."

"Good. There you go," Nadine says. "Will and Kate. That's how we roll."

I start to protest, but Patty smiles up at me. "Sweetie, we're just doing a backyard wedding. Mostly family."

"Oh, right."

"But you guys can bring friends if you want."

"What about dates?" Cassie asks.

"Ooh—do you have something to tell us, Kitty Cat?" Nadine grins and Patty presses her hand to her heart, and their expressions are just like they were on the night of our barf mitzvah, when Cassie slow-danced with Jenna Schencker.

"Okay, please don't make that face. You guys are as bad as Molly."

"We created Molly," Nadine says. "We made her bad." She leans forward, brushing my bangs aside.

"So tell us about her," Patty says.

Cassie bites back a smile.

"What's her name?"

"Mina."

"What's she like?" Nadine asks.

"Awesome."

"Yeah, I got that. But, okay. If this is your first real girlfriend, Kitty Cat, I'm gonna need details."

Cassie raises and wrinkles her eyebrows. "I didn't say she was my girlfriend."

"She's not?"

"All I'm saying is that I met her."

Nadine smiles. "And she's awesome."

"And she's hilarious and cool and pretty and kind of hipster, but not *too* hipster," I chime in, "and I like her."

"Oh, so Molly's met her." Nadine turns to me. "Hold up. Now I really want the details."

"Well, Cass hasn't told me anything," I say, and it comes out sharp. I don't mean for that to happen, but it does.

I feel suddenly off-kilter, like my limbs don't know how to act. I guess I'm the tiniest bit pissed off. Because it kind of feels like Cassie's teasing us. She wants us to know something happened with Mina. She just doesn't want us to know what. It's like those people who post vague, attention-grabby Facebook statuses.

Whoa—something HUGE is happening this wknd, LOL!

cannot believe u would do something like this. i will never forgive u, God will never forgive u, u will probably burn in hell but no hard feelings!!

Cassie and I live for these statuses. I just never thought she would become one of these statuses.

"You'd like her," Cassie says finally. "She's really cool and funny, and she knows a lot about music. And she loves fish. Not like to eat. Like as animals. She's really into aquariums," Cassie adds. "She has a French angelfish tattoo. Did you know the

French angelfish is monogamous? Oh, and she likes penguins. Mina likes all monogamous animals."

"Sounds like she's a romantic," Patty says.

"I guess so."

When I glance up, Cassie's looking at me with an expression I can't read.

And now I can't sleep. Not even close, though it's practically midnight. Cassie's hanging out with Mina at some party.

I feel so twitchy and strange and too hot and too cold. I'm reading my phone in bed, trying to ignore this suffocating feeling, but it's not working. I feel like I'm drowning in it. I sit up, suddenly, and then I stand up all the way. Because this is stupid. This is ridiculous. I'm taking my laptop, and I'm going downstairs.

I'm extra quiet in front of Xav's room, and I do my best not to creak on every step. There are yogurt-covered raisins in a container on the kitchen counter, so I bring them to the couch. But I don't even feel like watching TV. I don't feel like doing anything. I don't even know what I need right now. I just want to feel normal.

I open my computer and start clicking through some of the wedding blogs, most of which are very hazy and twinkly and dreamy and rustic. And I have to admit, it's soothing. Just something about the taste of yogurt raisins and professional photos of pies arranged on bookcases. We should definitely do pies on bookcases, and also one of those do-it-yourself photo backdrops. Maybe something simple, like a patterned piece of fabric and some distressed wooden picture frames. I should probably start pinning this stuff.

"Momo? Why are you still awake?"

I look up, and it's Nadine, wearing pajama pants and a T-shirt and this striped robe thing. She's disheveled and sleepy looking, and she keeps poking at the corners of her eyes. I must have woken her up.

"I'm sorry."

"Honey, what's up?" She gestures for me to scoot down on the couch, and she slides in next to me. "What's . . . are you looking at wedding blogs?"

"Possibly."

"Man, you're hardcore." She reaches out to tuck my bangs away from my eyes. "Hey. You okay?"

"Huh? Yeah."

"Mmmhmm."

"Mom, I'm fine."

She's quiet for a moment. And then she stands up. "Come on. Let's go for a drive. You and me."

"What?"

"Yup. Let's go. I just need some coffee."

"Um, it's midnight."

"Correct."

"I'm wearing pajamas."

"So am I." She grins down at me. "Momo, come on. Stop making the Molly Face. Just trust me."

It feels entirely surreal to be wearing pajama pants and sneakers, walking out to Nadine's car at midnight like we're sneaking out of the house. It's warm, even this late, and there's that buzzing insect sound that Patty says is cicadas. Nadine opens the car with her clicker, and I settle into the passenger seat. And then she backs out of the driveway extra slowly, like she's worried about pedestrians, but the streets are totally empty.

"Where are we going?"

"You'll see." She's staring straight ahead, one hand on the steering wheel, one hand on her coffee mug, but she's grinning. I relax into my seat, taking everything in—the streetlights, the porch swings, and the way my neighbors' houses seem to loom in the darkness. The Applebaums' cat stares at us through their living room window like the little creeper he is. And then he runs to another window to try to keep up with us. But we keep driving, onto Piney Branch, onto 16th Street. And we're quiet, but it actually feels nice. We're almost at Adams Morgan by the time Nadine finally says something.

"So. How are you doing, kiddo?"

"Good," I say.

She shakes her head. "You are such a little faker."

"What?"

"It's weird, right? Cassie having a girlfriend."

"She's not technically her girlfriend."

Nadine grins. "I give it a week."

That makes me laugh, but there's also this sad sort of tug in my chest.

"Yeah, it's weird," I say.

"I know. Oh man, Momo. This is a tough one." She nods, still looking at the road. "You know, growing up, my brother was such a dickwad, but your aunt Karen and I were really close. And I remember this. I remember when she got a boyfriend, and she just fell off the grid. It sucked."

"Yeah."

"And no one warns you about this. No one tells you how hard it is, because, yay, love! And we're so happy for them! But there's this sharp edge to it, right? Because yeah, you're happy for them. But you've also lost them."

My heart twists. I can't speak.

"But Mo, they come back to us. You know? You roll with it. It's weird for a while. But they come back. You'll get her back."

I tuck my knees up and stare out the window. We're almost at Dupont, heading downtown. And there are so many people out. There's this palpable energy in the air. It's the kind of night where strangers start hugging and everyone's drunk and loud and happy just to be in the middle of all of this. I bet people will remember today, even when they're old. I bet I will, too.

"Pretty wild," Nadine says.

"Yeah." I nod. And suddenly, I feel like crying, but not in a bad way. More like in the way you feel when someone gives you a perfect present—something you'd been wanting, but thought you couldn't ask for. It's that feeling of someone knowing you in all the ways you needed to be known.

"Hey," she says softly. "Look."

I look up, straight ahead, and I recognize it immediately from five million Facebook posts. It's the White House, lit up with rainbow lights. And it takes my breath away. Even though it's far away, even though we'd have to pass a million cars to get close to the actual house. I don't even think it's the front of the building. But still.

"Really cool, huh?"

I nod, feeling choked up.

"Just wanted to see it in person," she says.

"I'm so happy about it," I tell her. Suddenly, it feels so important to say that. "And I'm so happy about the wedding."

"Well, good. Because we need someone trolling wedding blogs at midnight."

"Oh, I'm on that." I smile. "But seriously, I'm just so glad this is happening."

"Me too," Nadine says, turning left onto a one-way. "You know what I think?"

"What?"

"I think this is going to be a really great summer for our family."

"Me too," I say, and I try to believe it.

10

BUT HERE'S THE PIECE I can't quite shake.

Nadine said they come back. That we'll be normal again. Cassie and me. And I get that. I mean, Abby came down to earth after Darrell. And Nick hasn't ruined us. Love doesn't kill friendship. It definitely doesn't kill family.

Except it sort of does, doesn't it?

Because we almost never see my aunt Karen. Because she's not Nadine's main person anymore. I think she used to be. But Nadine's main person is Patty.

And I don't know when that happened. Maybe this is how it starts.

Anyway, somehow Mina's coming for dinner on Wednesday, despite the fact that my grandma's coming in from New York that day. Patty's mom. Also known as the grandma who hits people with her car and then calls them bitches. So, I'm pretty sure this is going to be a shitshow. Like, a major, epic shitshow. But even though Cassie gave this plan a solid nope a week ago, today she seems really Zen about it. It's like she's so focused on the Mina-coming-for-dinner part that she's forgotten all about the with-Grandma part.

The thing about Grandma is that she doesn't always have a filter. So this should be interesting. I'm in charge of dessert.

I spend all weekend thinking about it, looking up recipes, and waking up at three in the morning wondering if Mina has gluten allergies or diabetes. Though there's no way Cassie would have forgotten to mention this. I'm pretty sure there's nothing Mina-related in the world she's forgotten to mention.

But oh. I'm so wrong.

Because on Monday, I get an Abby text with about five million exclamation points. No words, no emojis: just undiluted punctuational excitement. And at first I assume it's some new development with Nick, which throws me for a loop—because once sex has already happened, what could be worthy of five million exclamation points? Like, I don't think that's how she'd break the news if she were pregnant. I hope not.

Anyway, I figure it out pretty quickly when Abby follows up with, Why didn't u tell me about Cass?!?!

What are you talking about?

Um. Go check Facebook. Now.

So I tap into the app and go straight to Cassie's page. Which she never updates. Ever.

But she did.

In a relationship. With Mina Choi.

I cradle my phone in my hand and just stare at it.

She seriously didn't tell you? Abby writes. WTF is wrong with her?

No idea, I write.

She didn't tell me. Cassie's in a real-life relationship with Mina, and she didn't tell me. I found out on Facebook.

I'm Cassie's twin sister, and I found out on Facebook.

Do your moms know??

No idea, I write back. But she's coming for dinner on Wednesday.

Whoa. Cassie! Introducing her to the folks . . .

And grandma . . . I add.

OMFG. Your grandma Betty?

Yep. I add that emoji with the big, toothy, grimacing smile.

LOL. Should be quite a night.

Which makes me smile, a little bit.

I decide to make homemade edible cookie dough. When I tell Reid about it at work, he seems both impressed and confused.

"But how is regular cookie dough not edible?" he asks. We're in the back room, unboxing new inventory.

"Well, it has raw eggs."

"Oh, okay." He nods—but a moment later, he frowns. "And you're not supposed to eat raw eggs . . ."

"Reid, no!"

"I mean, I know you're not supposed to eat them *raw*, but what if they're mixed in with stuff?"

I side-eye him hard. "You know they're still raw, right?"

"I know, but they're neutralized by the other ingredients."

"That is not how eggs work." I bite back a smile. "I think you just have to try the egg-free kind. It's really good. I promise."

He leans backward on his palms and seems to consider this for a moment. Finally, he nods. "Okay. I approve."

"Whew." I stretch forward, pulling the last box toward me. We actually timed this well—we'll get the last stuff unboxed right at the end of the workday.

"So when is this happening?" he asks.

"Tomorrow, probably? I'll make a supply run to CVS when I leave here."

"To CVS?" He looks scandalized. "No, you have to go to the Giant in Silver Spring. It's the all-time best grocery store."

I look up. "Oh, really?"

"Yes." He gives one of those very serious Reid nods, but his dimple flickers.

"Is it on the Metro?" I ask.

"Oh. I don't think so."

I bite my lip. "Oh, okay. I don't have a car."

Reid is quiet for a minute, and I feel slightly awkward. It's funny: I don't really mind the car thing. I think it bothers Cassie more than it bothers me. But now I feel weirdly self-conscious about it, and I have no idea why.

"Do you want a ride there?" he asks.

"You don't have to do that."

"I don't mind. Seriously, it would be fun. I like grocery shopping."

"Really?" I shoot him the Molly Face.

He smiles. "Okay, not really. But I like cookie dough. And if I drive you to the supermarket, you'd probably have to give me some."

"Probably," I agree. Now I'm smiling, too. I can't help it.

So now I'm in Reid's car, and he's driving me to the grocery store. A very particular grocery store. Apparently the best grocery store, and I'll have to take his word for that.

An immediate perk of riding with Reid: he's placed a bag of Cadbury Mini Eggs open between us in front of the gearshift.

"You know what I love about Cadbury Mini Eggs?" I lean back against the seat. "Their simplicity."

"Right? No one appreciates that."

"I'm really over fancy desserts. Like, I'm sorry, but anything with citrus infusion and caramelized kumquats or almond and Cointreau, or anything like that . . . I mean, does anyone actually like that stuff?"

He laughs. "Nope."

"They just think they're supposed to like it because they're trying to look classy."

"Trying and failing," says Reid.

"Utterly failing."

We pull into the parking lot of Giant, and Reid picks a spot by the cart return. Then he twists off the ignition and looks at me with this solemn expression. "Are you ready for the grocery experience of a lifetime?"

"Well, I'm pretty sure I've been here before."

"But not with me," he says firmly.

"Not with you." I feel suddenly shy.

It occurs to me, as we're crossing the parking lot, that people probably assume we're a couple. Like maybe we're a college-age couple grabbing food for the night. Young lovebirds. Boyfriend and girlfriend. It's like when someone mistakes the random guy sitting next to you on the Metro for your dad.

There's a line of carts near the entrance, but as soon as I ease one out, Reid tugs the front end and guides me over to a bench outside the store. Then, he pushes the cart to the side and sits, looking up at me expectantly. I sit down next to him.

"So, now you need to take out your phone."

"Why?"

"You'll see." He pulls his own phone out of his pocket. "And get into your notes app."

"Okay." I'm smiling. He's being kind of bossy, and I'm sorry, but it's hilarious. It's like when your teacher leaves the room for a second and puts a Well-Behaved Kid in charge. Reid is a Well-Behaved Kid on a power trip, and it's so cute, I have to play along.

"You got it?" He peeks over my shoulder. "Good. Now write down the titles of three pop songs from the early 2000s."

"What? Why?"

"Because those are the rules."

"So I just write down . . . any pop songs?" I ask.

"Yup. But choose wisely."

I pause for a moment, finger poised above my keypad. I want to pick the absolute worst ones. I want the ones that almost ruined music. They come to me quickly.

1. Stacy's Mom
2. Sk8er Boi
3. I'm Not a Girl, Not Yet a Woman

"Excellent," Reid says.

"Let's see yours." He tilts his phone toward me, and I burst out laughing. Because in another life, I'm pretty sure Reid was someone's dorky dad. He even looks proud of himself.

1. Find me in da club
2. The one with the girl playing the piano singing about if she could fall into the sky
3. Justin Timberlake

"So now what?" I ask.

"Good question. The rules are as follows: if any one of your songs gets played, you get twenty points."

"If the supermarket plays them?"

"Yes."

"So, out of every song in the entire world, you think this supermarket will play one of the six random songs we happened to choose."

"Absolutely."

I laugh. "Why?"

"It's magic." He shrugs. "And because all grocery stores play early 2000s pop music. It's federal law."

I'm skeptical until the moment we walk into the store and "Stacy's Mom" is playing.

"Oh hey. Twenty points to me," I say.

Reid groans, leaning into the cart handle. "Beginner's luck." He eases the cart down the baking aisle, and literally makes it three steps before getting distracted by tubs of frosting. "Ohhh. Hey." He picks up some Duncan Hines chocolate. "Oh man. I would sit and eat this with a spoon, like yogurt. Is that weird?"

"Is that a real question?" Seriously, I want to know: is there anyone who *wouldn't* eat a tub of chocolate frosting like yogurt?

All of a sudden, I'm inspired. "Can I add a rule to our game?"

"Definitely!"

"Okay." I grin. "Quick challenge. Ten points to whoever

finds the grossest flavor of frosting in the next minute, starting . . . now."

I set the stopwatch on my phone, and we both fall silent. I'm feeling very competitive, for some reason, which isn't like me at all. Maybe this is what it's like to be Cassie. She used to win all the competitions at camp: hot dog eating, pig latin speaking, watermelon seed spitting, and all the other things I never really cared about.

But I care about this. I want the ten points—these ten nebulous points that count toward literally nothing. And it's exhilarating. I scan the shelves, and almost everything is pretty standard: home-style chocolate and Funfetti and cream cheese. There are a few contenders, like coconut pecan and key lime, but in the end, I have to throw my shade at Betty Crocker's Limited Edition maple bacon. Not okay, Betty.

Reid is flailing at the forty-five-second mark. "Molly, help! They all look good."

"You are joking."

"Maybe I just like all frosting?"

I shake my head sadly. "I don't even know what to say to that."

My phone stopwatch beeps, and I reveal the maple bacon—which Reid hadn't noticed. "Oh, that's really funny," he says.

"I know. I have to take a picture of this for my sister."

He laughs. "Will you send it to me?"

"Um. Yeah. If you give me your number." I feel my cheeks

grow warm. I hope he doesn't think I'm Asking For His Number. I don't *think* I'm Asking For His Number.

I'm just asking for his number.

"Oh, right!" He gives it to me, and I text him the picture and add him to my contacts.

Then he pulls out his phone to add me to his.

It's funny, but I almost wonder if he wanted us to exchange numbers. Because he totally could have snapped his own picture, instead of having me text mine.

For a second, I'm speechless.

But I'm saved by Avril Lavigne. "Sk8er Boi" starts playing, loudly and suddenly, and I finally exhale. "Twenty points," I say, grinning.

"What? How are you so good at this game?"

I shrug, palms up. I become the shruggie emoji.

"I'm psychic," I say.

God, this phone number thing. Not that it's a thing. It's definitely not a thing. And I don't know why I'm suddenly so breathless. I guess lungs are giant traitors. As are stomachs. As are heartbeats.

There's traffic on the way home, but it's still light out, and there's this quietness between us. In the supermarket, it was all jokes and teasing and games (which I destroyed, by the way—fifty points to zero). But in the car, I'm suddenly shy. And I think Reid is too.

"So you have a sister?"

"Yup." I nod. "A twin."

"Really?" He sounds surprised. Have I never told him about Cassie? But I guess when we're at work, we talk about random stuff. We talk about the things we like, rather than the things we are.

"We're fraternal," I add, because it's the first thing people ask.

"What's she like?"

"Cassie?" I pause. "I don't know. She's totally fearless."

"I don't think anyone's actually fearless," Reid says. And then he clicks on his turn signal, even though we're a block away from the turn. Even though the traffic's so thick, we're barely inching forward. It ticks like a metronome.

"Yeah, maybe," I say, and I smile. Because I remember the look on Cassie's face when she told me Mina was pansexual. When she knew she had a chance, but wasn't sure how things would go. Maybe she was a little scared. I guess she didn't need to be.

Then I remember the Facebook status update, which is starting to feel less like a gut punch and more like a joke. I mean, it's funny. Reid would probably think it was funny. And I should definitely say something funny right now.

"You want to hear something weird?" I ask.

"Always."

"Not like Tolkien weird."

"Okay, Tolkien? Is not weird," he says. "He's probably the most basic fantasy author you could have picked."

The funny thing is how much I want to tell him about Cassie. Not just about the Facebook thing and the funny parts, but about the other stuff too. About this strange, tiny shift between Cassie and me. I just have this feeling he'd understand, even though I have no reason to think that. Even though two minutes ago, Reid didn't know Cassie existed.

"I mean, if you want *weird*," he continues, "let me know, because—"

"Uh, no," I say, and I smile a little bit. I feel clenched up inside.

"So, Cassie just started dating her first actual girlfriend. And guess how I found out."

"How?" he asks, and I love that he doesn't bat an eye at the word *girlfriend*. Not that I expected less from a Takoma Park boy, especially one related to Deborah and Ari. But still.

"From a Facebook status update."

His eyebrows knit. "Oh."

"Yeah."

He pauses.

"How was she supposed to tell you?" he asks finally.

"Well, not from a status update."

I have this immediate sinking feeling. I don't know how I wanted Reid to react. I don't know why I even care about Reid's reaction. But something feels off. I'm not sure why I thought this would seem funny or cute. It's just awkward, and kind of sad. I turn quickly toward the window.

"Molly?" he says after a moment.

"Yeah."

We're stopped at a light now, and I feel him watching me, trying to decide if he should say something. I stare at my wrists, at my bright rows of friendship bracelets. I taught Abby how to make them in the spring before she left, and we both still wear them, always. But thinking about Abby right now gives me this little prickle of sadness.

Because she's in Georgia. And Cassie has a girlfriend. And everything and everyone are moving at a million miles an hour.

"You shouldn't have had to find out on Facebook," he says finally.

I shrug.

"I'd be sad about that, too," he adds.

And oh. There's a lump in my throat. That's another thing about me. If someone says I'm sad, or asks me what's wrong, or tells me not to cry, it's like my body hears: NOW CRY. Like a command, even if I'm not actually sad. But maybe there are always tiny sad pieces inside me, waiting to be recognized and named. Maybe it's like that for everyone.

"Anyway, it's fine," I say quickly, forcing a smile. "Obviously, I'm really happy for her."

"Oh. Okay." He looks confused. And I really wish I hadn't said anything. Now he thinks I'm a shitty sister. And a shitty person. And an all-around asshole.

I don't know why I'm incapable of shutting up around this boy.

11

I WAKE UP BEFORE SUNRISE on Wednesday, feeling jittery. My mind will not simmer down. It's just jumping from one thought to another.

I mean, there's Reid. And his glowing white sneakers. And his surprisingly low standards for frosting.

And there's Cassie. And Mina. And the Facebook status update. And the cookie dough. And the fact that Mina's coming when Grandma's here. The inevitable shitshow.

I try to hypnotize myself by staring at my ceiling fan, and when that doesn't work, I scroll through wedding inspiration blogs on my phone. But I can't focus. Finally, I just take my pill and head down to the kitchen, and I start pulling out my ingredients. You never think you'll be spooning egg-free cookie dough into tiny mason jars at five in the morning, until you are.

I've just gotten them into the fridge when I hear Xav babbling upstairs. I actually love being the one to get Xavier out of bed. I slip into his room, and when he sees me, he pulls up on the crib railing and does this bouncy little dance. Baby twerking.

"Hi, buddy." I scoop him into my arms, and he cups my cheek, grinning.

"Momomomomomo."

"That's right!"

Let it be known that Xavier is the actual cutest baby in the universe. He has these huge brown eyes and big, mushy cheeks, and the softest brown skin, and a little gap between his front teeth. He's perfect. I always loved the idea that we share DNA, even if it's on the donor's side. Maybe there are a bunch of mutual ancestors drinking ambrosia and spying on us right now.

"Hey, baby," I whisper into the crook of his neck, and he scrunches up and giggles. I hoist him onto my hip and carry him downstairs. I figure I'll set him up with his activity center in the living room and let my moms sleep in.

Except Nadine wanders down a few minutes later, yawning and smiling. "Well, look at you two."

"Oh, did we wake you up?"

"Aww, Momo, no. It was the boobs." These days, Nadine talks about her boobs like they're sentient beings. They're always waking her up or leaking through her nursing bras or demanding to be drained, like cows on a dairy farm. They have their own boobish agendas.

I pass Xavier to her, and she lifts up one side of her pajama shirt. Xav glomps right on. "So, I heard this rumor," Nadine says, sitting up straight against the back of the couch.

"About Cassie?"

She grins.

"How did you know?"

"The mom chain."

Otherwise known as Olivia's mom. Olivia tells her mom everything. And her mom tells my moms everything. It's a pretty foolproof system.

I settle onto the armchair with one of Xavier's toys. It's one of those interactive button-pushing ones that sings animal songs in an unnervingly chipper male voice.

"God, that thing needs to burn," says Nadine.

"We should burn it."

"Yeah, but you know another one will just spawn in its place. That's right, Xavor Xav," she adds. He's popped off the boob to grin at her. "Hey. Hey. We're spraying. Get back on there."

"I made cookie dough," I tell her.

"For dessert tonight?"

I nod.

"That's what you were down here working on?"

I nod again.

"Momo, you know you need to sleep every once in a while."

"I couldn't."

She tilts her head. "Aww, honey."

"I'm fine," I say quickly.

"Are you working today?"

I shake my head.

"Okay, well—oh, now we're vibrating." She scoots forward and gropes around for a minute under her butt. "I think I'm sitting on your phone." She pulls it out and hands it to me. "You're getting texts like crazy. Look at you, Miss Popular. Who's texting you at seven in the morning?"

"Um, probably Abby?"

But when I glance at my phone, there's this tiny hiccup in my chest.

I've missed two texts from Reid.

Need any help making cookie dough?

And by making, I mean sampling

Xavier's still on the boob, but he swings his arm back to make a grab for my phone.

"Nice try," I tell him.

Nadine snorts. "The kid wants an iPhone."

Okay, I feel like a jerk, because now I want Nadine and Xav to leave, so I can write back to Reid. It's funny, because Cassie texts girls at the table and in the living room and in the car, and everywhere. I honestly think she'd coordinate an orgy in front of all of us. On the couch between Nadine and Patty. As long as they're not actively reading over her shoulder, she doesn't care.

But I can't text a boy in front of my moms. I just can't. Not even Reid.

"So, Mina and Grandma tonight." Nadine yawns. "How the hell did that happen?"

I laugh. "I don't know. I think it was Mina's idea."

"Cannot believe Kitty Cat's allowing it."

"Maybe Grandma will be cool?"

"Mmmhmm, right." Nadine grins. "I'm excited to meet this girl, though."

"Yeah, you'll like her. She's—" My phone buzzes again, and I try to ignore it. But I've lost my train of thought. Sometimes not looking at my phone requires all my mental energy.

Maybe it's Reid again. Not that it matters.

Xavier finally finishes his boob, and Nadine readjusts her top, standing. "Okay, I've got to take this little dude to the supermarket before storytime."

Nadine never misses storytime in the summer. Patty says it's because whenever Nadine did baby stuff with Cassie and me, people assumed she was our nanny. Which I imagine is a shitty thing to hear when you're a mom.

As soon as they leave, I tap into my texts, and my heart feels like it's skipping. My body has no chill whatsoever.

There are the two cookie dough ones from Reid.

And the new text. From a Maryland number, not in my contacts. It says, simply: What's up. No question mark. Just two words, plus that little emoji with the dancing bee ladies.

So now I'm curious. A text from a mystery person. But it's got to be someone I know. I don't think you're allowed to drop the bee ladies on a stranger.

I Google the number, but Google doesn't know, and I feel dumb asking who it is. So I ignore it.

I mean, I try to.

Anyway, I still need to think of something to write to Reid. And it has to be funny and casual and badass. But it can't seem like I'm trying too hard.

I type: Too late. Dough is already made and sealed away. Sunglasses smiley emoji.

Though I may be able to part with some . . .

For a price.

Right away, three dots appear. And a moment later: For a price, huh?

And suddenly, I'm mortified. I don't know. It's just hitting me how that sounds. *For a price.* Like it's a sex thing. It reads like I'm flirting with him.

Fuck.

Must neutralize awkwardness immediately.

I accept payment in Mini Eggs.

I'M SO THERE, he writes. Where are you?

There's this prickle in my stomach. Seriously, this body. No chill.

I'm home, I write back. And I carefully press send.

Honestly, I wouldn't mind if he came over. I don't think that's weird. I mean, he's my coworker. We've been grocery shopping together. And he dropped me off here on Monday, so I guess he knows where my house is.

He doesn't write back.

But maybe he's on his way. He did say he was so here.

I should stop staring at my phone. I should probably relax. I probably shouldn't picture Reid standing in my doorway with his ridiculous sneakers and his cute almost-dimple.

I don't know why my mind keeps going there.

I try to empty my head. I put my phone on the end table. Patty talks a lot about mindfulness and being fully present in the moment, but that's actually really hard for me. I think I have a wandering kind of mind. When I'm able to rein it in, it's a pretty cool feeling—it's like, just for a minute, I stop wanting things. I didn't even realize how much time I spend *wanting.* And yearning, and crushing, and aching. It's like I have this perpetual sense that something's missing.

I keep turning my head toward the door.

It's a little ridiculous, but I think I'd really like him to show up.

Before I can stop myself, I open my chain of messages with Reid.

Wait, are you coming?

Three dots. He's typing.

Coming where?

So, he was kidding. And now I wish I hadn't said anything. I feel awkward and stupid. I try to play it off. To claim the cookie dough I originally saved for you but then totally just ate myself.

He writes back immediately with a very tearful series of emojis. I'm actually sort of surprised he does emojis.

Anyway, I don't care. I'm not going to care. I'm going to lean back on my hands and be very mindful about this.

I do not care.

I do not want.

Hours later, Cassie's completely freaking out.

"Oh my God. Where are they?" She has her whole face pressed to the window, much like the Applebaums' cat. Outside, it's raining so heavily, it seems to come down in waves.

"Probably stuck in traffic," Nadine says. "Rush hour and airport and rain, Kitty Cat. But they'll be here."

Cassie huffs into the living room and collapses onto the couch, and I sink down beside her.

"It's gonna be fine, Cass."

"Yeah, well, I really need Grandma to get here before Mina."

"Why?"

Cassie raises her eyebrows. "Because you know she's going to say something racist, and I need to, like, intervene before it happens."

I laugh. "Intervene how?"

"I don't know. Tell her not to say anything racist."

"She's going to anyway. She's Grandma."

"Yeah. Fuck." Cassie sighs. "What do I do?"

"I mean, it's not like it reflects on you. Just talk to Mina. Give her a heads-up."

Cassie leans back, laughing bitterly. "Right. *Hey, Mina. My grandma is probably going to act like you don't speak English, or tell you about the Chinese lady in her building, or something really awesome like that.*" She covers her face. "Fuuuuuck."

"Hey."

She slides one hand off her face and peeks up at me.

I hook my arm around her shoulders and hug her. "Gonna be okay."

She exhales. "I know."

"This is a good thing, right? You have a girlfriend. She's coming to dinner."

I try to say it nonchalantly, but my voice seems to snag.

Cassie rolls her head toward me. "You're pissed off that I didn't tell you."

"No I'm not!"

"That is such bullshit." She smiles.

"I was *surprised* you didn't tell me."

"And pissed off. Look, I get it." She leans into me. "I know I'm an asshole."

"No you're not."

"This is just weird for me, you know? And talking about it

is weird. It's fucked up. Like, it's so easy for me to tell you about some random hookup, because who cares? And we can laugh about it and whatever."

"You know I'd never laugh at you about Mina, right?"

"No, I know. It's just." She shuts her eyes. "Like, I don't know how to say this without sounding like a dick, but, like, maybe it's one of those things you're not going to understand until you get a boyfriend."

For a moment, it just hangs there.

"Oh," I say.

"Okay, that came out wrong, but you know what I mean."

"Yup," I say, standing abruptly.

I mean, it's pretty clear. Cassie's had a girlfriend for two days, and now she's the expert on the wonders and mysteries of true love. Whereas I clearly understand nothing. I guess I'm some kind of naïve, sexless child.

"Molly, come on. I'm sorry, okay? I told you it came out wrong." She sighs. "Can you give me a break? Just this once?"

Suddenly, her phone buzzes on the coffee table. A text. She picks it up.

"She's here!"

"Grandma or Mina?"

But already, Cassie's sprung off the couch and out the front door, running through the rain. There are only a few yards between our door and Mina's car, but Cassie's soaked within moments. She doesn't seem to care. She slips into the car on the passenger side, and they lean toward each other over the gearshift.

I blush and turn away.

Patty and Grandma pull in about thirty minutes later, and then we all settle around the dining room table. And the first thing Grandma says is this: "Cassie, you didn't tell me your girlfriend was Oriental!"

"Grandma!" Cassie hisses. She shoots Patty a desperate look.

Patty winces. "Mom, you can't say that."

"I can't?"

I shake my head.

"Grandma, Mina is Korean American," Cassie says. "Okay? You can't say Oriental."

"Unless you're talking about rugs," I add.

"Well, they just keep changing the terminology on me." She laughs. "Mina, dear, I hope you don't take offense. It's so nice to meet you."

"Nice to meet you, too."

Mina definitely looks overwhelmed.

Nadine brings out this giant turkey—the kind you roast for Thanksgiving. It's the kind they always label *young turkey*, which makes you wonder how epic old turkeys must be. Everything gets passed around, and I feel strangely self-conscious. I think it's sympathetic self-consciousness. I think I feel it on behalf of Cassie. Or maybe Mina. God. Poor Mina.

"So, you live in Bethesda?" Nadine asks. "That's a fun place."

Mina smiles faintly. "I don't know if I'd call it fun."

"Mom, fun is like H Street," Cassie says.

"Not true," Nadine says. "Fun exists wherever you make it. Am I right, Xavor Xav?"

Xavier is currently mashing a slice of peach into his hair.

"He looks a lot like you," Mina says, looking back and forth between Xav and Nadine.

"Aww—thanks," Nadine says.

"Told you," Cassie says. "He's her mini-me."

People notice that all the time. Xavier looks so much like Nadine, and Patty's old pictures look exactly like Cassie. I'm the oddball. I secretly think I must look like the donor, but I've never seen a picture of him. Of course, Grandma always says I look like her. I don't exactly see it, but she loves to bring it up.

And sure enough: "You know, Molly is the spitting image of me at seventeen. But, of course, I was very thin at that age."

She loves to bring that up, too.

"I used to be a model for Macy's department store. Can you believe it?"

"Oh, wow," Mina says.

"And I always tell Molly: you're a little zaftig, of course, but you have a lovely face. Isn't she lovely?"

"Definitely," Mina says, nodding, but Patty says, "Mom, stop it," in this warning tone. So, Grandma makes a big show of snapping her mouth shut and winking at me.

And I think I might cry. I might actually cry. I can't believe I'm sitting at this table, pretending things are normal while my grandmother calls me fat. Right to my face. I know what *zaftig* means. She's even called me that before. But saying it in front of Cassie's gorgeous new girlfriend makes it a million times worse.

"You know, my friend Sylvia's granddaughter is at Columbia," Grandma says quietly, leaning in close. "She's a beautiful girl. Her name is Esther."

"That's great."

Grandma rests a hand on my elbow. "In New York. You know, Columbia's in Manhattan, dear. And in New York, they have this exercise program. I think it's on the DVD. And Esther just puts it on and does it right in her dorm room."

"Okay."

"She just loves it."

I nod slowly. I think every cell in my body freezes in place. I notice Cassie and Mina are listening in.

"You should think about it, mamaleh. You know. I'll tell you what I wish someone had told me," she says. "It gets harder and harder to lose."

Grandma does this sometimes. Half the time she's totally cool, and half the time she makes me want to disappear.

"When you're young, it's easy," she continues. "Just be a little more careful. Leave half of everything on your plate. And you should talk to Esther! She really loves her program. You know, she lost twenty pounds?"

"Okay."

"And now she has a boyfriend."

Cassie swallows a chunk of turkey and drops her fork with a clatter. "Yeah, no. That's not okay."

My cheeks are burning. "It's fine."

"It's not fine." She raises her voice. "Grandma, stop saying this shit to Molly. You can't. I'm sorry. You can't talk to her like that."

"Molly doesn't mind, right?" Grandma says, patting my arm.

"I don't mind," I say.

"Yes, you do," Cassie says quietly.

And I do. It's seriously stupid, but I do mind. It's just that every time Grandma says this stuff, I freeze up.

But now Nadine and Patty have caught wind of the conversation. "Mom, stop it. We've talked about this."

"I'm just trying to be helpful."

"This isn't helpful."

"Patricia, it's a health issue. You know that."

"Betty," Nadine says, setting her fork down. She glances at Patty.

Cassie presses her foot against mine under the table, but I can barely process it. I feel hot and cold all at once. It's hard to explain.

I mean, I know I'm fat. It's not a secret. Kyle Donner used to whisper the word *gorda* in my ear every day of eighth-grade

Spanish. And once, Danielle Aldred asked me if I was worried I'd crush a guy during sex. In seventh grade. She actually asked that.

So, I should be used to it. Still, it always throws me a little bit when people say stuff about my body. I guess I want to believe no one notices I'm fat. Or that I'm somehow pretty and fat all at once, like a Torrid model. I don't know.

Anyway, Cassie's still fuming, and Mina's staring awkwardly at her plate, and now Patty is escorting Grandma into the living room. I can't hear what she's saying, but I can hear snippets of Grandma's replies. *Small portions. Something to think about.*

"Let's pretend that didn't just happen," Cassie says, shaking her head.

"Want to help me clear the table, Momo?" Nadine asks.

I nod and start stacking plates. Nadine wraps me in a one-armed hug as soon as I step into the kitchen. "Hey. You okay?"

"Yeah."

"That was some pretty fucked-up shit from Grandma. Don't even listen to her, okay?" She shakes her head. "Let it roll off your back."

Mina starts bringing in plates and dishes, even though Nadine tells her to go relax. But she insists on helping. It's that dance people do. Like when I was little, and we'd go to restaurants with our relatives, and Nadine and Uncle Albert would argue over the check. Abby and I thought it was the funniest thing. Our parents would go back and forth, more and more insistently, and *MY GOD. YOU FREAKING GROWN-UPS. IT'S A FREE MEAL. LET IT HAPPEN.* But I get it now. Maybe I'm more of an adult than I realized.

Cassie follows behind Mina, holding Xavier. "So, Molly made us cookie dough in mason jars," she says. She opens the fridge to show Mina.

"Oh my God. You made these?"

I smile shyly.

"Aren't they so cute?" She sets Xav down, holding his hands up while he toddles. "Like, if it was me, I'd have put a big glob of it in a Ziploc bag and been like *here you go.*"

"It was super easy," I say.

"This is literally the greatest dessert I have ever seen," Mina says, looking awed.

We end up carrying all the jars and a bunch of spoons into the living room, and I feel my cheeks go red when I see Grandma. Like, now I'm supposed to eat dessert in front of her. Though there's a part of me that wants to plant myself beside her and make her watch me do it. Dare her to say something.

But it's cool to see how excited Mina is about the cookie dough. Sometimes it's so easy, I almost feel bad. Honestly, the secret to impressing people is this: individual portions, packaged in mason jars. I even remembered to leave room on top for vanilla ice cream.

I squeeze all the way up against the armrest of the couch to make room for Cassie and Mina. Except it ends up being pointless. They kind of perch there for five minutes, until Cassie says she has a book she needs to find for Mina.

Funny how this task seems to require both of them.

Even funnier how they come down half an hour later, with no book.

I'll be staying in Cassie's room for a few days until Grandma goes home. We actually used to share this room. Cassie never got rid of her bunk beds, so when we have houseguests, I reclaim my bottom bunk. It's like stepping back through time.

But, of course I can't sleep. Again. My mind won't stop churning. I fluff up my pillow and stare at the underside of Cassie's bedframe. Which is still lined with glow-in-the-dark animal stickers. And probably decade-old boogers. I wasn't the classiest child.

I roll over, and the bed creaks, and I hear Cassie sigh.

"Molly, go to sleep."

"I'm trying."

"Try harder."

For a moment, we're quiet.

"I know you're still awake," she says.

"So are you."

"But I have an excuse. I'm lovesick."

I draw up into a sitting position, cross-legged beneath my blanket. "How do you know I'm not lovesick, too?"

"Wait, what?" She swings her torso down over the side of the bed, peering at me, upside down.

"I'm kidding."

"No you're not. Oh my God. He texted you, didn't he?"

"Who are we talking about?" I ask, trying to sound nonchalant. But my heart starts fluttering wildly.

I don't know how she knows Reid texted me. Unless she's actually talking about the mysterious dancing bee ladies.

"So here's the thing," she says. It's dark, but I can see her twist of a smile. She whips her head back up, but moments later, her feet dangle over the side of the top bunk. She pushes off with her arms and lands neatly on the ground in a crouch.

There's a ladder. She never uses it.

Another fundamental difference between us.

"Mina and I *might* have given Hipster Will your number."

"What?"

"Oh man. I really thought he was going to text you." She sinks onto the end of my bed, tugging her pajama shorts down. "He wimped out, huh? What a dipshit."

"I don't . . . understand."

"Molly, this is part of the mission. The boyfriend thing. I told you. We're making this happen." She shakes her head. "I can't believe he didn't text you."

I blush. "Um. I think he did."

"WHAT?"

I push my bangs out of my face. "I don't know. I got a text from a random number. But I didn't know who it was."

"Holy shit. What an idiot. He didn't tell you it was him?"

I shake my head.

"What did he say?"

"I don't even know if it was actually him." I paw around the floor for my phone and tug it out of the charger. "Here."

I pull up the text and hand her my phone.

She laughs. "Yeah, that's Will. He sent you the bee ladies?"

"Apparently."

"Oh my God. I'm dying. I have to tell Mina." She rubs her cheeks. "That's so fucking great. You should write him back."

"And say what?"

"Anything. Seriously, it doesn't matter. You just have to keep it going. She leans back against my pillow and sighs. "I love this. I'm dating Mina, and now you're going to date her best friend."

"Um, I don't think that's happening." I feel warm. I must be utterly, inhumanly red right now.

"Look. I'm just saying he's a good target for our boyfriend mission, okay? I really like him for you. He's sweet, he's cool, he's artsy, and he has great taste in music. And he's cute, right?"

"Yes," I say softly.

"And he's Mina's best friend."

"I know."

"We always said we were going to marry best friends," Cassie says.

"You and Mina are getting married? Wow."

"Fuck you. You know what I mean." But she's blushing.

"I'm just saying. He's Mina's friend. That's very convenient for us. And I really think he likes you, Molly."

I shake my head. "No he doesn't."

"Okay, you know what's fucked up?" She looks me straight in the eye. "That you don't even seem to think that's a possibility."

Well, I don't.

But I do.

I mean, I honestly don't know.

12

AND NOW CASSIE WON'T STOP talking about it. The Will thing. She's being a little too hardcore. I know for sure she's consulted with Abby, Olivia, and Mina. It's really pretty embarrassing. It would be nice if I were the kind of person who didn't require a battalion of wingwomen to make this happen.

I just feel like I'm a really defective girl in some ways.

So, now I'm wearing this black top I got a couple of weeks ago, with an empire waist and a black lace overlay. I've worn it before, though always with a camisole underneath and a cardigan over. Except Cassie has forbidden both the camisole and the cardigan. And she pulled me into the bathroom for smoky eyeshadow, and then Olivia made my hair wavy, and the attention of them dressing me felt strange. But not bad.

"You look *so* pretty," Cassie had said. "Doesn't she look so pretty?"

And Olivia paused for a moment, before agreeing. "Yeah, you really do."

I felt this warm, happy flutter when she said that. And when I glance at myself in the window of the Metro, I actually think they're right. I look okay. I look better than okay. I feel strangely brand-new.

We get off at Woodley Park and cross the bridge to Adams Morgan, and Mina and the boys are already waiting for us in front of the bar. Will is holding a man-purse. But he's more pissed off than I've ever seen him. "Okay. This. This is ridiculous." He runs a hand through his hair and huffs. "Since when is there an age limit for music?"

"It's a bar," says Cassie.

"But it's not about the booze," says Will. "It's about the *music*."

"Look, I get it."

"Why doesn't *he* get it?" Will stabs a finger in the general direction of the bouncer and, honestly, growls.

"Whatever. Fuck him. You can still kind of hear it out here," Cassie says.

"Not the same."

"Here. Drink." Cassie reaches into her purse and pulls out a thermos, passing it to him.

"What's this?"

"Lemonade," she says.

Will sips it and turns to her, grinning.

"With peach schnapps," she adds.

"I want." Mina reaches for the thermos. "And I want Jumbo Slice," she adds, smiling extra contagiously.

Twenty minutes later, I'm packed tightly onto a wooden bench with Cassie, Mina, and Olivia, and I'm holding the most epic slice of pizza. And a Coke. And the boys are sort of hovering over us. There's this couple a few yards away gazing at each other really intensely, and Max is pretending to narrate their thoughts. And Cassie and Mina are trying to seem casual about the fact that they're holding hands, but their expressions are like sunshine through window shades. I feel happy. And a little lonely. But they're cute. And it's nice. I can't explain it. I guess it's this feeling of *rightness*. Like I'm saying the right things, and I'm in the right place. Like I'm the right person.

I wonder if that even makes sense.

I lean over to whisper to Olivia about it, but then there's a nudge on the toe of my flat.

"Hey," Will says. "You never wrote back to my text."

"Oh. I didn't . . ."

He laughs. "I'm just kidding. It's fine."

"I didn't know it was you," I say.

Cassie snickers, and I realize she and Mina are both listening.

"Well. Now you know." His blue eyes meet mine, and I feel myself blush.

I clear my throat. "Is there any more schnapps?"

As it turns out, Will's man-purse is full of fifty million

miniature bottles of booze. No more schnapps, but he dumps an entire tiny bottle of rum into my Coke.

"Um, okay, that's . . ."

Cassie leans over to steal a sip. "Wow, that's strong."

To be honest, I don't have much to compare it to—I don't think I've ever had more than a sip of anything. I'm not supposed to, with my pills. But I just need something tonight. I need to not feel like myself for a minute.

I'm wavy hair Molly. Cardigan-less Molly. Rum and Coke Molly.

"I think the street is tilting," says Cassie. "Do you guys see that?"

"Oh," Mina says, "you are not sober."

"Nope." She nudges her head into the crook of Mina's shoulder.

My head's a little fuzzy, and my chest is warm, but it's a cozy feeling. I like it. And when I look up, I see that Will is watching us and smiling. Oh my God. I could sit for five million hours and analyze the angles of his smile.

"Are all of you drunk?" he asks.

"Maybe," I say. But out of the corner of my eye, I catch a glimpse of Olivia, who suddenly looks like a kid dragged to a cocktail party. She's shuffling her feet on the edge of the bench and fidgeting with her napkin.

I turn toward her to say something, but Cassie flings an arm around me. "Drunk Molly. I never thought I'd see the day."

"I like Drunk Molly. She's cool," Will says.

"I know, right?" says Mina.

"Need a refill?" Will asks.

And Cassie gives me this look like she wants to mention the Zoloft.

I ignore her.

"Yeah, okay," I say, and Will tilts his head and smiles down at me. He has a really bright smile. And I kind of like the way he's looking at me. I can't believe this messy-haired hipster boy in skinny jeans is looking at me like that. I feel this little surge of adrenaline or attraction or alcohol or something. It makes me nervous.

"Why are you making zombie faces?" he asks.

"What?"

"Just relax!"

"Zombies are relaxed."

He laughs. "You are so freaking funny."

I feel like this conversation is spinning too quickly, but maybe that's a good thing, and when I look up at Will again, his smile is smaller but better. More intimate. And I'm blushing so hard, I think my face is burning off.

So, maybe Cassie was right about the cardigans, and maybe this is how it happens. Maybe this is actually happening. But I don't see how it could be. Because Will is so cute and so cool, and I'm just me. And I'm way out of my depth. It's like trying on a dress that doesn't quite fit.

"I'm telling you. It's on," Cassie whispers. Except it's not really a whisper. Because, oh my God. Drunk Cassie. Is so fucking loud. I'm 100 percent positive Will can hear her, and Max can hear her, and all of 18th Street can hear her and probably people in Antarctica can hear her. If there even are people in Antarctica. Are there people in Antarctica? Maybe a small settlement of explorers. I feel like Reid would know this. I have no idea why I think that. And I don't know why I'm even thinking about Reid. Especially when I'm sitting in the glow of Will Haley's tiny sunbeam smile.

"I like him so much," Cassie adds, not so quietly. "He's your best crush yet. I approve. Team Will."

"Cass. Stop." I cut my eyes toward her. I feel so self-conscious. I feel like I'm naked on a giant circular stage with an audience extending out to infinity in all directions. It's a little unbearable. More than a little. "Yeah, I think I'm gonna go," I say.

"What? No!" Cassie says. "Don't leave. I'm not ready."

"You can stay. It's fine."

"And you're just going to Metro home by yourself?" Cassie asks. "Molly, you're drunk."

"So are you."

She stares me down.

"I'll go with her," Olivia says, after a moment.

Cassie narrows her eyes at both of us, but I know she's not going to argue. She wants to stay too badly. "You better text me when you get home," she says, squeezing my hand.

"Sure," I say, trying not to laugh. Because the protective sister thing is cute, but I'm pretty sure Cassie's not going to be sitting here waiting for my text. It's probably hard to check your phone when you're suctioned onto Mina's face.

"We'll leave soon, okay?" she says. "I'll see you at home."

Another thing I'm not sure I believe.

The farther we walk from Adams Morgan, the more Olivia relaxes. "Sorry. I'm just feeling kind of off tonight," she says as we approach the bridge. "I think I just need to get home and into pajamas, so I can Netflix and chill with Titania."

Titania. The dog.

I press a hand to my mouth. "Olivia, you cannot Netflix and chill with Titania. That does not mean what you think it means."

"Wait, I'm confused," she says.

"I think you Netflix and chill with Evan," I say, letting my eyebrows explain the rest.

"Oh."

"Yeah."

"I mean, I just want to watch Netflix." She looks slightly traumatized.

"I know. Oh God. Me too."

And it's true. Even hearing the word *Netflix* has a way of centering me. Netflix means not having to suck in your stomach or think of anything smart or adorable to say. It means a whole night of not wondering what people think about you. No alcohol, and no flirtation, and no confusion, and every organ calm and settled.

Perfect.

Exactly what I want.

Except there's this tiny, perverse part of me that wants to run back down 18th Street to hear Will Haley say I'm so freaking funny. Even though that's the quickest way to unsettle my organs. And it's the literal opposite of Netflix. But that's me. I always want opposite things.

"Um, Molly?" says Olivia. "You're sort of zigzagging."

"Oh! Oops."

"You sure you're okay?"

"I'm totally okay."

"Okay . . ." She bites her lip. "Hey, do you mind if I call Evan really quickly? I want to catch him before he goes to bed."

Here are the facts about Evan Schulmeister: he falls asleep at ten thirty, with earplugs and a retainer, and wakes up at five to run three miles. Every day.

"Totally, totally fine," I say. I think I'm saying *totally* a lot. I'm totally saying totally a lot. This must be a special feature of Drunk Molly. Just like regular Molly, but with 150 percent more *totallys*.

Olivia pulls out her phone and walks a few steps ahead of me, and I take my phone out, too. My head feels funny: light and spinny and wobbly, but my brain still works well enough to text.

Abby what are you doing rightt now? I really really kiss you!!!

Haha miss you not kiss you, I add.

And now I'm walking along the bridge, and Olivia's still talking to Evan—even though she's seeing him on Sunday. I mean, she's literally driving up to Pennsylvania to see him in two days, and she's still cradling the phone like every second on the line is precious stolen time.

That Evan Schulmeister.

So I just amble along behind her, pulling out my phone every few seconds to see if Abby's written back. Which she hasn't. I text her again.

ABBY MY LOVE WHERE ARE YOU?

Then, I almost bump into someone. But I feel my phone buzz, finally. And it's Abby! Except it's not actually Abby, because the text says: Hey! Sorry—this is Simon. Abby fell asleep. Want me to wake her up?

Oh, hi Simon!!! That's okay

This is her cousin Molly btw

I check the spelling a few times. I don't want to be incoherent, Drunk Molly for my first conversation with Simon. THE Simon. Abby's new best friend. My replacement. HAHAHAHAHAHAHAHAHAHAHAHA.

Ha.

Yeah. It's not funny.

Hi, cousin Molly! Simon writes.

I can't believe she's asleep already, I say.

I KNOW! She fell asleep watching Harry Potter. Side-eye emoji.

I write back frantically. WHAT? That is the worst. She is the worst

She's a squib, he writes. Which makes me smile all the way to Woodley Park.

Olivia doesn't hang up until we step onto the escalator, and she's quiet for a few minutes. She's always like that after talking to Evan. I think it takes her a minute to shift back to the regular world. Probably because he's such a sex god. REIN IN YOUR HOTNESS, EVAN SCHULMEISTER. For Olivia's sake. For *the world's* sake.

But we get on a train almost right away, and we even get a seat together. It's a miracle. It's the neighbor guy from *Kimmy Schmidt* saying *it's a miracle*. It's that miraculous. Except I think I need to vomit, and that's probably not allowed. Not on the Metro. Not on Olivia. I breathe in and out until the wave of nausea passes.

Just a few more stops.

I keep replaying the night in my mind, trying to make sense of it, and my hand trails across my breastbone. All that skin. Patty calls it "décolletage." It's kind of a sexy thing, even though *sexy* isn't a word I usually associate with myself. But I kind of felt like that tonight. I actually think Hipster Will was flirting. With me.

The train passes Rhode Island Avenue, and Olivia tucks her knees up and rests her chin on top of them. Which is a pretty impressive position to assume in a Metro seat, especially when you're six feet and change. She tilts her head toward me and smiles. "So, Will texted you?"

"Um. Sort of?"

"How do you sort of text someone?"

I close my eyes and lean back. "I don't know. Well, I think Cass and Mina forced him to."

Olivia giggles.

"No, I mean it," I say. "I'm pretty sure Cassie made Mina harass him until he did it."

"So Cassie forced Mina to force Will to text you."

"Exactly."

Olivia's tiny smile. "Yeah, you might be overthinking this."

But here's the thing Olivia doesn't get. I'm not trying to overthink things. I'm trying to be less careful. But you have to be your heart's own goalie.

And if I'm going to be rejected, I want to see it coming.

13

I WAKE UP TO MY phone buzzing: four texts from Abby.

Were u drunk texting Simon on my phone last night?!

And I'm not a squib!!!!

(What's a squib??)

Did u seriously get drunk?

I can't move yet. I stare at my light fixture. I've never noticed this, but it's collecting a thin layer of dust. And a bulb is burned out. I should fix that, eventually. Maybe when I'm slightly less catatonic.

But I really should get out of bed. It's the Fourth of July. That's actually a pretty big deal in our neighborhood. There's a parade, with papier-mâché animal heads and clowns and entire floats dedicated to composting. That is a thing here: moving platforms decorated to honor decayed perishables.

Cassie's rustling in the bunk bed above me. "Oh hey," she says finally, her voice thick with sleep. "You up?"

"Kind of."

She laughs. "Me too. Ughhh. Last night was . . . something."

I'm scared to know what she means by that. Maybe something happened after Olivia and I left. Maybe Drunk Cassie evolved into Drunk-as-Fuck Cassie, or even the ultimate Shitfaced Cassie.

I don't even want to imagine what Shitfaced Cassie might have said about me to Will. Shitfaced Cassie is not known for her carefulness.

I squeeze my eyes shut and try to think of something neutral. Anything. My Fourth of July outfit: a pale denim shirtdress over navy leggings with white stars. And I don't care if anyone side-eyes me for wearing leggings in July, because I am not here for chub rub. Also, they're very patriotic leggings.

But then Cassie shifts, and the bed creaks, and I'm nervous all over again. I feel like the two negative ends of a magnet. Like there are parts of me that can't come together. If Cassie did say something to Will, I want to know. But also, I *never* want to know.

"Hey, so I invited Mina to the parade and fireworks and stuff," Cassie says suddenly.

"Oh, okay."

"Are you cool with that?"

I sit up slowly. "Why wouldn't I be?"

"Because . . . I don't know." I hear her yawn. "I know that's usually our thing."

And it's true: normally Cassie and I watch the parade together. And yes, under normal circumstances, the idea of Mina tagging along might bother me a little. But I'm so preoccupied by boy drama right now that it barely even registers.

It occurs to me that this may be exactly why Cassie wants me to have a boyfriend in the first place.

She hoists off the top bunk a moment later, sliding in beside me under my blanket. "Anyway, you and Will were so cute last night."

"Um. Okay." I hug my knees.

"For real. He was totally flirting with you. Mina gave him so much shit after you left."

"What did she say to him?" I blurt.

Cassie just smiles, and I feel this wave of quiet panic.

"Cassie! What?"

"Oh my God. Stop worrying!"

"Why are you smiling?"

"Because you actually like this guy, and it's so fucking cute. Crush number twenty-seven, right?"

"I don't have a crush on Will."

Cassie laughs. "Okay."

"Wait. Did you tell him I did?"

"Molly. No. Stop freaking out."

"Okay."

And for a moment, she's silent.

"But, like, okay. Real talk," she says finally. "This boyfriend thing. Do you actually want this to happen?"

"I don't know. I guess so."

She rolls her eyes. "That's a yes. And that's great, okay? You're allowed to want this."

I bite my lip.

"But at some point, you have to put yourself on the line. You know?"

Okay. I know she's right. I mean, my brain knows it. But I can't seem to get the rest of me on board. It's like trying to hold my breath. There's this protective thing inside of me that opens my mouth, unpinches my nose.

"I know," I say.

"Like, say Will knew you were interested. What's the worst that could happen? He'd reject you? So what? You move on to crush number twenty-eight."

Move on. So what.

But there's this awfulness that comes when a guy thinks you like him. It's as if he's fully clothed and you're naked in front of him. It's like your heart suddenly lives outside your body, and whenever he wants, he can reach out and squeeze it.

Unless he happens to like you back.

I don't want to third-wheel it with Cassie and Mina, so I end up going to a parade-watching party near the Dance Exchange with my moms. And Xav. And Grandma. Wild times. It's hosted by these people Nadine knows from baby group, so the party is full of babies.

I am seventeen years old, and this is my social life.

Xav immediately starts climbing on some other baby's stroller, and my moms and Grandma drink lemonade on the front steps. All the adults are super relaxed. There are boobs out all over the place, and half-naked toddlers with foam pool noodles, and cloth diapers everywhere. I recognize a few of the adults, who seem to know I'm one of Xavier's sisters, but don't know which one. I don't think they actually care which one I am. They mainly seem interested in where I'm applying to college.

I mean, maybe I should start carrying flyers with my list of schools, ranked by preference. Or maybe—*maybe*—these random adults should reflect on why they give a shit in the first place.

"Hey," Nadine says, catching my eye. "You okay?"

"What?"

"You seem, like . . . kind of surly."

"I'm feeling kind of surly."

"Okay, well, now you're smiling," she says. "Way to ruin it."

But she's right: I am surly and moody and not quite myself. This must be a hangover thing. Or a Cassie-making-my-brain-hurt thing. Either way, I am clearly unfit for human company right now. But then I glance across the street, just in time to see Reid step onto the sidewalk.

Reid Wertheim. Here, of all places. And he looks as surprised to see me as I am to see him. I cross the street to greet him. "What are you doing here?"

"I live here." He points to a little blue bungalow.

"No way." I grin.

He grins back, and for a minute, we're both quiet. But my heart beats really quickly, and it's actually kind of nice.

"So, what are you doing here?" he asks.

"I'm, uh." I glance across the street at the party house, and of course, Patty, Nadine, and Grandma are all watching me. BREAKING NEWS: MOLLY IS SPEAKING TO AN ACTUAL BOY. TUNE IN NOW AS THE STORY UNFOLDS. I mean, at least my moms have the dignity to glance away when I catch them. Grandma gives me a thumbs-up.

I turn to Reid quickly. "Want to take a walk?"

"Oh. Sure!" He does this flush-cheeked kind of smile. "But I have to be back at the store in about forty-five minutes. I was just grabbing lunch."

"Wait, I don't want you to miss your lunch."

"I don't care. I'd rather walk around with you. Really."

Oh. My heart is pounding. Why is my heart pounding?

We walk up Maple, and I feel tongue-tied. Not even tongue-tied. I mean, my tongue isn't the problem. It's my brain. It's like this:

Me: Hey, brain. Let's think of something cool to say!

Brain: UHHHHHHHHHHHHH.

Me: Okay, it doesn't have to be cool. Just something semi-coherent . . .

Brain: UHHHHHHHHHHHHHHHHHHHHHHH.

Me: COME ON, BRAIN, GIVE ME SOMETHING.

Brain: *white noise*

Shit. Shit. Shit.

"Hey, how'd the cookie dough turn out?" Reid asks finally.

"Oh!" I laugh. "I actually did save you some."

"Really?" His eyes light up behind his glasses.

"Really! And it came out awesome." Finally, finally—something unlocks in my brain, and I'm me again. "I think it tastes better than regular cookie dough. The consistency's slightly different. But in a good way. You'll like it."

"I know I will."

"We can grab it right now, if you want. It's just at my house."

Which is two blocks away. I live two blocks from Reid.

I have to admit, there's something quietly thrilling about this. I'm bringing a boy to my house. For cookie dough purposes. Totally platonic. But still. A boy. My house.

"You know, I didn't put this together before," Reid says, following me through the back door, "but I actually walk by your house sometimes with my cat."

I smile up at him. "With your cat? Like on a leash?"

"Yeah, it has a little harness thing on it. But just the gray cat. Elefante." He shrugs. "The other ones aren't into it."

"I can't believe I've never noticed you walking a cat in front of my house."

"Maybe I should stop wearing my invisibility cloak."

I laugh and head toward the kitchen. "So, the cookie dough is in the fridge. Do you want vanilla ice cream on top?"

He tilts his head. "Do I?"

"I think you do." I open the fridge and dig it out from behind Patty's extensive Greek yogurt collection.

He beams when he sees it. "You put my name on it?"

I did. Which, of course, necessitated a very brief trip to Facebook. *Not* to stalk. Just to confirm the spelling: *Reid*, as opposed to *Reed*. But yes, Reid Wertheim has a Facebook profile. And yes, Reid Wertheim is Single. Not that it matters. I just happened to notice.

"Oh, right—you need ice cream," I say quickly.

"I'm pretty sure I'm about to be ruined for all other food, Molly."

And I'm about to make a wiseass comment about Mini Eggs, but there's a sudden burst of laughter from upstairs. I'm so startled, I almost jump. I definitely thought Reid and I were the only ones home.

But then I hear Cassie's voice, and Mina's low, husky laugh, and oh.

OH.

And all I can think is this: DEAR GOD. PLEASE LET THIS NOT BE SEX. Is that even a thing? Daytime Fourth of July sex? Because I'm pretty sure I won't survive overhearing sex in the presence of Middle Earth Reid.

I look at him. He looks at me. And then I hear the familiar

creaking thud of Cassie's footsteps on the stairs. She and Mina appear in the kitchen doorway moments later.

Fully clothed. Holding hands.

"Whoa. I didn't know you were home," Cassie says.

"We just got here."

"Aww, Molly, you look so cute and patriotic," says Mina. And then she looks up at Reid. "Oh hey!"

Reid looks startled. "Hey, Mina."

I look back and forth between them. "Wait, you know each other?"

Reid nods. "We go to school together."

Cassie peers up at him. "But I don't know you."

"Oh. This is Reid," I say, trying to sound casual. Which shouldn't be this difficult. This should be an effortlessly casual situation. "And this is my sister, Cassie."

"Ohhhh. You're the guy from work," Cassie says.

There's this hanging pause, during which Reid nods, and I blush, and Mina looks at Cassie, and then the freezer starts beeping. So, I shut it quickly, and pass the ice cream to Reid.

Super casual.

Though now Reid knows I've mentioned him to Cassie. Which is pretty great. Let's just add him to the list of guys who now think I'm obsessed with them.

"Anyway, Olivia's meeting us at the cheesecake place," Cassie says. "Come with us."

"Right now?"

She nods. "Put some ice cream in there, and let's go."

Reid has to go back to work, but he walks with us up Tulip Avenue, hugging the jar of cookie dough to his chest. He and Mina end up talking about this teacher from their school, and I'm still kind of thrown by the fact that they know each other. It's not like I mind. But it's this little shift in my head.

And I guess it kind of sucks that he seems to have forgotten about me. I mean, maybe this teacher they're talking about is a really interesting person. None of my teachers are that interesting, to be honest.

But when we get to the cheesecake bakery, Reid turns to me suddenly. "Okay, well," he says, and his hand hovers close to me, like he's about to rest it on my shoulder. Or maybe he's about to hug me.

Maybe.

It would definitely be cool if my brain could keep functioning right now.

But there must be a force field around me, because Reid whips his hand back and wraps his hands around the mason jar like a baseball bat.

"Cool. Well. I guess I'll see you at work," he says, waving briefly. Then he grips the mason jar even tighter and starts walking toward town.

"I can't believe you work with Reid Wertheim," Mina says, pushing through the door of the bakery. She holds the door for Cassie and me. "I've known him since first grade. He's so sweet."

"Just like someone else I know," Cassie says, grinning and elbowing me. Because that's the word I get, too. *Sweet.* I'm pretty famous for it, actually. Every yearbook I own is filled with: *Ur the sweetest. Stay sweet.* Sometimes spelled like "sweat."

"He's kind of cute," Cassie adds. "What's his deal?"

"Reid?" Mina asks.

"Yeah, like is he single?" asks Cassie, and my whole body goes on high alert.

I mean, Reid's Facebook profile said Single. Capital *S* Single. But maybe he's one of those people who never updates his profile. Not that it matters.

"Oh my God, this place is cute," Mina says, peering up the staircase at the front of the bakery.

"Right?" Cassie says, taking the steps two at a time. Mina and I follow her up.

"So, this is literally a cheesecake bakery," Mina says, laughing. "How did I not know about this?"

"I guess you should hang out here more or something," Cassie says.

"I guess you're right." She smiles. And Cassie threads their fingers together, just for a minute. Probably no one even notices but me.

I look quickly away, eyes on the display cases. WHAT'S UP, CHEESECAKES? I'M JUST GOING TO STARE AT

YOU FOREVER. Because when a tender moment happens between any two people, I turn into an eleven-year-old boy. It is my most consistent talent.

I don't think I've ever been so happy to see Olivia show up.

We order some cheesecakes and bring them to a table. "So, wait. Back to Reid," Cassie says, leaning toward her. "We still need the info on him."

I could hug her.

Not that I care. I'm just curious. But still.

"Right," Mina says. "Well, he's definitely single. Oh God. How to explain Reid . . ." She tilts her head. "Like, he's one of those Ren Faire guys. Season pass, full costume."

Olivia smiles. "Aww. I love Ren Faire guys."

"Yeah—I don't know. I'd say he's the kind of guy you marry, but not the kind of guy you date. Or have sex with." Mina wrinkles her nose.

Which pisses me off. Are there really people who just aren't the sex type? I mean, obviously there are asexual people, but that's different.

I guess I'm wondering this: can a person be fundamentally sexually repulsive? I mean, maybe Reid's not cool or muscular enough for sex. And if I like him anyway, what does that say about me? Is it because I'm scared to like someone hotter?

I'm not saying I like him. But *if* I did. Hypothetically.

I mean, Abby dates geeks. But when you're that pretty, you can date anyone, and people know you picked the geek on purpose. Like, you could have had the hot guy, but you didn't want him. But when you're a fat geek who likes another fat geek, everyone assumes you're settling.

I feel a little sick. I can't explain it.

"Anyway, Will was seriously flirting with you last night," Mina says.

"Um. Okay."

I feel my face grow warm. I don't know. I can't entirely process the idea that someone like Will was actually flirting with me.

"It's so perfect, too, because even if the boyfriend thing doesn't work out, you could always hook up with him. He's great about that. I promise, he wouldn't even be weird about it the next day."

I just look at her. To be honest, I kind of wonder how she knows that.

"Well, Molly would be weird about it," Cassie points out. And under the table, she presses her foot against mine, side by side.

"I would *not*."

"You would," Olivia says.

I mean, they're right. I'd be super weird. I'd get quiet and self-conscious, and I'd probably wonder for the rest of my life what Will thought about my kissing abilities. Or lack thereof.

I feel really jittery, all of a sudden, and I need to do something with my hands. I take out my phone, and I have two missed texts from Reid. I take a bite of chocolate cheesecake and tap into my messages.

Okay, so my official assessment of the cookie dough is:

Cat emoji with heart eyes. Thumbs-up emoji. Trophy emoji. Beefy muscle arm emoji. Blissful eyes-closed smiling emoji.

And there's that same soft prickle in my abdomen.

He's pretty good with emojis.

Olivia leaves to hang out with her mom, but Cassie, Mina, and I spend the afternoon wandering around the back streets. Just the three of us. I feel a little strange, like maybe I'm vag-blocking them just by being here. But every time I try to leave them alone, they follow me.

I have to admit, it's kind of nice. I guess they actually want to spend the day with me, even if it means fewer opportunities for making out. Maybe my company is even better than making out—which is pretty much my goal as a human being, honestly.

After dinner, we walk down to the middle school for fireworks. The field behind the school is already packed with people—on lawn chairs, on blankets, eating organic kale chips and jiggling babies. We spread out our moms' big "Fear the Turtles" blanket, and we settle in together, and then Mina takes a group selfie. And then I fold my hands behind my head and let my eyes slide shut, just listening. There's this jumble of sounds: people laughing, kids shrieking, and my heart beating along with the community marching band. I feel almost electric.

"Hey." There's a tap on my arm. I open my eyes. "Look at this." Mina stretches her arm over Cassie to pass me her phone.

"What am I looking at?"

"Just read it," she says, grinning.

It's a text from Will. I guess she sent him the selfie, and he wrote back: BRB, just sulking forever.

"Why is he sulking?" I ask, heat rising in my cheeks.

"Uh, because there's a cute girl here, and he's stuck at home babysitting."

I can't wrap my mind around it. The idea that not hanging out with me would drive Hipster Will to sulking. And if it's true, I can't decide if it's thrilling or terrifying.

It's funny. A few hours ago, I was obsessing over Reid.

Maybe *obsessing* is the wrong word. But running into him did something to my heartbeat. And when I thought he might hug me, I kind of definitely almost lost my shit. It's like I'm thinking about him as a crush, not a coworker.

But suddenly, there's Will.

It's hard to know what to make of this. I've always been a very monogamous crusher.

But my head's all mixed up about this. When I close my eyes, it's so easy to picture Will beside me. The bright blue eyes and the wildly red hair, both dimmed by the sunset. Dating Will would feel like a seat belt clicking into place. Everything lined up just as it should be. Mina and Cassie. Will and me.

It's just strange that my mind keeps circling back to hazel eyes and stupidly white sneakers.

Cassie nudges me suddenly. "Hey, they're starting."

I open my eyes.

And the first thing I notice isn't the crackling streak of the first firework.

It's Mina's leg, draped over Cassie's. It's their hands, laced together, resting softly on Mina's stomach.

14

MY EYES SLIDE OPEN AT sunrise, and I feel a little unmoored. It's still surprising, waking up on the bottom bunk. Above me, Cassie breathes softly. Not a snore. Just those Cassie sleep sounds she's made since we were little.

It's funny, the things that change and the things that don't.

I wander downstairs in my pajamas, to find Nadine in the kitchen, sipping coffee. "Xav's still sleeping?" I ask.

"Never." She scoffs. "He's in the living room with Grandma."

"She's leaving today?"

"Tomorrow morning," Nadine says. "How were the fireworks?"

"Literally the best ever," I say.

She laughs.

I smile faintly. "What?"

"Nothing's ever just the best. Gotta be *literally* the best."

There's a sudden, loud wail from the living room.

"Eeep—there we go," Nadine says, setting down her mug. I follow her into the living room, where Xavier has flung himself backward in Grandma Betty's arms, sobbing.

"What's going on, baby?" Nadine asks. "What is so terrible?"

"It's this terrifying pigeon," Grandma says, holding up a picture book.

"Hey," Nadine says, raising a finger. "Don't you diss Pigeon."

Grandma laughs, and I sink onto the couch next to her. "How are you doing, mamaleh?" She strokes the back of my hair.

"Pretty good."

"Now, you're not working today, are you?"

I shake my head.

"Good. You girls work too hard. I think you should just take the day and relax."

"Well, I need to get started on wedding centerpieces."

"You're doing the centerpieces?" Grandma asks. I nod. "Well. That's very ambitious. How can I help?"

And she actually does seem up for it—so I let her cover the dining room table with newspapers while I grab mason jars and paint from the basement.

I hand her a paintbrush. "So, I saw this in a tutorial on YouTube."

"Now, is that like the band?" she asks.

"What?"

Nadine pokes her head in the doorway, grinning. "She's talking about U2."

"Ohhh. No. This is different. YouTube is like . . ." I trail off. I mean, how does a person explain YouTube to her seventy-year-old grandmother?

I give up, and start organizing my paints. I have these totally badass, magical Martha Stewart paints in pastel colors, and you can use them on anything—even fabric. Sometimes, I paint tiny flowers on the collars of my cardigans. My theory is that it's impossible to plan a wedding without Martha Stewart paints, and I suspect there are studies that prove this.

"These are lovely," Grandma says.

I show her where to paint, and how thickly to coat it, and we settle into a sort of quiet rhythm.

"You've gotten to be so artistic."

It takes me a minute to realize why I'm blushing. But then I remember—I've had this conversation before.

With Will. And Cassie, being mortifyingly unsubtle, as usual.

"You know, my mother was artistic. Your bubbe. She was a wonderful seamstress." She leans forward. "She had a model 201 Singer sewing machine, and she sewed all our clothing. They were beautiful pieces. The girls at school used to ask me where I bought my dresses."

I nod, feeling like I should say something.

"She'd be so proud of you, mamaleh."

I have this sudden vision of my great-grandma high-fiving my other ancestors in Cassie's reality TV version of heaven.

"Now, tell me, do you have a sewing machine?"

I shake my head. "I just use a needle."

"Oh, well, we'll have to do something about that. Molly, it will change your life."

"Okay." I smile.

Suddenly, I hear Cassie's footsteps on the stairs.

"Hey, I'm heading out!" she calls.

"Hold up." Nadine steps into the living room, Xav balanced on her hip. "Where are you going?"

"To Mina's."

"Okay, but I need you back by dinner. It's your grandmother's last night."

"Um. Okay. We were gonna—"

"Nope. You're gonna be right here with your butt in this chair by six o'clock. Got it?"

Cassie starts typing on her phone and doesn't respond.

Nadine shakes her head. "Yo. Put the phone away. This is not how conversations work."

"I'm texting Mina—"

"Uh, yeah. I know."

Cassie's eyes flash. "Okay, I was literally texting her to say I need to be home at six. Which you'd know, if you just gave me a second without interrupting—"

"Whoa," Nadine says. "You don't get to talk to me that way. Now you're not going anywhere."

"What?"

"You just earned yourself a day at home with your family." Nadine shrugs.

"Are you kidding me? Because I sent a text? That's fucking ridiculous."

"Yeah, your language? Also not okay."

Cassie throws her hands in the air. "Since when do you care?"

"You know what—" Nadine starts to say, but Cassie interjects.

"This is bullshit. Where's Patty?"

"She's delivering a baby," I say.

Cassie huffs and sinks into a chair.

"Do you want to help us paint mason jars?" I ask, after a moment.

Cassie laughs harshly. "Um, no."

"Wow," I say.

"Jesus Christ. Molly, stop."

"I'm not doing anything."

"Ugh—you're looking at me like . . . no. I mean, no offense, but do I want to paint fucking mason jars with you and Grandma? Or do I want to hang out with my girlfriend?"

There's this awful, throbbing silence. My chest tightens and my throat gets thick, except I'm not going to cry. Not right now.

But my eyes start to sting. I stare at the floor.

"I just have to say, I love these Apple phones," Grandma announces suddenly. "You know who I love? Siri. Have you tried asking her about zero divided by zero? She's a hoot!"

Yeah, I don't even want to know how Grandma Betty knows that.

But I get what she's doing, and it's working. I think the air in the room just became 50 percent more breathable.

"You have an iPhone?" Cassie asks, eyes narrowed.

"Oh, I have an iPhone," Grandma says, "and I have an iPod and an iMac and an AirMac . . ."

"An AirMac?" I ask, and she gives me this exaggerated wink.

"Betty, you're so full of shit," Nadine says—which makes me laugh, despite myself. Despite everything.

Grandma wags her finger. "I'm proud of my shit."

"Unbelievable," Cassie says. She rubs her temples, like she's the longest-suffering, most profoundly wronged human on the planet. Then, she turns on her heel and charges back up the stairs.

15

OF COURSE, CASSIE SHOWS UP for dinner acting totally normal, like her standoff with Nadine never happened. Like she didn't throw a tantrum about the prospect of wasting a Sunday with me. And I kind of want to give her the silent treatment, except she's basically immune to it. She just retaliates with a Double-Silent-Stinkeye-Attack, and somehow, I'm the one who ends up apologizing. Clearly, I should just forget about it.

I wish I were better at forgetting about things.

We settle in around the table, and Cassie straps Xav into his high chair—but Grandma and my moms are so deep into their conversation that it's like they don't notice us.

"I don't know," Nadine says, with this tense little shrug. "She just said she can't make it." Then she pours herself a glass of wine and chugs it like it's lemonade.

Um. Nadine. Wow.

"Well, maybe it's a money thing . . . ," Patty says.

"Or maybe she's a homophobic asshole."

"Who's the homophobic asshole?" I ask.

They all startle, looking up at me.

"Oh, sweetie. I'm sorry," Patty says, glancing quickly at Nadine. "Maybe we shouldn't be talking about this at dinner."

"Need me to beat someone up for you?" I ask.

Cassie makes a face. "It's Aunt Karen, right?"

"Yep." Nadine nods.

Cassie rolls her eyes. "Yeah, I'm not even surprised."

"She's not coming to the wedding?" I ask.

Patty purses her lips. "Yeah, she's being . . . you know. She's Karen."

It's funny—Nadine and my aunt Karen have been close since they were kids. Way closer than Nadine is with Abby's dad, my uncle Albert. Karen's never been married and has no human kids, though she has four rescue dogs. But even though Nadine and Karen talk every week, and even though she just lives in Annapolis, Cassie and I have only met her in person a handful of times. She always just happens to visit when Patty's at work. And she kind of pretends like Patty doesn't exist.

In other words: homophobic asshole.

"My goodness. That makes me so sad," Grandma says. She picks up her fork and waves it around. "Love is love!"

Cassie snorts. "Thank you, Grandma."

"I'm telling you: life is too short for this bullshit."

"I'll toast to that," says Nadine, and she chugs her drink again.

But hours later, I'm still restless. So, I wait until everyone's gone to bed, and then I slide out of the bottom bunk as quietly as I can.

"What are you doing?" Cassie asks.

"Going to pee."

"No, you're not," she says.

I have no idea how she knows this. Sometimes Cassie knows exactly what I'm thinking, and I literally can't think of any explanation other than twin telepathy.

"I'm eavesdropping," I admit.

"Ooh—I'm coming with you." She slides her legs down and lands on the floor beside me with a thud.

We creep down the hall to the bathroom, and I pull the door shut slowly. Years ago, Cassie and I figured out that the vent in the upstairs bathroom is a direct portal to our moms' room. We used to bring snacks up and line the bathtub with pillows, so we could really settle in for some quality eavesdropping. And then it occurred to us that we were at grave risk of overhearing mom-sex.

So, we shut down that operation pretty quickly.

But tonight, Cassie puts the toilet lid down and sits on it like a chair, and I settle in with a pillow in the bathtub, and it's exactly like it used to be. Right away, I hear them.

"—not calling her," Nadine's saying.

"She's your sister."

"She's an asshole."

"I'm just saying we should hear her side of this."

"She doesn't get a side." Nadine's voice cracks. "She's missing our *wedding*."

Patty sighs. "I know."

Nadine says something else, but it's too quiet to make out.

"Deenie, I know," Patty says again. "I know."

"It's just messed up," Nadine says.

"But Albert and Wanda and the kids are coming."

"Yup, they're coming." Nadine sighs. "I just never thought Karen would be the one with issues, you know? And Al's the chill one. What fucking universe are we living in?"

"Nadine sounds so upset," I whisper.

"Well, yeah. I mean, even Grandma thinks it's fucked up." Cassie shrugs. "Like, that's a pretty clear sign we're wading into some problematic shit."

"Yeah." And I get that feeling, all of a sudden, where I could honestly start laughing or crying. It could go either way.

But I guess you have to hand it to Grandma. She has issues with weight, and she's maybe kind of racist, but she's never once had a problem with Patty being bisexual. When Patty came out, the first thing Grandma did was try to set her up with the cantor's daughter. Who is actually straight, but Grandma gets thrown off when women have short hair.

Anyway, Grandma tries. And at least she'd never miss the

wedding. Even Uncle Albert would never miss it. I just don't understand how you could miss your sister's wedding. If Cassie got married, you'd have to kill me to keep me away. And even then, I'd show up as a zombie. I'd be the Zombie of Honor. I'd lurch down the aisle with my face oozing off and my eyeballs popping out into my bouquet. But I would never, ever miss it. So this Aunt Karen thing doesn't compute.

Cassie must be thinking the same thing, because she whispers, "You'd never do that."

"No way."

"Because I'd kill you," she says, smiling.

"I'd deserve it." *And I'd still show up!*

"And I promise not to blow off your straightsie wedding."

"Straightsie?" I ask.

"Straightsie. Hetsie."

"Oh, I like hetsie."

"Of course you do. It sounds like Etsy."

I grin. "That's what I was thinking!"

"Yeah, I know. You're really predictable. Come on." She stands up. "Let's stop hanging out in bathrooms."

"Me hanging out in bathrooms is the reason you have a girlfriend," I say.

"Touché."

I feel this bubble of happiness. It's nothing, really. Just a moment. But it's the most normal moment Cassie and I have had all day. Out of nowhere. In the bathroom. Just us being us.

So, maybe we'll be fine.

16

I'M UP BEFORE CASSIE, AND I've got hours before work, so I heft a bunch of fabric down to the living room. I'm making a garland. I've seen them all over Pinterest—scraps of mismatched fabric tied onto a ribbon in colorful strips.

Though I'm having trouble focusing. My mind keeps getting stuck on what Cassie said yesterday. *No offense, but do I want to paint fucking mason jars with you and Grandma? Or do I want to hang out with my girlfriend?*

It's just a dumb thing she said when she was angry. And we're fine now. I should clearly let it go.

But there's something about being lumped in with Grandma as one of the undesirables. Like I'm an annoying little sister here to rain on Cassie's parade. It's just not how twins are supposed to operate.

I try to focus on the crisply satisfying *snip* of scissors through fabric. I try to be mindful. But my brain is such a whirlpool that I barely notice anything. I don't even hear Patty's footsteps until she's standing above me. "Oh wow. What's all of this?"

I almost jump. "Hi."

She pushes a throw pillow aside and perches on the edge of the couch. "Can I see?"

"Sure. Yeah, it's for the wedding." I show her a picture on my phone.

"That's gorgeous."

"It's really easy to make. I'll definitely finish it this week."

"Perfect." She makes this sound that's halfway between a laugh and a sigh. "Less than three weeks, huh?"

"Are you nervous?"

"About being married? Nah. But this wedding thing. Let me tell you."

I settle in next to her on the couch, feet tucked up. "And the drama with Aunt Karen."

"Ahh. Yeah. I feel bad for bringing it up in front of you guys."

"Don't feel bad. We would have found out anyway."

"How?"

"Eavesdropping," I tell her.

"Oh really?" She laughs. Then she presses her hands on her thighs and leans forward, sighing. "Yeah. It's—you know. It is what it is. Your mom is pretty sad about it."

"Has she talked to Karen?"

"I don't think so."

"I don't think I could get married without Cassie there," I say.

"Aw, sweetie." She sweeps my hair to the side and rubs the back of my neck. "Yeah, it sucks. But it's just one of those things. And as you get older, it's not quite so . . ." She trails off, thinking.

"Quite so shitty?"

She smiles faintly. "It's pretty shitty. It really is. This stuff is incredibly hard." She tilts her head. "But it's not quite so *raw*. You know, when you're seventeen, everything feels like the end of the world. Or the beginning of the world. And that's an awesome thing."

I nod.

"But, you know. It's been really complicated with Deenie and Karen for a long time. Obviously, she's never been cool with Nadine being gay. And they're not as close as they used to be."

"Oh."

"And sometimes that's just what happens. People grow apart."

Her words just sit there. And they leave this hollow ache in my gut.

Not as close as they used to be.

People grow apart.

And it makes me think of Cassie.

Even though Cassie and I would never do what Aunt Karen's doing. We'd never fall that far apart. But we'll drift. Siblings always do. They marry other people and have their own families and forget the way they used to whisper in bunk beds. It's as inevitable as an airplane landing.

But there's this sonogram picture of Cassie and me, where we're pressing up against our little sacs, as close to each other as we can get. Apparently, we wouldn't sleep in separate cribs. We held hands in our car seats. We started walking on the same day. Cassie first, and then me.

Now it feels like all we do is take tiny steps away from each other.

Toward crushes.

Toward girlfriends.

I'm not saying I want to be like those hundred-year-old Delany sisters. I always pictured us both married, with our own homes and spouses and a bunch of awesome kids. I just never thought about the in-between time. The part where we turn from *we* to *she and me.*

I mean, Cassie's so ridiculous with her *let's date best friends* plan. But maybe she's right. Because Cassie's gone. Her train has left the station. And all I can do is try to catch the next one in the same direction.

Or I don't. And we grow apart.

"I hate that phrase," I say. "*Growing apart*. It reminds me of plants."

Patty laughs. "What do you have against plants?"

"I just hate it."

"I know."

She hugs me around the shoulders and sighs.

When I get to work, Reid's at the front of the store, taking down the Fourth of July display. Or, at least he's making it a little less conspicuously red, white, and blue. He leaves the burlap tablecloth and vintage Coke crates, but he's stacking the Americana painted mason jars into a cardboard box. It's pretty interesting watching Reid work. He gets really hyper-focused and methodical, like he's in the zone. He doesn't even notice me until I'm literally standing next to him.

"Hey—you're here!" He lays the final mason jar down in a nest of bubble wrap and nudges the box aside with his shin. "Okay, I have to tell you something. Your cookie dough was the best thing I have ever tasted in my entire life."

"Really?"

"It's all I can think about."

I laugh. "Oh wow."

"Molly, I am not joking. I don't know how something so wonderful even exists on this earth."

"You know there's still a few left over, right?"

"What?" He clutches his heart.

"You should come over after work," I say.

And then I immediately regret it.

It's not the fact that I'm being extremely uncareful. That's a good thing. Uncareful is exactly what we're going for.

Except the person I'm supposed to be uncareful around is Will. Because Will takes me a step closer to Cassie. Reid takes me further away.

But still. My heart is beating so quickly. I open my mouth to speak again but the words fall away. My entire brain empties in a single whoosh. Like driving through a tunnel in a rainstorm.

And now I should probably say something, but that would involve words, and WHAT EVEN ARE WORDS, and he's looking at me with the hazelest eyes and the softest, most upturned mouth.

I can't.

But I'm saved. By Deborah, who corners us, smiling. God, she even looks like Reid, sort of. I think their mouths are similar. I don't know how I didn't notice this.

"Hey. Sorry to interrupt," she says, "but I need some heavy lifters. Someone bought that vanity. You guys up for it?"

I don't know why I feel so nervous.

"Sure. The white one?" Reid asks.

"Yup. She's pulling her car around now."

Reid and I head over to the back corner of the store, where there's a wooden vanity table painted a distressed white, with a big, rectangular mirror. It's one of my favorite pieces in the whole store.

"You ready?" Reid asks, gripping one side, bracing for its weight.

"Ready."

We lift it on three and carry it a few feet before setting it down slowly. Then, we lift it again, walk, and stop. Lift, walk, stop. And as it turns out, Reid and I are pretty good at carrying heavy stuff together, even though he's over half a foot taller than me, and I'm the least athletic human on the planet. I think it helps that we take it slowly.

We set it down again, and he looks at me. "So, your sister's dating Mina Choi?"

"Yeah. They're kind of inseparable these days."

"Oh, that's cool."

We pick up the vanity again and walk a few steps.

"So, what's she like?" I ask when we set it down again.

"Mina?"

"Yeah. Like, should a protective sister be worried about this?"

"Oh, I don't think so. She's pretty cool. She's artsy, I guess? I don't know her that well." He shrugs.

We lift the vanity again, and this time, we get it almost to the door—and then it takes two more lift-walk-stop cycles before we reach the woman's car. She has a big, open SUV with all the back seats folded down, and the three of us manage to wedge it in there somehow.

Then the woman drives off, and Reid brushes his hands on his jeans.

"Okay, that was really impressive of us," I say. "Right? Like, as a feat of strength?"

"It was a feat of strength," he agrees, smiling, and I think he likes the way I phrased it. Then he pauses. "Okay, question."

"Yup?"

He tilts his head. "Are you serious about this cookie dough situation?"

"You mean the situation of extra cookie dough existing at my house?"

His dimple flickers. "Yes."

"Oh, I'm serious. I am dead serious."

"That is very good to know."

"And there may also be vanilla ice cream," I say, "if you're willing to help me with my moms' wedding centerpieces."

"I see." He grins. "Okay, but I'm not very artistic."

"I can talk you through it," I say—and there's this quiet little yank below my stomach.

When our shift ends we take the back streets to my house, and Reid tells me about this fireworks-viewing party he went to at his parents' friend's condo. Which has a rooftop. Because of course Deborah and Ari go to rooftop parties downtown.

"And it was interesting," he says, "but it was basically a bunch of adults drinking craft beer and asking me where I'm applying to college."

"Oh my God. Why are adults so obsessed with that?"

"I know." He shrugs. "Anyway, my friend Douglas lives near Capitol Hill, so my brother and I snuck off to his house to play World of Warcraft."

"You missed the fireworks?"

He looks sheepish. "Yeah . . ."

"Not very patriotic, Reid."

"I know."

"But hey—you're wearing red, white, and blue today."

"I am?" He looks down. He doesn't remember what he's wearing. I love that. "Oh, I am." He pauses. "But where's the white?"

"What?"

"On my outfit. I've got a red shirt, blue jeans . . ."

I grin up at him. "Your sneakers."

"Ohhhh." We step into the crosswalk.

"They're very white," I tell him.

"Yeah, that's actually funny," he says, "because one of the only real conversations I've had with Mina Choi was about that."

"About your sneakers?"

"Yup."

"Really? What did she say?"

"Oh, you know." He blushes. "It wasn't a big deal."

Okay. So now I'm curious. What in the world did Mina say about Reid's sneakers?

"This is your house, right?" he says.

"Yup! Are you ready to paint centerpieces?"

He looks slightly unnerved. "I think so," he says, with a serious nod. Then he pushes his glasses up. "Yes."

"All right. Let me give you some newspapers, and maybe

you could cover up the porch? And then I'll run in and get the supplies."

"I can do that."

"And I'll also grab your cookie dough," I add.

He beams. "Awesome."

I set Reid up with our recycling bin, and by the time I return with the mason jars and paint, he's got the whole porch covered with newspapers.

"This is great," I tell him. "It's the perfect workspace." I set the first batch of jars down on top of it.

"And you're painting these?" he asks, brow furrowed.

"Yup. And then I'll fill them with flowers. It'll be really cute and simple."

"So, I don't want to throw you off your game or anything," he says, "but you realize they're already painted, right?"

"Yes." I make a face at him. "They get a second coat."

He settles cross-legged onto the newspaper with his cookie dough, while I pick up my paintbrush. And somehow, it's this perfect sigh of a moment. It's cloudy and sort of breezy. I line up my brushes and begin squeezing different colors of paint into an egg container. And the funny thing is, I know Reid's not looking at me. But I sense him looking at me. It doesn't line up.

I should say something, though, before the silence takes on its own life force. Silence does that sometimes.

"So you're really not going to tell me what Mina said?"

"What Mina said?"

"About your shoes."

He laughs. "It was really nothing."

"I want to know."

He shrugs. "Okay. I don't know. It was during prom, so she might have been a little drunk, but we both ended up outside at one point. And she came over and sat next to me—which was a little surprising, just because, you know, we'd never really—anyway, she put her arm around me and got a very serious look on her face and said, 'Reid, I'm going to give you some really, really important advice. Okay?' And I said, 'Okay.' And she said, 'Those sneakers are a liability.'"

"A liability?" I ask.

He nods and takes a quick bite of cookie dough. "Yeah. Like with girls." He blushes. "With dating. Like my shoes are a turnoff."

"Oh God." I cover my cheeks. "Mina."

"Yeah, it was kind of weird," Reid says.

But oh—there's a tiny, secret part of me that knows: Mina's right. Sort of. It's hard to explain, but the sneakers are awful. They are so bright white. They're so loudly, defiantly uncool.

Not that it matters. It totally doesn't matter.

But come on: he wore the sneakers to prom?

"But you kept them," I say, nudging his sneaker with the toe of my flat.

"Yeah." He smiles. "I don't know. I just don't care that much?"

"About impressing girls?"

He blushes again. "No. It's just . . . I am who I am, you

know? I'm not ever going to be cool." He shrugs. "But it doesn't really bother me."

"I think you're cool."

He laughs. "Thank you."

"I'm just saying." I turn a mason jar over in my hands and try not to smile.

Because I have to admit: there's something really badass about truly, honestly not caring what people think about you. A lot of people say they don't care. Or they act like they don't care. But I think most people care a lot. I know I do.

Like, if someone had told me an article of my clothing was a liability? I'll be honest. I'd probably burn it. But Reid wears those sneakers every single day.

And there's something interesting about that. Unsettling, but in a good way, like when a stranger looks you right in the eye.

I feel suddenly nervous.

"I need to stick these in the oven," I say, standing abruptly. "The paint needs to set."

There's this springing in my chest. My pogo stick of a heart.

When I step back outside, Reid suggests going on a walk. If I want to.

And yes, I want to.

So we do. We fall into pace together, our strides adjusting automatically. It's getting grayer outside, with heavy-hanging clouds like wet diapers. That's how Nadine describes it.

"So, are you doing any other projects for the wedding?" Reid asks as we come up on Laurel Avenue. He reaches out to press the walk button.

"I'm making a fabric garland for the ceremony space."

"A fabric garland." His dimple flickers. "Are we sure that's a real thing?"

"Oh, we're sure."

"I need a visual," he says.

I pull out my phone. And then I text him the link to "Let Me Google That for You."

He stops walking to check my text. I don't think he's actually capable of texting and walking at the same time.

"Psshhhh—very funny." He grins. And then he hugs me. It's kind of a one-armed, sideways, squeezy hug. It's over before I can process it, but now my insides are one big shaken Coke bottle.

"So, I—" he starts to say, but then the sky dims so suddenly, it's like someone flipped a switch. The first few raindrops plunk down slowly.

Then the sky splits open.

"Um," I say.

"Should we make a run for it?"

"I think we have to." I look up at him—his hair clings slickly to his forehead, and rain slides down his nose and his cheeks and the lenses of his glasses. "Can you see?"

He laughs. "Can you?" And then, carefully, he reaches

forward, pushing my wet bangs to the side. My breath catches in my throat.

"Okay, let's run," I say quickly.

He grabs my hand, and there's this pulsing tightness below my stomach. We run all the way back to my front porch, our clothes soaked through, hands still intertwined. The rain is still coming down so forcefully, the drops seem to ricochet back up off the pavement. It smells wet. And it sounds like stepping into the shower.

He laughs. "So, that was—"

Don't be careful.

But then the door opens. Our hands spring apart.

It's Cassie. And her eyebrows are raised to unprecedented heights. "What is this? A wet T-shirt contest?"

"Yes." I grin. My heart's still pounding.

"You both lose," she says. But she looks at me quizzically.

And I can read her thoughts as clearly as if she said them out loud.

17

AND NOW I CAN'T STOP thinking about it. The rainstorm. All of it. My brain has turned the whole thing into a hazily lit movie reel, Valencia-filtered, to a soundtrack of Bon Iver. I keep remembering the way our hands looked, laced together. My arms, covered in goose bumps. Reid's fingertips on my forehead, sliding my bangs aside.

This is crazy, but I almost think he might have kissed me. Or I could have kissed him, and he would have kissed me back.

So this is what it's like not being careful.

I feel vaguely nauseated. Like a weirdly pleasant norovirus. Kind of the halfway point between vomiting and becoming a sentient heart-eye emoji.

Which means it's probably time to officially declare it: crush number twenty-seven. Reid of the Sneakers. Reid of the

Cookie Dough Obsession. Reid of the Year-Round Mini Egg Relevance. I mean, I don't even know how to explain him.

It's too soon. I'm too in the thick of it.

I want him to text me, even though I know he's at work. He's probably unpacking picture frames at this very moment. But I can't stop checking my phone.

Nothing. Miles of nothing.

I try to lose myself in my garland, cutting slits into the ends of the fabric. The cool thing about cotton is that you don't have to cut the entire strip. If you rip it in the right direction, it comes apart in a straight line. I need approximately fifty billion fabric strips for this garland. Which is good, because my hands need fifty billion distractions. If I'm ripping fabric, I'm not sending embarrassingly honest texts to Reid.

Reid, I don't think your sneakers are a liability.

Reid, you should have kissed me in that rainstorm.

Maybe I should have kissed you.

The weirdest thing is this compulsion I feel to say it out loud. I want to yell it into the tunnels of the Metro and make it my Facebook status. I want to look Reid right in the face and say it. *Reid, I just like you, okay?*

I think he might like me, too.

Except maybe I'm misinterpreting. Or maybe he does like me—but what happens after that? We'd kiss. Okay. We'd have sex. I don't know. Even if he likes me, I'm not sure he'd like me naked.

I hate that I'm even thinking that. I hate hating my body. Actually, I don't even hate my body. I just worry everyone else might.

Because chubby girls don't get boyfriends, and they definitely don't have sex. Not in movies—not really—unless it's supposed to be a joke. And I don't want to be a joke.

I'm not scheduled for work on Wednesday, so I end up tagging along with Cassie to Mina's house. And it's slightly weird, because Mina's parents are home. I don't mean that her parents are weird. They're actually really cool. Mina's mom is a psychiatrist, and her dad's a psychologist, but they're the type who don't want to be called "doctor." Especially her dad, who almost seems like a hippie. Which I didn't expect from a guy in Bethesda named Eugene.

We end up making small talk in the kitchen. Mina's mom pokes at something on the stove, while her dad flips through a stack of mail on the counter.

"Hey, I hear you live in Takoma Park," he says. "I did my post-doc right near there."

"And now they're in private practice together," Mina says. "Isn't that so sweet?" She rolls her eyes.

But Cassie nods eagerly. "It is!"

Oh my goodness. She is sucking up to the parents, and she's sucking hard.

"Do you have a specialty?" Cassie asks.

"A little bit," Mina's mom says. "We get most of our referrals through insurance, so we end up seeing a nice variety, but we work a lot with anxiety."

"Nice," Cassie says, beaming at me, as if to say HEY, MOLLY, YOU HAVE THAT. What a cool, totally-not-awkward coincidence.

"So, the guys are already downstairs," Mina's mom says, "but can I get you anything to eat? I've got an egg and ramen almost done here."

"We're good," Mina says quickly.

"Or do you need some drinks to bring down there?"

For a minute, I think Mina's mom means booze. Maybe they really are hippies. But then she opens the kitchen fridge and hands Mina a few bottled waters.

"Really nice to meet you, Molly," she says. "I'm just so glad Mina's made some more girlfriends."

Oh. Okay. So, I don't think Mina's mom was using the word *girlfriend* in the my-daughter-makes-out-with-this-person way. Unless she thinks Mina's actually dating both of us. Now I wonder if they even know Cassie's more than a friend. I mean, I assumed Mina was out, but now I'm not sure. And I feel strange asking.

"What was your mom making?" asks Cassie as we follow Mina downstairs.

"Egg and ramen? Have you never had that?"

"Uh, no, but it sounds amazing."

"Oh, it is." Mina pauses at the bottom step to smile up at

her. “I’ll make it for you someday.”

In the basement, the boys are absorbed in an old-school Nintendo game. Will’s perched on the love seat, jabbing a controller.

“Is this Mario?” I ask.

“Yes.” Will’s eyes never leave the game.

Don’t be careful. And don’t think about Reid.

I sink into the cushions beside him.

“He’s scary good at this,” Mina tells me.

Onscreen, Will’s Mario eats some kind of leaf, which turns into a raccoon. You have to wonder, sometimes, what these old-timey video game inventors were smoking.

I let myself zone out, watching Mario leap over cliffs and sink into pipes. Zoning out feels good. I just need to step outside myself for a minute. I feel so crowded in my head. I can’t seem to shake this perpetual awareness of being Molly.

Sometimes I’m a confusing person to be.

My phone buzzes with a text. Abby.

We got our plane tickets for the wedding! she tells me. And I’m bringing a plus one.

Nick’s coming? I write.

Yes!! AND HE’S GONNA WEAR A SUIT.

OMG, he doesn’t have to. He’ll be the only one, I say.

I don’t care, I want to see him in a suit. Are u bringing anyone? Winky emoji. Kissy-face emoji.

Why, yes, I write. If by “someone,” you mean eighty-four mason jars and a zillion buttercream cupcakes

And a handmade fabric garland, I add.

Molly, u are pinterest af, she writes.

I grin at the screen of my phone. Why, thank you

But u should bring a date. You should ask Hipster Will.

God. I don't know what made her latch onto that. Especially when I've been spending so much time thinking about Reid.

Reid's rain-soaked glasses. Reid pushing my wet bangs out of my eyes.

"Who are you texting?" Cassie asks, from the couch. She's lying with her head on the armrest and her feet in Mina's lap, while Mina makes some pretty halfhearted efforts as Luigi.

"The fuck, Mina," Will says. "You missed an extra life."

Cassie sits up suddenly. "Are you texting Reid?"

"Wait, is this the Reid I know?" Max interjects, looking up from his phone. "Husky pants Reid?"

I feel my whole body burn. "I'm texting Abby!"

Her eyes narrow. "Why are you blushing?"

"Shut up."

My phone buzzes again, and I glance at it.

I notice u've gone mysteriously silent. I also notice there are no objections to the Will idea, Abby says.

I OBJECT, I type quickly.

Too late. Smiley emoji.

I look up, and Cassie's expression is unreadable.

Unreadable. Even to me.

18

REID TEXTS ME ON FRIDAY.

Hey, so my friend Douglas and I are going to Medieval Madness.

I write back, That's awesome.

Want to come? Smiley emoji.

Oh.

My heart thuds. I'm so sorry. I can't!

Oh, no problem, he writes.

I'm going to a party with Cassie and Mina

Three dots.

Oh, okay, he writes.

I'm sorry.

Why are you sorry?

I don't know!

But I am. And it's stupid, because God knows what Medieval Madness even is. Something where you drink from flagons, probably. And wear tunics. Something so Reid. I really shouldn't care.

But I do care. It sort of ticks in the back of my mind all evening.

We Metro to Bethesda after dinner, and Mina picks us up from the station. She and Cassie kiss in the car. Just a quick kiss, like parents do. And it occurs to me, suddenly, why they call it the Kiss and Ride.

"So, Max's parents aren't home?" Cassie asks.

"Yeah, they travel a lot."

"There aren't going to be adults?" I blurt. I feel like I'm Xavier's age.

"Well, his sister is eighteen," Mina says, catching my eye in the rearview mirror. "So, in the eyes of the law . . ."

Cassie twists around to grin at me. "Stop making the Molly Face."

"I'm not," I say, but my cheeks are warm. I shouldn't be freaked out by the idea of a house party. It's not like it's an orgy. I don't think it's like an orgy.

Mina parks on the street, at the end of a long line of cars. I can't believe how many cars there are. I have to admit, I had no idea house parties were even a thing. I fold my arms across my chest and try to act nonchalant.

But there's something about tonight. Everything feels a

little surreal. For one thing, it's surprisingly chilly out. I'm actually wearing a jacket in July.

"Molly, you look so cute," Mina says, putting an arm around my shoulders.

Which makes me blush.

"I'm cute, too," Cassie says.

Mina smiles up at her. "You just look like you're cold."

"A.k.a., you're a wimp." Cassie grins. She's wearing a tank top and these short yellow shorts. She's just one of those people. She can throw on anything and look adorable. Whereas I'm completely camouflaged in careful layers. Under my jacket, I've got this belted dress—green, with tiny birds on it—and a camisole, and boots.

We've timed our arrival pretty carefully. It's late enough that we're not the first ones here, but not so late that everyone's sloppy drunk already.

"Should we text Will?" Mina says.

Cassie shrugs. "Is he here?"

"He should be."

The way into Max's basement is through the backyard, which still has one of those giant playhouse structures, with swings and a rock climbing wall. And it's perfectly maintained. Even though Max doesn't have younger siblings. Parents are funny like that.

But inside, it's not quite what I expected. Not that I had any idea what to expect. I guess I thought it would be more like a movie, with a beer pong table and a keg in the corner and guys in well-worn baseball caps. And yes, there are plenty of guys in well-worn baseball caps, but other than that, it's just a normal basement. There are two Ikea-looking futons and a bunch of chairs, a foosball table, an air hockey table, and a giant drum set. The lights are dim, and there are lots of people holding red plastic cups.

"Mina!" someone shouts. It's a girl I've never seen before, and she's ridiculously gorgeous—tall, with light-brown skin and wide hips and a very twee blue patterned dress. She nudges a fallen hoodie aside with her toe as she walks toward us. "Hey! You must be Cassie."

She's talking to me. "Oh, I'm—"

"I'm Cassie," says Cassie.

"This is Samar," Mina says.

"Oh, *you're* Samar," Cassie says.

And now I'm wondering what planet I must have been living on, because I'm pretty sure I've never heard of Samar. But Cassie's greeting her like she's famous. I hate that. I hate feeling so utterly out of the loop.

"Oh, well, hi! I don't know you," Samar says to me.

"This is Molly," Cassie says, with no point of reference. Just Molly. Like I'm some random girl.

"Are the boys here?" Mina asks.

Samar nods. "Yeah, Max is hooking up with someone, and Will—I just saw him. He's . . ." She cranes her neck. "Oh, he's by the booze table. Predictably."

There's a desk at the back of the room that's been totally overtaken with little glass bottles and half-full liters of Coke and orange juice. And there's Will, pouring Sprite into a red cup, his red hair perfectly tousled. His eyes light up when he sees us walking toward him.

"You guys made it!" He grabs my hand. "Molly, let me make you a drink. What do you want?"

"Um."

"There's vodka, Jack, rum, and gin, I think?"

I hesitate. "I guess rum?"

He pours a rum and Coke and hands it to me, and I realize with a start that Mina and Cassie are gone. They've been absorbed into the crowd. There's someone waiting to pour a drink, so Will and I step to the side, in front of a futon. My legs are heavy with nerves, and I kind of want to sit, but people aren't really sitting. I guess you're not supposed to.

Okay, so being alone with Will is making it very hard to keep my cool. Maybe it's just Abby getting into my head, but there's this prickling sense of possibility. It feels like something could happen between us—something other than me blushing a lot and drinking a rum and Coke with record-breaking slowness.

"I can't handle this music," Will says.

"Who is this?"

"I don't know. Maroon 5. That Adam guy."

"Ah, yes. That Adam guy."

Will grins at me. That's the other thing about Will. He makes you feel like you're the only person in focus. Like everyone else is just background noise. I'm pretty sure it's not personal. Probably every girl who enters his orbit feels this way, at least for a moment. Still, I can see how people get swept up in him.

It's just so hard to believe this is my reality right now. I'm at a party in Bethesda, and my sister has vanished, and now I'm alone with a very cute boy. Well, not alone. But we might as well be. I think his calf is touching mine. I wonder if people watching me right at this moment think I'm part of a couple. With Will. That's sort of thrilling.

But I can't shake the thought that I could be at Medieval Madness right now with Reid. Like there's some alternate universe Molly drinking from a flagon right this second—and yes, it just occurred to me that flagon rhymes with dragon. And yes, I really want to text Reid to tell him. But I probably shouldn't text Reid when I'm standing with Will.

"You must be hot," Will says, startling me.

He means my jacket, but I blush anyway.

"I don't know if there's a place to put my jacket," I say.

"I'll take it." He sets his drink on a coffee table.

"You don't have to do that."

"No, I've got it. I'll find a spot for it."

I unbutton it, feeling strangely like I'm in a movie. Undressing.

"I like your dress," he says when I hand the jacket to him. "I love it."

"Thanks." I can't even look at him.

"So, I'll be right back."

I nod. But as soon as he leaves, I feel a hundred times more self-conscious. I sip my drink faster, my other arm curling across my body. It occurs to me that Will could peek at the tag of my jacket and see my size. Which makes my heart jump so high in my throat that I almost run after him.

But suddenly, someone's beside me. A random boy. "Hey, want to hear something crazy?" the boy says, as if we've known each other for years. I've never seen him before in my life. He's pretty cute—kind of athletic looking, with super-short brown hair.

"Okay," I say.

"So, like, we're in this little town," he says. "Like, in England. And there's this big stone wall next to the street. Like, just this big-ass wall. And so we're pretty fucked up at the time, and my dude Jones has to pee."

I don't know who Jones is or why I should care about his bodily functions. But maybe this is how parties work. Maybe there's some kind of drunk etiquette I don't know about.

"So he pees on the wall, but then . . ." He sips his drink again, and then says, "Shit."

"What?"

"I'm gonna need a refill. You want something?"

And I don't know how any of this works, but I'm pretty sure I'm not supposed to let strange guys fill my drink.

"I'm fine?" It comes out sounding like a question. I hate that.

"No worries," he says. "So like—well, I gotta tell you this part. There were these giant fucking—"

"Hey."

I look up. And Will's back.

"Hey, man," says the guy.

Will narrows his eyes at him.

"Oh, are you guys, like, together?"

"Yes," Will says quickly.

My heart almost stops.

"Oh, okay, cool. That's cool," the guy says. "Okay, well, have a good night." He chugs the last of his drink and starts to leave—but then he turns back to face me, suddenly. "Okay, I just gotta say it." The guy touches my arm. "You are fucking gorgeous for a big girl."

I freeze.

"It's a compliment!"

I look at him. "Fuck you."

I've never said that before. At least not out loud. It feels kind of amazing. My heart pounds wildly.

"Whoa. Okay. Not trying to . . . whatever." He tilts his hands up defensively. And as he drifts back into the crowd, I hear him mutter, "Fat bitch."

Will looks at me. "Okay, that was the hottest *fuck you* moment I've ever witnessed."

"Um. Thanks."

"Do you even know that guy?"

"Nope."

"Wow. Just a random dickhole."

"I guess."

I can't think straight. I can't think of anything other than the fact that Will said we were *together*. And I know he was just trying to get rid of the random guy. But still.

He sinks backward onto the futon, patting the cushion beside him. I sit and tug my skirt down closer to my knees.

My heart won't stop pounding. I take a tiny sip of my drink.

He leans back, eyes flicking toward me, and he opens his mouth like he's about to speak. But I cut him off with a question. And I almost don't realize I'm asking it until it tumbles from my mouth. "Why did you tell him we were together?"

"Oh. Shit." His eyebrows shoot up. "Sorry. Were you trying to . . ."

"No! God. No. He was shady."

"Yeah, you looked really uncomfortable."

"I did?"

Will laughs. "Yeah, your body language was like . . ." He sits up rigidly straight with crossed arms and a look of utter terror on his face.

"I did *not* look like that!"

"I mean, I thought you were going to vom. That's kind of your thing, right? Public barfing?" He grins.

"Touché." I smile back at him.

God. He really is so beautiful. His eyes are supernaturally blue. And he's funny and nice and smart and all the other things boys should be. Not to mention that he's best friends with my sister's girlfriend. It would make a lot of sense for me to fall for him.

Much more sense than Reid, for example.

I lean back against the cushions and squeeze my eyes shut. When I open them, I catch a glimpse of yellow shorts and tangled legs on an armchair across the room.

It's Cassie and Mina.

The funny thing is, Cassie's always described her hookups in glorious detail, but I've never watched one happen. I've never actually seen her make out with someone.

It's weird.

And sort of sweet.

But mostly weird.

They're completely intertwined. That's the main thing. It's not even that they're kissing continuously, but there's no space between their bodies anywhere. I watch as Cassie tucks a lock of Mina's hair behind her ear, and Mina's lips twitch into a smile. Then Cassie says something, and Mina laughs, and they kiss again, and Cassie's hand cups Mina's cheek.

I definitely shouldn't be watching this. Though I guess I'm

not the only one. At least three dudes are blatantly staring at Cassie and Mina like they're the Super Bowl.

The futon creaks, and I suddenly remember Will is sitting beside me. He's tucked one of his legs up, bent at the knee, and he's tugging at his shoelaces. And looking pointedly away from the armchair.

"Are you freaked out by it?" I ask, and my voice comes out quiet.

He looks up at me with a start. "By Mina and Cassie?"

"I don't know." I smile slightly. "I guess?"

He leans back, staring at the ceiling. "I think they're good together."

"Oh, well, yeah. I just mean the fact that they're making out in front of us. It's like watching your parents make out, you know?"

He laughs. "Sort of."

I sneak another glance at them. They seem so separate from this room. Like they're on a piece of driftwood, floating. And I feel so lonely, all of a sudden.

Maybe I should reach for Will's hand or scoot closer or say something uncareful. I could do that, I think.

But then my phone buzzes.

I shouldn't check it. Not right now. It's just a text. Probably from Abby. Or from Olivia, who's still in Pennsylvania with Evan Schulmeister.

I will not be vag-blocked by Evan Schulmeister.

It buzzes again, and I lose my train of thought.

"Anyway, I should probably find Max," Will says, patting my arm quickly, before hoisting himself up. "You're okay, right?"

"Yeah. Definitely." I nod.

It's funny. I feel less disappointed than I thought I would.

As soon as Will walks away, I peek at my phone.

It's Reid.

I guess I kind of had a feeling.

So I'm sitting here with Douglas outside of Medieval Madness

And this place is an orgy.

Wait, Douglas would like me to clarify that Medieval Madness is not an orgy. King Street is an orgy.

I lean back into the cushions and giggle quietly. That is hilarious, I write, because I'm at an orgy, too.

He responds right away. Oh, really?

But it's a classy orgy. Mostly kissing/groping.

And texting . . . he writes.

Which makes me blush. I'm not sure why. And texting.

I really love texting, he writes.

Me too.

Three dots. He's typing something. I glance up, and it's funny—I feel sort of invisible. There's this party happening all around me, and I'm entirely separate. I'm a total ice cube. But in a good way.

You know what would suck about living in the Middle Ages? he writes finally.

The bubonic plague? I reply.

Yes. But also. No texting.

Three dots. He's typing something else.

But imagine if there WAS texting in the Middle Ages.

I smile. Oh, you're really thinking about this, I write back.

Yes.

So, what would medieval people have texted?

Three dots.

Chaucer quotes. Codpiece selfies.

Yeah. Holy shit. This boy is funny over text.

I can totally see you sending a codpiece selfie to Queen Elizabeth, I write.

Wrong time period, but yes. G-d yes.

AND HE DOES THE JEWISH THING WITH GOD'S NAME. FUCK.

That's cute.

Step it up, Molly.

"Elizabeth. R U a virgin? Luv Reid" I type.

He writes back immediately. "Nope." Winky-face emoji.

Uh, wasn't she the virgin queen?

Not if I'd been alive, he writes.

Sorry, but who is this boy? Because I'm pretty sure he's flirting. And I did not realize Reid Wertheim knew how to flirt.

I bite back a smile.

And I'm about to write back something *very* uncareful when Cassie collapses on the couch beside me. "There you are! Hey. Okay. Guess what." She leans her head on my shoulder and smiles up at me. "You, Molly Adele, get the Lexus tonight!"

I just look at her.

"Why are you making the Molly Face, Molly Face?" She giggles.

"Okay, how drunk are you?"

"Just a little," she says, and sighs. "Molly." She nuzzles into the crook of my neck. "You always smell so flowery."

I laugh. "It's our shampoo. You literally use the same kind. From the same bottle."

"Yeah, but I don't smell it on myself. Anyway." She pokes my arm. "Aren't you excited? You get to drive Mina's Lexus."

"I'm not driving Mina's Lexus."

"Okay, well . . . ," she says, and I start to reply, but she covers my mouth. "No, hear me out. So I know Mina wasn't going to drink, but we ended up playing Kings, and she's not drunk, but she's like a *little* bit drunk, so we're just going to play it really safe and crash here. So, if you want to drive it home, you totally can. We just need you to pick us up here tomorrow morning."

"Okay, that's not—"

"And park on the street, just so Nadine and Patty don't get freaked out, okay?"

I look at her. "Cass, I can't. I had a drink."

"Okay." She tilts her head. "Just one drink?"

"Cassie, I'm not driving."

"I'm just asking."

"Are you seriously asking me this?" I sit up straight, pulling away from her. "Are you asking me if I'm going to risk my life by driving home after having alcohol for the second time ever, which I'm not even supposed to combine with Zoloft, by the way—"

"Okay." She laughs, but kind of harshly. "Then why'd you do it?"

"Why did I drink?"

"If you're not supposed to drink on your meds, why do you keep doing it, Molly?"

"Are you kidding me?" I feel this tightness in my chest and this ache in my cheek, and I realize I've been clenching my jaw. "Fuck you."

It's the phrase of the night.

Cassie's eyebrows shoot up. "Whoa."

"So now you're going to judge me for drinking? Are you serious? You guys were my ride. And now your big plan is to completely ditch me so you can spend the night making out with your girlfriend, and I get to be your chauffeur?"

Something in her expression seems to snag, and my throat thickens. "And, like, you don't even care if I'm safe to drive. Just as long as you get your awesome hot night with Mina."

"Are you joking?" she asks. "You're seriously going to give me shit for this?"

"Forget it," I say.

I wish I hadn't said anything. I don't want to have this conversation. Not here. Not ever.

"I mean, do you want to talk about this?" Cassie says, scooting closer to me.

"Can we not?" I grip my cup tightly.

"Molly."

I look up at her, and her eyes are shining. Okay, that throws me. Cassie doesn't cry. Cassie doesn't even almost-cry.

"You think I'm ditching you for Mina?"

"What do you think?" It's something I'd normally never say out loud, but I guess that's the thing about alcohol.

"Like, you know she's my girlfriend, right?"

I stare at my knees. I keep picturing Cassie's lips pressed against Mina's ear. I can't stop thinking about that.

"Molly, why are you doing this?"

"You think I'm doing this?" My jaw tightens, because this is what Cassie does. She twists things around and acts like I'm coming at her out of nowhere. As if she hasn't spent the last few weeks completely absorbed in Mina wonderland.

"Oh my God. Just stop," she says. "You are so goddamn—"

"Oversensitive, I know."

She throws her hands up.

And I feel this wave of calmness. I know that's strange.

But even though I hate when she calls me oversensitive, I like that I knew she would. I understand Cassie better than I understand myself. And I don't think Mina will ever know her like I do.

"I think I'm going to go," I say.

She leans backward, laughing, hands over her eyes. "So, what? You're gonna walk to the Metro now?"

I'm suddenly aware that people are looking at us. Not in a blatant way, but there's some not-so-subtle glancing. People love a shitshow.

I shrug.

"Molly, come on."

"I mean, what were you thinking?" Now I'm fighting tears. "Like, you just decided to get drunk, and you assumed I'd be able to drive home by myself?"

I cannot cry. I cannot start crying.

"Okay, to be honest? I kind of thought you'd be getting a ride with Will tonight anyway, so . . ."

"Yeah, he's drunk, too."

She sighs. "Or crashing here with Will. Molly. Please don't pretend you don't understand what I'm talking about."

"I'm not." I exhale and rub my forehead. "I'm not hooking up with Will."

"Yeah, I noticed. Which is why I thought you'd want the fucking Lexus. Look, you want to leave the car? Great. That saves us some hassle tomorrow morning. I just thought you might not want to Metro tonight. Thought I was being nice. But whatever."

There's this pause. I look up, and the light seems a little dimmer, and everyone's a little blurrier around the edges. I catch a glimpse of Max across the room, talking to a girl I don't recognize, and he's laughing, and his bangs are clipped back from his face with a plastic barrette.

"And what's the deal with Reid?" Cassie says, and I almost flinch.

"With Reid?"

She rolls her eyes. "Or not. I don't know. Just kind of got a vibe the other day on the porch."

"We're friends."

"Look, I just want you to be happy, okay?" She grabs my drink and takes a swig of it. "And I thought you wanted—okay, this is really warm and gross." She takes another sip. "I mean, it seemed like things were going really well with Will, but then I look over here and he's totally gone, and it's like, okay. I don't know what's up. But then something seems to be happening with you and Reid, which is great, fine, whatever—"

I swallow. "Yeah, well, apparently Reid's not the kind of guy you date. Or have sex with."

"What are you talking about?"

"Mina said that. She said Reid's the kind of guy you marry . . ."

She laughs. "God, Molly. You shouldn't give a shit about

what Mina thinks. Look how bad her taste is." She pats her own chest and grins. "Come on. It's all so subjective. Like, look at that girl. Purple dress." She gestures with her chin. "Are you sexually attracted to her?"

I shake my head.

"Okay, well, guess what. I think she's hella cute, and I would *totally* have sex with her."

"I'm sure Mina would be thrilled."

"Oh my God. I'm just making a point. We like who we like. Who cares if someone else doesn't get it? That's a good thing. That's less competition."

"I don't know if I—"

"If you talk yourself out of liking Reid because of your goddamn ego, I will punch you."

My ego. I don't have an *ego*. If I had such a giant ego, why would I have such a hard time believing Reid actually likes me?

Except, if I'm totally honest, I do believe it. Reid likes me. And I like that he likes me. But I'm not used to this game. It's this totally new way of seeing myself. Like I'm some hazily lit dream girl from a movie. I've never been that girl before.

I really like being that girl. So, maybe I am some kind of egomaniac.

There's just something terrifying about admitting you like someone. In a way, it's actually easier when there's no chance of anything happening. But there's this threshold where things suddenly become possible. And then your cards are on the table.

And there you are, *wanting*, right out in the open.

It's so many things. It's everyone knowing you're attracted to a guy who wears electric-white sneakers. It's that little twinge of shame you feel when someone thinks he's not cute. Even though he is cute. He's actually really fucking adorable. I actually really fucking like him, and none of the other stuff should matter.

19

I WANT MY NORMALCY BACK.

I feel so undone. It's like stringing beads and realizing you forgot to knot your thread. I don't feel like me. I'm not a girl who curses out one boy, pretends to be dating another, and can't stop thinking about a third.

And I've never fought with Cassie so often in my life.

There's been this carefulness between us all day. She ended up crashing with Mina in Max's guest room, and Mina's friend Samar drove me to the Metro. But we haven't talked about any of it since—not Reid, not my giant ego, and especially not the other thing. The ditching-me-for-Mina thing.

"Hey." Cassie appears in my doorway as I'm putting away my ribbon garland. "Mina's here, and Olivia's working, so we're going to go keep her company and paint pottery."

"Great."

"Thought you might want to come."

"Okay." I wind my ribbon garland into careful loops—over my thumb and under my elbow, and back around again. "I don't want to bust in on your date."

She laughs flatly. "It's not a date. Jesus. Olivia is literally going to be there the entire time."

I don't reply.

"Okay, I get that you're feeling really, really sorry for yourself, but I kind of think you might want to come. Have you talked to Olivia recently?"

"No . . ."

"So you don't know what's going on with Evan?"

I look up. "What's going on with Evan?"

"Well, I was hoping you knew. Abby doesn't know either, but something's up. She just got back from Philly." She shrugs. "Anyway, we're leaving now, so if you're coming, let's go."

I hesitate.

"Okay, look. Don't come. That's fine. But I don't want to hear this shit about me ditching you for Mina."

"I'll come," I say quickly.

It's like Cassie and I are partners in the world's most complicated dance. Everything feels really fragile. If I take a wrong step, it could throw us off completely.

Cassie slides into the front seat of Mina's Lexus, and I take my spot in the back. We spend the whole ride to Silver Spring pointedly not speaking to each other. Which brings out this pressured kind of chattiness in Mina. I remember her saying she talks too much when she's nervous.

"Have you guys ever done this before? It's like they have plates and mugs and everything already made and fired up and ready to be painted. It's really fun. I mean, I suck at painting, but still. Molly, I think you'd like it."

"Yeah. I mean, Olivia works there, so . . ."

"Oh. Right," Mina says. "Duh." She slows to a stop at a stop sign.

"But it's been awhile," I add.

She tucks a lock of dark-purple hair behind her ear. "Yeah, I'm thinking I'm going to do like a penguin design? Like penguins in love? I want to try to make something for your moms as a wedding gift. But only if it turns out okay."

"You know they'll love it no matter what," Cassie says. "They're obsessed with you."

"Aww—really?"

"Yeah, I think they're grateful you didn't dump me after that night with Grandma."

Mina giggles, and Cassie turns toward her and smiles. It's pretty awkward watching this from the backseat. They're not even being mushy or gross, but there's this feeling like they're the adults, and I'm a little kid. I should be in a car seat, holding a sippy cup.

We end up parking on the street a block or two away from

the pottery place. I walk half a step behind Mina and Cassie. I'm not talking much. I guess I feel a little self-conscious. So then, of course, the act of talking starts to feel like this huge, impossible thing. I get like this sometimes. I get locked into a cycle of not speaking. It's like every time I think of something awesome to say, I rehearse it in my head so many times, I forget whether I've said it out loud yet. And I think it goes without saying that awesome one-liners are decidedly less awesome when you repeat them by accident. Better not to risk it.

"So I honestly have no idea what we're about to walk into," Cassie says, walking backward for a moment like she's our tour guide.

"You mean with Evan?"

"Yeah. I don't know any details. At all. Abby just said something was up." She shrugs. And then she pushes through the entrance.

The pottery place is quiet for a Saturday, and right away, I see Olivia. She's actually sitting at one of the tables painting a plate. There are two little girls working on ceramic piggy banks with their mom, but other than that, we have the place to ourselves.

"Oh hey," Olivia says, without getting up. We walk over to her. And she looks normal. I mean, she's wearing an awesome purple shirt with a gnome on it, and she doesn't look like she's been crying.

"What are you working on?" Mina asks, peering at Olivia's work in progress.

"Oh, it's dumb. It's just something to put up as a display."

But it's not. It's not dumb. I stare at Olivia's plate, feeling stupidly jealous. God, I always forget how artistic she is. Like, every once in a while, I fool myself into thinking I am, too, but I'm not. Not like this.

Olivia's plate is stunning. She's covered the background in the palest green paint, with a thin line of gold around the outer edge. And in the middle, there's a half-finished dragon, exquisitely detailed, with carefully defined scales.

Reid would flip over this. Holy shit.

"Can I take a picture of this?" I ask.

Olivia looks confused.

"The dragon," I add. "It's beautiful."

"Oh, thanks."

"I'm serious."

"I mean, it's not done, but sure."

I snap a picture with my phone. Then we settle in at Olivia's table, and she sets us up with plates and paint and brushes. First, we're supposed to sponge the plates down with water. Then, Olivia reminds us to do three coats of the background color.

"Look how hardcore she is," Cassie says. "Don't even try to skip one of the coats. She will lose her shit."

Olivia nods. "Shit will be lost."

It's like, I'd almost say she was acting normal, except for the fact that I know something's up with Evan. So now I can't help but read sadness and heartache into every single paint stroke. I kind of want to just ask her. I can't believe Cassie hasn't.

But instead, we work in almost total silence. I cover the full surface of my plate with three coats of white paint, which feels slightly ridiculous. When it dries, I leave the entire middle of the plate white, but fill in tiny colorful flowers around the edges. Mina's across from me, working on her penguins, leaning forward on her elbow. And Cassie appears to be trying to copy Olivia's dragon design. It's not going well.

"This looks like it was painted by a fetus," she grumbles.

Mina rests her chin on Cassie's shoulder. "I like it," she says.

Cassie smiles. "You would."

"So, you guys went to a party last night?" Olivia asks.

"Yeah, it was all right. And you just got back from Philly, right?" Mina asks.

I give her a huge internal high five. I cannot believe how quickly she just brought the conversation around to Philly. She is truly the child of psychologists.

"Yeah, I got back last night," Olivia says, and then she sighs.

Cassie jumps in. "You okay? What's up?"

"Well." Olivia shrugs. "Yeah. So, Evan broke up with me."

"Oh, Livvy."

"Yeah." She gives me this wavery smile.

"Oh my God. What happened?"

She shakes her head calmly. "I honestly don't know."

Then she shrugs again.

Then she bursts into tears.

"That *fucker*," says Cassie.

And then Olivia tells us everything. "I was just going to stay until Wednesday. And, like, I don't know." She sniffs. "Everything was normal, for the most part. Like, I guess he was acting sort of distant, but I didn't realize it at the time, you know? Just in hindsight."

"This was at his parents' house?" Cassie asks.

"Yeah." She nods. She takes a deep breath. "Yup, I mean. His parents were there, his sister was there, so it wasn't like there was drama."

Evan Schulmeister's parents. I'm pretty curious to know what they're like. Also, maybe this is really nosy, but a part of me wonders how this all works. Like, what happens when you visit your long-distance boyfriend at his parents' house? Do you just not have sex? Or do you risk it and hope his parents don't bust in? Because something tells me Evan Schulmeister's family is very, very involved. Though that's strictly speculation. And it's clearly beside the point.

But then again:

"Did you have sex?" Cassie asks matter-of-factly.

Olivia blushes. "I mean, yeah."

"So he had sex with you and then he dumped you."

"I guess so."

"I will fucking destroy him," says Cassie, and Mina nods solemnly.

"I don't even understand," I say.

Olivia fidgets with her paintbrush. "I don't either. Everything was fine, you know? He asked if I could stay until Friday, so I even rearranged my work schedule . . ."

Cassie practically hisses. "This is so fucked up."

"And I guess it was because he was planning to break up with me, but hadn't worked up the nerve yet? Like he needed an extension."

"ARE YOU KIDDING ME?"

Across the store, the two little girls and their mom look up from their piggy banks abruptly.

"Shit. Sorry." Cassie drops her voice to a whisper.

"It's fine," Olivia says. "Yeah. I'm not even kidding. So, yesterday morning, he comes into the guest room with tea and a bagel and everything, and I thought it was sweet. He'd never made me breakfast in bed before, you know? But then he literally waits until my mouth is full of bagel and says, 'So I wanted to talk to you.' And I'm like, 'Okay.' And he says, 'I don't think I'm ready to be exclusive.'"

"Jesus Christ," Cassie says. "You've only been dating since eighth fucking grade."

"I know." Olivia shrugs.

"So then what?"

"I mean, it's not like I was going to argue with him."

"I cannot fucking believe this."

"Oh, there's more," Olivia says. "So, I'm basically quiet this whole time, and he keeps saying he's very concerned that I'm not reacting."

"Which is bullshit," Mina interjects.

"Right? So he finally says he's going to leave me alone to *process* this."

"Ugh." Cassie snorts.

"Except right before he leaves, he seriously turns to me and says, 'I just want you to know we can still hook up.'"

This makes me gasp. "He did NOT."

"Oh, he did."

"Fucking Schulmeister," says Cassie. "Tell him I'll hook him up with my fucking fist. This motherfucking *douchebag.*"

Holy shit, I forgot how terrifying Cassie is when she's really, truly angry. I don't think I've seen her like this since middle school. Since the boner-deflating *womp womp womp* guys. And I guess that's the thing about Cassie. She has zero tolerance for this kind of cruelty. She will smack boys down, with no hesitation.

It's kind of heroic. I kind of love that about her.

And now she catches my eye, maybe by accident, and I feel my lips tug upward. I can't help it.

She smiles back. Just a little.

And I feel this twinge of relief.

Cassie's already gone when I wake up on Sunday, but my moms talk me into going to the farmers' market. So, I wander down there on my own. It's one of those days when the crowds are sort of overwhelming. I claim the end of a bench and sit cross-legged, fidgeting with my friendship bracelets.

There are little kids everywhere, wandering among the booths of vegetables and freshly cut flowers. It's the kind of thing that normally makes me feel really nostalgic.

Today, I'm mostly just tired.

So now I'm officially that person sitting on a bench in perfect weather, surrounded by neighbors, zoned out on my iPhone.

I text Abby. Did you hear about Schulmeister? Angry-face emoji.

And then I pull up my photo of Olivia's plate and text it to Reid before I can talk myself out of it. So, my friend Olivia painted this. You love it, right?

Okay, there's something terrifying about typing the word *love* in a text to a boy. Even in this utterly neutral, dragon-related context. I mean, now I can't stop looking at it. It's as if I typed it in bold, with a heart for the *O*.

Oh, I totally love it, he writes back immediately.

And then, a moment later: How's the farmers' market?

Okay. Wait.

He texts again: Psst: look up!

And it's him. He's right here. "Hey! What are you doing here?"

"Getting vegetables?" he says, his voice rising like a question. He hoists up a reusable grocery bag to show me.

"Right." I smile.

God, he just looks so *Reid*. He's wearing brown shorts and

a *Game of Thrones* shirt—but it's a totally different *Game of Thrones* shirt, which means he clearly has a collection of them. And his sneakers. Are so, so white. There's this feeling in my stomach like ribbon curling.

"Hey, guess what," I say quickly.

Of course he actually tries to guess. "You found a tiny chocolate chicken inside a Mini Egg."

I laugh. "Um, no."

"That is a shame." He sits beside me on the bench. "So, what is it?"

"What is what?"

"What am I guessing?"

"Oh! Now it feels anticlimactic. It's just, I realized something the other night that made me think of you."

"What?"

"Have you ever noticed that dragon rhymes with flagon?"

"Um. Yes," he says, smiling.

"I guess it seemed funnier on Friday," I say. "Told you it was anticlimactic."

"I think it's climactic!"

Climactic. Okay, that word. Jesus Christ. It can't be possible to blush this hard. I can't keep acting like this around him.

"Hey, I have a question," he says suddenly. He clears his throat. "Do you feel like working today?"

"Oh. Sure. Do you need me to cover your shift?" I tuck my hair behind my ear.

"No, I just want company."

"Really?"

"Really. And," he adds, "I'll pay you in Mini Eggs."

"You must think I'll do anything for Mini Eggs."

"Yes."

I grin at him. I don't know how to explain the way I'm feeling. It's equal parts terror and contentment. Which makes no sense. I know that.

"Let me text my moms so they know."

"That's very responsible of you."

We walk down Carroll Avenue, and Reid tells me about a new shipment at Bissel. Except I'm having trouble paying attention. To be honest, I'm a little bit obsessed with my hand. And his hand. And the space between our hands. I don't know if I should swing my arm or clasp my hands or let it hang. Every movement feels weirdly deliberate. It's a little ridiculous. If you turned me into a pie graph, the obsessed-with-hands part would look like Pac-Man.

"So, we're left with the greatest quantity of bubble wrap ever to exist in one room," he concludes.

"What about the bubble wrap factory?"

"We have surpassed even the bubble wrap factory."

I pantomime pinching a bubble between my fingers. *Pop.*

"Pop," Reid says. I look at him, and he's smiling.

We walk right past Cassie—I don't even notice her until she calls out to me. She's on a bench with Mina and Olivia, and they're all holding cups of gelato with tiny plastic spoons. Cassie's legs are tucked up cross-legged. "Hey! Where are you guys going?"

"I tricked Molly into helping me work," Reid says.

"No, I tricked him into *thinking* he tricked me."

Mina giggles, and Cassie rolls her eyes, but not in a mean way.

"Have you guys met each other?" I say. "Olivia, Reid."

"Hey." Reid smiles at Olivia, and she smiles back. I feel almost apprehensive. Maybe it's the particular way he's smiling, or the way her cheeks have gone pink.

"Wow. I love your shirt," Olivia says.

Reid looks delighted. "Wait, are you into *Game of Thrones*?"

"Am I into *Game of Thrones*?" she asks incredulously. "Am I a human being with a beating heart?"

"Yes!" Reid pumps his fist.

And my twist of dread turns into a tidal wave of panic. Because I've already seen this exact kind of moment unfold. At the 9:30 Club. With Cassie and Mina, and Mina's Georgie James shirt.

And for the first time in four years, Olivia is single.

No. No. No.

I've never been someone who gets the urge to hit people. I'm not actually imagining smacking Olivia across the face right now.

My sweet, faerie-loving, ocean-calm friend Olivia! Who

just had her heart broken. By Evan Schulmeister. I think I must be going crazy.

Because this is *Olivia.*

I mean, I can't be this shitty of a person.

"We should get down there," I say quickly, and Reid nods.

"Okay, well, hey," Cassie says. "We were thinking about having a sleepover tomorrow night. With us and Will and Max. Do you guys want in?"

I don't even have to look at Cassie to know that she's mortifyingly twinkle-eyed right now. I can hear it in her voice.

I look up at Reid, and he shrugs. "Okay. Yeah." He smiles.

And Olivia smiles, too.

I can't tell if the lurch in my stomach is excitement or dread.

20

PATTY AND NADINE ARE ALL about the sleepover. I think they'd be twitchy if it was just Mina. I guess they recognize the rest of us for the vag-blockers we are.

I don't even think they worry about me around boys. So, that's a little sad.

Anyway, Nadine digs out some old sleeping bags from the linen closet, which is essentially an official endorsement. Mina's eyebrows shoot up. "Your parents are so cool."

"So are yours!" says Cassie.

"Mine are like low-key cool," Mina says. "Not this cool. Do your parents let you drink?"

Cassie and I glance at each other. "Not technically," she says.

Mina bites her lip. "Should I tell the boys not to bring vodka?"

"We'll be discreet." Cassie grins, and my heart beats faster. I've never felt quite so seventeen.

We carpet Cassie's floor in sleeping bags. Our entire upstairs used to be an attic, so the rooms aren't exactly huge. Cassie's isn't the biggest, but it feels like it is, because it's the only room where the ceiling peaks high enough to fit the bunk beds.

Mina stays for dinner, and Nadine has picked up those giant double-fried Korean chicken wings from Bonchon to impress her. And honestly, I can't decide if it's a sweet effort, or if we're wading into Grandma Betty territory. But Mina laughs it off. "That's awesome," she says.

"Well, we think you're awesome," Nadine replies.

But everyone's acting awkward. Except Xavier, who's doing drum solos on his high-chair tray with a plastic spoon. But the rest of us. I can't explain it.

"So, who's coming tonight?" Patty asks. "Olivia . . . ?"

"And Will and Max and Reid," Cassie says.

"That's a lot of dudes," Nadine says.

We're all silent for a moment.

"Yes," Cassie says finally.

"So, are you guys feeling ready for the wedding?" Mina asks.

"I think so." Nadine shrugs. "It's very casual. We've got about thirty-five people coming, so it's just about making sure we feed everyone."

"And we'll have kosher, gluten-free, vegan, everything," Patty adds.

There's another random silence. I don't even know why. Maybe we haven't found our rhythm with Mina.

"And our nephew is arranging the table and chair rentals," Patty says.

"Isaac?" I ask. That's Abby's brother, and I'm having trouble picturing him on the phone with a wedding rental facility. He's ridiculously smart—smart enough to get a full scholarship to Howard. But he loves to party, and not in the way that involves rented Chiavari chairs.

"He has hidden depths," Nadine says.

"Maybe we should have a backup plan."

"Right, what's the plan if it rains?" Mina asks. "My mom was wondering that." She takes a bite of her chicken wing and puts it down, reaching for her napkin.

"Our plan is to deny the possibility of rain," Nadine says. And Xavier bangs his tray loudly, as if to add an exclamation point.

Everyone comes over after dinner, and I cannot get my mind to simmer down about this. Spending the night in Cassie's room, with everyone. With Reid. I'm not entirely sure how to navigate this. I'm a certain version of myself when I'm around Reid. And I'm a different version when I'm around Mina's friends. I'm not good at collisions of worlds. I feel jittery and on edge.

"This is a cool neighborhood," Will says. "I'm jealous you can walk to the Metro."

"It's definitely convenient." Cassie settles in next to Mina on the floor, their backs against the bedframe. Everyone's leaning against something: Will and Max against the drawers of Cassie's desk, Olivia against the door, and Reid and me against the wall. We're all in a rectangle on the outer edges of the floor—but if we stretched our legs out, I think everyone's feet would touch.

Will unzips his famous man-purse and pulls out a bottle of vodka—it's the fancy kind, with frosted glass and a blue top. I have no idea how he gets all this booze. Maybe he has a fake ID. Maybe everyone does except me. I feel like I'm in a movie.

Cassie has a carton of orange juice from the Co-op, and the first thing she does is pour some into a big plastic cup. That's Cassie's favorite hack. If you make enough room, you can mix vodka right into the carton.

"I'll drink that," I say quickly. "I'll have the plain cup."

"Can I share it?" asks Reid, and I smile up at him. I had a feeling he wouldn't drink.

But everyone else does, even Olivia. And it's funny. I never really imagined myself as a person who would go to a boozy slumber party. Or a boozy house party. And definitely not both in one week. But I guess that's the thing about being seventeen. You never know what you'll do until you do it.

"So, guess what I read today," Cassie says. "Did you know orgasms strengthen your core?"

"Sweet." Max pumps his fist.

Olivia bites her lip. "I've never had an orgasm."

And here's the funny thing: when she says it, I actually feel this twinge of envy. Not because she's never had an orgasm (which, go figure. Evan Schulmeister). I mean, it's probably obvious that I haven't either. And lack of orgasms aren't something to envy. But I wish I were the kind of person who could just admit it out loud.

"Olivia," Cassie says. "You are missing out."

Does that even need to be said? It's an orgasm.

"But I hear it's like sneezing," Olivia adds.

"Orgasms?" Cassie laughs. "Says who?"

"Says the internet."

"Is that why you used to sniff cumin powder all the time?" Cassie asks.

"Scientific inquiry."

Mina giggles. "Olivia, you are so cute."

"You know what it's like?" Cassie says suddenly. She leans back, her arm draped around the bedframe. "It's like Super Mario Brothers. It's like when Mario eats the leaf, and then he runs and runs and then he's flying." She zips her hand up into the air.

Will and Max start laughing so hard I think they both might choke. But Olivia looks reflective. "That's sort of beautiful," she says.

"Olivia, that's not what it's like. Orgasms are not like video games," Max says.

"Oh, okay. You're the expert. I'm sure you're the only person in the world who's ever had one." Cassie rolls her eyes.

So, I'm a little freaked out. This whole conversation is making me unravel. Sometimes I think I'm the last virgin left in the entire universe. Everyone else is having incomprehensible amounts of sex. Everyone's naked and touching and kissing. Except me. I know it's not true. But that's how it feels.

Will chugs his drink with a giant gulp, and immediately refills it. "Don't you dare get sloppy drunk," Cassie warns him.

"I'm not drunk."

She narrows her eyes at him.

"Look," he says, pulling up onto his feet. "Want me to walk in a straight line?"

He walks in a straight line, directly toward me.

"See. Perfectly sober." And then he slides down the wall next to me. Right beside me—one entire side of his body is pressed against mine. And Reid's on my other side. Honestly, it's kind of thrilling, being sandwiched between two boys. Even though I don't like Will. Not like I like Reid.

Will asks if Cassie can turn on some music, and then he leans in to ask me what I want to listen to. It feels like a test.

"Florence and the Machine," I say uncertainly.

"Ah." He nods, and it's impossible to read his expression. This is a little overwhelming. Cassie puts on the Florence + the Machine album, and then everyone starts talking about sex again.

"Okay. I have a theory," Reid says, leaning toward me.

"A theory."

"Yes." He pauses, and lowers his voice to a whisper. "I think they're all virgins. I think everyone is full of it."

I turn to smile at him. "Oh, really?"

He nods emphatically. "It's a huge conspiracy. I think everyone insinuates they're having sex, but really they're just at home on the internet."

"Telling all their internet friends how much sex they're having," I add.

"Exactly." He smiles.

"Okay, but how do we explain pregnancy?"

"Immaculate conceptions."

"Hey." Will nudges me. "What are you whispering about?" And then he gently grabs my wrist and cradles it in the palm of his hand. He seems strangely intrigued by the texture of my friendship bracelets, tracing his fingertips along their knots and ridges. I feel suddenly short of breath.

"Who are these from?" Will asks.

"My cousin." I swallow. "Abby. She's my best friend."

"Let me guess. She has matching ones."

"Maybe. Definitely."

I feel Reid watching me, watching Will, and I almost think he might be jealous. I mean, I could be imagining it. But I just have that feeling. And it's not a bad feeling.

I am definitely, definitely a shitty person.

Later, when we settle into our sleeping bags, I'm in between Reid and Will again. And Will scoots up extra close beside me—so close that I don't know how I'll get up to go to the bathroom without jostling him. That thought alone makes me have to pee, urgently, but I don't want to move.

I'm lying next to Hipster Will.

And Reid.

I don't think my heart wants to stay in my chest.

I wake to the sound of rustling fabric—Will rolling over. Though he's still passed out and snoring softly, his lips slightly parted, and Max is curled up in a ball next to him. Cassie and Mina are tangled up in blankets on the top bunk.

But the bottom bunk is crisply made. I guess Olivia's up. And Reid's sleeping bag is empty, too.

I have this sudden jolt of fear, but I try to shake it off.

I slip out of my sleeping bag and stop by the bathroom—and then I walk quietly past Xavier's room and down the stairs. The living room light is on, but only dimly. When I look through the doorway, I see two heads of rumpled hair over the back of the couch. Sitting very close.

"Hi." I step into the room. My brain is buzzing.

"Oh, hi!" Reid says. And I could be imagining this, but I swear he looks startled. Maybe even guilty.

Olivia smiles up at me. And she's practically tucked into him.

I feel numb.

"Have you guys been up for long?" I ask slowly. I perch on the armrest of the couch.

"Maybe an hour?" Reid says. "We've just been hanging out."

I'm trying not to stare at them. I'm trying. But I have to take inventory. Olivia's under a blanket, and I can't see her hands. I can't see his either.

Numb. Or maybe the opposite of numb.

They're holding hands under the blanket. I'm almost sure they are. Which is bullshit and extremely uncool. Not that I care who Reid likes. I should not fucking care. And I don't. I don't care.

Except, then Olivia stretches, her hands clasped together, and I almost sigh with relief.

They're not holding hands.

That's good.

I need to catch my breath.

"I was just telling Reid about the different types of lenses," Olivia says.

"Yes. Apparently there are lenses. And you can pop them off the camera."

"Apparently, cameras exist outside of iPhones." Olivia grins.

Reid's dimple flickers. "So you claim."

I can't stay here. I can't watch this.

"I should get dressed," I say.

Imagine if getting dressed took five hours. Because that's how long I spend in my bedroom. If I could stay in there forever, I would.

But eventually, Patty appears in the doorway. "Do you have a minute?"

I'm in bed. And I do not have a minute. Today's schedule is devoted entirely to Facebook—*Reid Wertheim became friends with Olivia Lambert*—and checking my phone for missed texts. Of which there are none. Of fucking course.

But I shrug. And when Patty pushes my door all the way open, I see that Nadine and Cassie are behind her.

"Family meeting," Nadine announces. "Mind if we sit?"

I shake my head. "Where's Xav?"

"Mina's watching him." She scoots onto the foot of my bed, and Patty takes the chair. Cassie slides in next to me and hugs my pillow to her chest.

"So yeah," Nadine says. "I'm just going to come out and ask you guys. Was there alcohol last night?"

I feel Cassie stiffen beside me. I don't say a word.

Nadine purses her lips. "Let's start with this. Want to explain why Will was puking in our bathroom at four in the morning?"

"He was puking?" asks Cassie.

"Oh yes."

Cassie shoots me a look. *Did you know?*

I did not.

A perfect telepathic conversation.

"I had no idea," Cassie says.

"I'm not asking if you knew. I'm asking if you know why."

Cassie hugs the pillow tighter and nods. I should deny it. I should point out that I actually just had plain orange juice. This time, anyway.

"I don't think we have to tell you this is unacceptable." Patty shakes her head. "We give you girls a lot of leeway."

"We trusted you," Nadine interjects.

"I'm sorry," Cassie says quietly. "This is my fault."

And maybe this is unfair, but I don't contest it. Because, yeah. It actually is her fault. She's the one who invited everyone over. She's the reason we're probably about to get grounded forever. And she's also the reason Olivia and Reid are sending flirty Facebook messages right this minute. Probably. Undoubtedly.

I'm not going to cry.

"Molly, we need to hear from you, too," Patty says.

"What do you want me to say?" I feel my eyes prickling, and I shake my head fast. "If you're going to ground us, just ground us."

"Excuse me?" Nadine says.

"Just tell me what to do, and I'll do it. You want my phone? Here." My voice cracks. "I don't care."

"You know what? No. That's not how we're doing this. You

want to drink like an adult? Fine. Then you're going to sit here and discuss it like an adult."

"Yeah. I'm sitting here." I fold my arms.

"Molly," Cassie whispers. I turn away abruptly.

Patty scoots the chair closer. "Molly, what's going on? Talk to us."

My thoughts are racing. I can't seem to catch hold of them.

"I guess I don't get why this is such a big fucking deal?" I trip a little over the curse word. "We'll be in college in a year. We're turning eighteen in five months."

"Which means you get to drink and sneak around?" Nadine's voice is quiet, but it thunders. "I don't think so."

"Why does it matter?" I whip back. "Why does any of this matter?"

It's like an anvil falling. Everyone stops. Everyone looks at me.

"Uh-uh. What has gotten into you?" Nadine stands.

But I'm too far gone to stop. "Into me? Literally nothing. Nothing's gotten into me. Nothing happens to me. So maybe you should talk to Cassie. Maybe you should ask her what an orgasm feels like."

Cassie gapes at me. "Are you kidding me?"

"Molly, that's not okay—" Nadine starts to say, but I cut her off.

"Whatever. I'm done." I stand abruptly, pushing past her, out the door, and down the stairs.

Mina steps out of the kitchen, holding Xavier's hands up while he wanders. "Oh hey," she says.

I barely return her hello. I don't even stop to hug Xav. I slip out the door, and I don't care that it's drizzling, and I don't care that I'm in pajamas. I curl up on the steps and take out my phone. I call Abby.

She answers on the first ring. "So funny—I was just talking about you!"

My heart sinks. If she was just talking about me, she's not alone. Which means I'm about to lose my shit in front of Nick or Simon or one of Abby's millions of other new best friends. Perfect.

"Molly?" she says.

"Hi." It comes out like a choke.

"Are you okay? Molly, what happened? Wait, hold on. Let me just . . ." I picture her gesturing to Nick, maybe smiling apologetically. "Okay, I'm heading upstairs. What's going on?"

I really want to tell her about Reid liking Olivia, but I can't. Which is ridiculous. I mean, it's Abby. She's not going to make fun of me. Except she might. I don't know. Maybe Cassie told her about Reid. Maybe she told her what Mina said. That sex with Reid is unfathomable. Which means sex with me is probably unfathomable, too. Because nerd sex is a joke. Fat on fat. Dweeb on dweeb. *Womp womp womp.* And no one seems to see how cute Reid is, except me.

And fucking Olivia.

Reid fucking Olivia.

I seriously want to scream.

"Molly, talk to me. Are you okay?" she asks again.

"I'm okay."

"No you're not. What's going on?"

I need to breathe. I need my lungs to get it together.

"I'm just . . ." Deep breath. "Cassie's really mad at me. And so are my moms."

"Okay." There's a smile in her voice. "That's it?"

"It's not funny."

"No—oh, Molly. I'm not laughing at you. I'm just—do you know how often Isaac is mad at me? Or my parents? Seriously, my dad is mad at me literally every day. That's how parents are."

"Not my parents."

"That's because you never screw up."

"Are you kidding me?"

She laughs. "Well, what happened?"

So I tell her. And, honestly, talking about it makes me feel calmer. I guess the situation is a tiny bit hilarious. I mean, I actually left Cassie there to explain how orgasms feel. To our mothers.

"So Hipster Will blew it for you guys, huh?"

"He totally blew it."

Abby giggles. "He's so not getting the Molly makeouts now."

"Never."

As if the Molly makeouts are such a hot commodity. As if

guys are lining up at my door. I actually hate that expression. Grandma says it sometimes. Like, that's supposed to be the goal: to have a whole line of guys desperate to date you or have sex with you or whatever the endgame is. Like, I should want to collect boys like Pokémon.

I don't want that. I don't want to break hearts. I just want Reid.

It's scary to even think that.

I want Reid. And maybe I'm crazy, but I was sure he liked me, too. The way he looked at me in that rainstorm. The way he sits a little closer these days. The way he looked at me when I was talking to Will.

I was so sure.

I was so not careful.

And now I know what rejection feels like. It's a whirlpool of suck.

21

"HEY! YOU'RE NOT GROUNDED," REID says when I walk into work.

"Not yet. I don't know." I settle down next to him on the floor of the baby section. There are baby shoes everywhere. "What happened here?"

"Toddler rampage."

"Uh-oh."

"This place is literally birth control," he says.

I smile faintly, settling in beside him to stack a few shoe boxes.

"Seriously," he says, after a moment. "Is everything okay? Mina told Olivia you seemed upset."

"You talked to Olivia?"

"She texted me."

My stomach drops. "Right."

There are approximately fifty billion things I want to ask him right now, like: *When did you and Olivia exchange numbers? Do you like her?* And especially this: *Do you like her better than me?*

"Hey, guys." I look up, and it's Deborah. "Is my muscle team available? We just sold the barnwood bookcase." She pumps her fist.

"We're on it." Reid jumps up and extends his hand to me.

I take it.

He squeezes my hand softly before letting go. And Olivia doesn't exist right now.

Until I see her by the checkout, her blue-streaked hair perfectly tousled. She's wearing a T-shirt and jeans, and carrying what looks like a camera case.

"You bought a bookcase?" I ask.

She laughs. "Uh, no. I'm looking for a picture frame. And saying hi."

"Hi," Reid says, smiling.

"The woman's just pulling her car around." Deborah rests her hand for a moment on Reid's shoulder.

We carry the bookcase in silence, and I sense Reid looking at me quizzically. But I don't want to speak. I don't trust my voice right now. I can't believe Olivia's here. She's here. And I don't think it's because of me.

"Did you find your frame?" Reid asks her when we step back inside.

"I did! What do you think?"

Of course she picked my favorite frame in the entire store. I mean, she's Olivia. It's wood, painted pale blue, with clusters of tiny hand-painted flowers.

"It's for your moms," she says. "Did you hear I'm taking pictures at the wedding? Actually, I'm heading over there in a sec to take some test shots. I've got my Canon." She pats the case at her hip.

"Your cannon?" Reid asks. He pantomimes an explosion.

"My camera."

"Oh, right," he says. "So, hey, I was just thinking. My friend Douglas is kind of a techie, and he's starting to get interested in cameras and photography. I was wondering if maybe you could talk to him?"

OKAY, IS FUCKING EVERYONE INTO PHOTOGRAPHY THESE DAYS?

"Totally," Olivia says.

"Actually, Will also does photography, and Mina's learning, too." I smile tightly. "So Douglas has a lot of options."

"Oh, cool," Reid says. "But if you're up for it, Olivia, maybe the four of us could find a time to get together or something." He glances at me. "I think Molly suspects Douglas doesn't actually exist."

"That is true." I can't help but smile a little.

"Well, I'm definitely up for it."

"Oh, great! Let me text him." He looks up at Olivia. "And hey, my shift's ending in a minute. Do you want me to walk you to Molly's house?"

"Aww, that would be great."

Oh my fucking goodness. So, this is happening. Right before my eyes.

I mean, that's how it's going to be. It's that easy for Olivia. Maybe this is what life is like for most girls.

I should smile. I should act normal. I should melt into the floor and disappear.

I pull out my phone as soon as they leave. I never did write back to Will's dancing bee ladies. I've never even considered texting him. But I will literally-not-literally-almost-literally explode if I have to sit around tonight imagining Reid with Olivia.

Kissing. Holding hands. Making out. Discovering orgasms.

What are you up to? I write, and then immediately delete it. I don't know how to do this. I don't know how to make this not sound like a booty call.

I swear this isn't a booty call.

Hey, Will? It's Molly. I tap send.

Here's what I know: I shouldn't wait for a response. I should close the app, lock my phone, bury it in the zipper pouch of my bag, forget about it forever. I think messages from boys are like Santa Claus or Buzz Lightyear. They won't happen if you're watching them. But I can't help but watch. I have such perfect laser focus, you'd almost expect the screen to crack.

A moment later, the screen refreshes, and a new message appears. A tiny miracle. Right as I'm staring at my in-box.

Oh hey what's up?

A million competing thoughts: He wrote back. Right away. And he asked what was up. Like he's wondering what I'm up to. But not in a booty call way. Or maybe this is a booty call. Maybe this is exactly how booty calls work.

At work, but—I take a deep breath—I was wondering what you're up to later?

Three dots.

But then the dots disappear. I think he's ignoring my question.

Oh God.

But. This is fine. Mortifying. But fine. I'm breathing. I'm okay.

God, he's probably sitting with Max right now. No question. And Max is reading over Will's shoulder and laughing and giving Will shit about the fact that I'm obsessed with him. Like, I'm 100 percent positive Will thinks I'm obsessed with him. And now he's so freaked out, he doesn't know how to respond.

Except.

Three dots.

Not much, want to hang out? When do you get off?

Oh.

Oh shit.

My brain goes foggy. Sure! Off at 4:30

That works, he writes. Want to meet at the takoma metro? I have an idea . . . And then he throws down the big cheesy smiley emoji.

Whoa.

What's your idea? I write.

Wouldn't you like to know, see you soon! he replies.

Will's wearing a bow tie. I know that's absurd. Even more absurd is the fact that he's really cute in a bow tie.

"You have excellent timing," he says, enveloping me in a hug. "I was home and bored as fuck, and Mina never replies to her texts anymore . . ."

So, Mina's not available. And that's why he's hanging out with me. I don't know how I should feel about that.

"She's probably with Cass."

Will smiles and shrugs.

We step into the Metro station—and for the second time in my life, I'm on an escalator with Will Haley. A train pulls in as soon as we step onto the platform.

"See? You have the best timing," he says.

It's crowded. I guess it's almost rush hour. I end up mashed between a giant double stroller and a woman reading her phone. Will's fingers are about an inch above mine on the Metro pole. Which is probably something I should obsess over.

Very cute boy. An inch away from holding hands.

I definitely shouldn't be thinking about white sneakers in this moment.

We get off at Silver Spring, and step outside, and I don't know how I managed not to notice how warm it is today. I probably don't need my cardigan. But I wear it, like armor. Will walks down Georgia Avenue, smiling at me sideways, and then he stops in front of a store.

"Joe's Record Paradise," I say out loud.

"Yup. Paradise," he says. He pushes the door open, and a bell jingles as we walk through. "*This*," he says. He looks back over his shoulder, eyes meeting mine. "Take a look."

There's vinyl everywhere—organized on racks and shelves down long, narrow aisles. And in the back, the walls are, surprisingly, bubble-gum pink. They're covered with framed band posters and album covers.

"Awesome." I flip through a rack of albums without really noticing any of them. "You have a record player?"

"Of course I have a record player." Will steps closer. We aren't looking at each other, even a little bit. But there isn't any space between us. I try to breathe normally. I have to admit, he has this ability to totally unsettle me. More important, he has the ability to make me forget Reid for almost five minutes straight. I timed it. Though, purposefully not thinking about someone might be the opposite of forgetting him.

"Wow," I say quickly, pulling an album off the front of a rack. There's a couple on the cover, and they're completely naked. Pubic hair and everything.

"That's John and Yoko," says Will. He reaches out to take it, and then he turns it over to show me. The back of the album is a picture of their butts. "Pretty edgy, right?"

He hands it to me, and I flip it back over. The album is

called *Unfinished Music No. 1: Two Virgins.*

Honestly, I don't think they look like virgins.

Also: I guess this means John Lennon is officially the first guy I've ever seen naked. I try not to stare at his penis. I wonder if all penises look like that.

"You're blushing!" He beams.

"I'm not blushing!"

"Oh, you so are."

My mind is spinning. I think I might throw up. Because I can't help it. I'm thinking about sex. Sex with Will Haley. Sex in general. The thing is, I can't make my brain turn the idea into something sexy.

Isn't that ridiculous? It's *sex.* It's inherently sexy.

But not to me. Because in hazily lit movies, when the girl pulls her shirt up over her head, she stops being me. The hazily lit girl is never me. She has a flat golden stomach and cute little boobs, and you can see the boy falling for her. You can read it on his face.

Under my shirt, there's no flat stomach, and there are no cute little boobs, and there's no hazy lighting. It's just a lot of me. Way too much of me.

But the best thing about Will is that you can have a complete internal breakdown in front of him, and he doesn't even notice. He's chatty and goofy on the Metro. He offers to walk me home. And he doesn't even live in Takoma Park. Not even close. He'll have to walk all the way back to the Metro and take it back to Bethesda.

I can't figure out what that means. Abby would definitely say he likes me, but maybe he's just being nice. Maybe he just likes walking.

I tell him not to worry about it.

"Seriously, Molly Golly. I want to," he says. "It's getting dark."

So I let him. We walk up Carroll Avenue, past the park, and my thoughts are a jumble. *Will is walking me home. He basically insisted. And maybe that's a really good thing. Maybe this is how it happens. Maybe we'll kiss. This could be exactly how I stop caring about Reid. Maybe I should just. I don't know.*

Stop being careful.

I stop in my tracks, and Will stops a moment later. "You okay?" he asks.

I nod, dazedly. Deep breath. We're right next to a gazebo. That's probably a sign.

"Hey. So." I squeeze my eyes shut. Open them again. And he's looking at me with his eyebrows knit.

"Molly?" he asks. He takes a step closer. "What's up?"

"Do you want to go in there?"

"In where? The gazebo?"

I nod.

He shrugs. "Sure."

God, my heart. I can *hear* it.

He follows me inside, and when I turn to face him, he's biting his lip. Doesn't say a word. I don't know if that's a good thing. But I step closer. I don't know how this works. I don't know if I'm supposed to tilt my head up, or press my lips out, or do something with my hands. Where do my hands go?

But.

Don't overthink this.

Don't be careful. Don't be careful. Don't be

I take another step closer.

"So, I've been meaning to talk to you," he says. Kind of loudly. Way too loudly. He steps back.

And oh.

There it is. Like a kick in the gut.

The first thing I feel is panic. Not disappointment. Not even humiliation. Just nausea and heartbeat and a total inability to catch my breath.

I don't even want to run away. I want to evaporate.

"You okay?" he asks quietly.

Breathe.

"I'm good." *Sound happy. Sound normal.* "Great."

"Do you want me to go?"

"No!" Oh my God. "No, no. You're good!"

He shuffles his feet. "I'm really sorry."

"Why are you sorry? Don't be sorry. I'm just." I shake my head quickly. "I mean, I wasn't trying to . . ."

"Oh. Okay." He nods. "Right."

And then it seems like we're silent for hours.

"So, what were you about to say?" I ask finally. *Before I tried to kiss you. Before you rejected me. Totally, completely, unambiguously rejected me.*

"What do you mean?"

"You said you wanted to talk to me about something."

"Oh." He scratches his hair. "Um. It's not a big deal. We can talk about it another time."

"No, tell me," I say, maybe too forcefully. *Let's erase the last five minutes. Let's just rewind.*

He presses his lips together. "Okay. Um," he says. "It's about Mina."

"Okay."

"The thing is." I watch him inhale. "I've known Mina since kindergarten. I fucking love that girl."

"Oh." I'm sort of stunned. "So you . . . and Mina . . ."

"No," he says quickly. "No, we've never. Ever. You know."

"But you like her," I say. It comes out like a breath.

He shrugs. "Doesn't matter." His cheeks flush. "It's just—she *really* likes your sister. So Cassie's got to be careful, okay? No heart breaking allowed."

"Well, Mina's not allowed to break Cassie's heart either."

"I'm serious," he says, stepping backward. He sinks onto the gazebo bench. "I'm just saying. She's very . . . tenderhearted." He lowers his voice. "And here's the thing. Mina's never dated anyone before, never kissed anyone before. I don't know if

Cassie knows that. Just. Tell her to be nice."

"What?" I gape at him.

"But you can't tell anyone I told you that."

I nod. "Okay."

"Seriously, I will lock you in a room and make you listen to Maroon 5 for twenty-four hours."

I actually laugh. "I don't think I hate Maroon 5 like you do," I say slowly, but my mind is still spinning. I can't quite wrap my head around it.

So, Will likes Mina.

I mean, of course he does.

But the fact that Mina's never kissed anyone before Cassie? Mina, who seems like she was built to fall in love. I've seen her talk about sex a million times without freaking out. But maybe, in her head, she was freaking out right alongside me.

Or not. Maybe she's totally cool with it.

It's just that this whole entire time, I thought I was the last virgin standing.

"I don't think we have to worry. Remember them on the armchair?" I say.

"Yeah." He blushes.

"Oh. Geez. I'm sorry."

"No, it's fine." He smiles slightly. "I just want her to be happy."

"Yeah."

He pauses, looking up at me. "Molly, I'm really sorry. I feel like an asshole. I totally get why you thought . . ."

"Oh my God. Don't worry. It's fine."

"I just feel bad. I know I'm kind of . . . flirtatious, I guess, and it's probably really easy to misinterpret that."

I stare at my feet.

"I'm so sorry. I really like you, Molly Golly. I so want to be your friend."

"Yeah. Definitely."

My phone buzzes in my pocket. A text. But I try to ignore it.

"Can we hug it out? Would that be weird?"

I swallow. "It's fine."

He grins and stands and wraps his arms around me. And he hugs me so long, I'd almost think it means something. Except for the part where I know it doesn't mean anything.

"You should head home," I say. "Seriously. I'm fine."

"Are you sure?"

He hugs me again, quickly, before heading back toward the Metro. And for a minute, I just stand there, in the center of the gazebo.

I mean. That counts. No question. I'm officially rejected.

And it's surprisingly . . . okay. Definitely awkward. But not earth-shattering.

I kind of wish I could tell Cassie.

I slide my phone out of my pocket, and I suddenly remember the buzz in my pocket. The missed text.

I wonder if it's Reid.

But it turns out to be Abby, randomly sending me a

left-pointing magnifying glass emoji. That's something we do. We send each other the underutilized emojis. Just to help them find their purpose.

I respond immediately as I'm walking home: aerial tramway emoji.

Floppy disk emoji.

Leaf fluttering in the wind emoji.

I think I'm okay.

Except when I walk in the door, the first thing I hear is Cassie's voice. And Mina's voice. And Olivia's voice. It turns out they're all at the dining room table, which is covered in newspapers. Xavier's still awake, and he's on Olivia's lap, holding a paintbrush.

Cassie turns her head away as soon as I walk in. Of course. She's been avoiding me since yesterday.

"Oh hey," Mina says. "I heard you were with Will! How was that?"

"It was fine. Great."

God. Will probably told her everything. The gazebo, the kiss attempt, the shutdown.

"Well, I think it's awesome." She smiles. "So, you want to see something amazing?"

She picks something up from the table and holds it out to me.

"An elephant?" I ask.

Oh hey. The fucking elephant in the room.

Mina nods happily. "We're painting animal figurines for the centerpieces. Olivia found a whole blog about it."

"Oh."

"Yeah, so, we're doing them all white, but then we're decorating them with patterns," Olivia says. "I was actually inspired by the plate you painted! And Xav is helping—aren't you, bud?"

I just stare at her. There's this pounding in my chest.

"I thought you hated crafts," I say to Cassie.

"Oh, right," Cassie says. "I forgot you're the expert on me."

"Cassie."

"Should we get Nadine and Patty in here, so you can tell them how I feel about crafts?"

Mina and Olivia exchange glances. I feel my cheeks burning.

"Cass, I'm sorry, okay?"

"Do you want us to give you a minute?" Mina asks quietly.

Cassie smiles tightly. "Oh, we're done."

I swallow. "I'm heading upstairs. Want me to take Xavier?"

"Oh, no worries! I've got him." Olivia grins. "Xavor Xav."

Olivia's smile. All of a sudden, my chest swells with rage. And a part of me knows it's unfair to put this on Olivia. Because I'm pissed at Cassie, too, for giving me shit right now. And Will, for making me think he liked me. And Reid, for I don't even know what.

Making me fall this hard. Not falling for me back.

But all I can think about right now is Olivia. Her audacity, calling Xav by his family nickname. Holding him in her lap and painting with him. That's supposed to be my thing. And the fact that she's sitting here making centerpieces for *my* parents' wedding. Not even asking if I was cool with it. Not even caring that I have an actual design vision for this wedding.

The really messed-up part is that I love painted animal figurines, and they'll be perfect next to the mason jars. Still. I'd really like to throw a tiny painted elephant at Olivia's stupid face. And I don't care if she just had a breakup. I don't care if that makes me a shitty person.

I text Reid as soon as I get upstairs. So, how was your walk with Olivia?

It was good!

Great. With a period. Even though I'm perfectly aware that a period in this context is essentially like saying FUCK YOU FOREVER.

Three dots. He's hesitating. Is everything okay? he asks.

Yup.

Okay, well, good.

My throat feels thick. I stare at my screen.

Three dots. Then no dots. Then three dots again, like he's deciding whether or not to say something else.

Then another text: How was your afternoon?

Awesome. And clearly, I'm an asshole or an idiot or both, because I add, I hung out with Will.

Yeah, Olivia mentioned that.

My heart twists. Guess they've been texting.

Looks like things are going well with you and Olivia, I type. I stare at it for a second before pressing send.

For a moment, time stops.

Then, suddenly, he's calling me.

"Hi." I sit on the very edge of my bed, feeling jittery. I don't even take my shoes off.

"Molly?"

"Yeah."

"Should we talk?" he asks. His voice is so quiet.

I swallow. "Okay." My chest tightens. I don't know why this feels so much like fear.

"Are you mad that I walked Olivia to your house?"

"No," I say quickly. "Why would I be mad?"

"I don't know."

We're both quiet.

"It just seems like you are," he says finally.

"Well, I'm not." I squeeze my eyes shut. "So, did you guys make out, or something?" I try to sound breezy.

"Um. No. She went to your house. I went home and played World of Warcraft."

"But you like her."

"Do you like Will?" he shoots back.

"So, you do like her." My whole body freezes.

"I didn't say that."

"You didn't deny it."

He pauses. "Neither did you."

We're both silent. And there's this thickening lump in my throat. I feel nauseated. I actually think I might throw up.

"This is really unfair," he says.

I need to just breathe. "What's unfair?"

"You're hanging out with Will, but you're angry at me for hanging out with Olivia? I don't get that." There's this catch in his voice.

"I'm not angry."

"Okay, then why are we having this conversation?"

And before I can stop it, I'm crying. It's the quiet kind. I don't even bother to wipe the tears from my cheeks. I just let them slide down. I'm a fucking mess.

"Molly?"

I take another deep breath. "Like, I don't get where this came from. You just met her this week."

He pauses. "Are you crying?" His voice cracks.

"No."

He does this quiet little sniff, and my heart beats wildly.

"I'm not dating her. Nothing's happening." I hear him swallow. "And I don't understand why you care."

"I don't."

"Okay." He's quiet.

"I mean, I care."

"It's fine."

"I just—"

"I'm going to go."

"Reid."

He hangs up. And it's like some kind of dam bursts inside of me. I flop backward on my bed, and I just start sobbing. I sob until I can barely catch my breath.

22

I WAKE UP TO A bunch of missed texts. From Olivia, of all people. And they're so perfectly normal and friendly and sincere. I almost feel guilty.

Okay, quick question

So Cass thinks we should do a few animals in gold, but I wanted to check with you first before I bought gold paint.

Whatever you want to do, I write.

God. This is so gross and awful. Things have never been complicated with Olivia. But maybe I owe that to the neutralizing, retainer-clad presence of one Evan Schulmeister.

I fucking *hate* Evan Schulmeister.

Cool! I'll probably get some, just so we can try it out. Yay! Olivia writes.

I'm dreading work so much, I almost can't get out of bed.

I have another shift with Reid. I don't know what I'm going to say when I see him. Maybe there's a protocol for this. It's the kind of thing other girls always seem to know. What do you say to a guy after you awkwardly, tearfully call him out for liking another girl?

I shouldn't care who he likes.

The bell on the door jingles when I open it, and Ari waves at me from behind the register. It's early, but there are already a few moms browsing with their babies in ring slings. At first I don't see Reid, and I'm so relieved I could weep.

But then the door to the storage area nudges open, wide enough to fit a giant coffee table made out of reclaimed local stump wood. With Reid pushing it.

"Hi," I say.

"Hi." For a minute, we just stand there, not quite looking at each other. There's this tuft of hair winging out above his ear. I have to shut my eyes. My heart and brain are jumping all over.

"Can we—"

"Molly, it's fine."

"Okay. Yeah."

"Sorry." I see him swallow, his Adam's apple pressing outward. I cross my arms over my chest. He looks up at me, finally, and says, "I don't want to talk about this here."

"Okay," I say again. I can't catch my breath.

Then Ari calls him over to the register, and we don't talk again for the entire workday.

. . .

He doesn't walk me out. Our shifts end at the same time, but at the last moment, he disappears into the back room.

I take the back streets home, feeling heavy and dazed. My phone buzzes in my pocket, and it takes me a second to even register it. I feel almost like I'm floating. I'm barely aware of the weather and my body and my stiffly plodding feet.

It's a text from Abby: Are u there? Can we Skype?

15 min, I type. Almost home.

As soon as I get there, I head straight to my room, settling onto my bed with my laptop. I log into Skype and dial Abby's computer.

"Hey!" she says, her face super close to the webcam. And when she leans back, I see she's not alone. "Molly, this is Simon!"

The famous Simon. He looks just like he does in photographs: messy blond hair and twinkly eyes behind hipster glasses. "Hi." He grins.

"Hi." I feel shy.

"Okay, so I don't have a clue what any of this means," Abby says, rolling her eyes, "but he has something very important to ask you. Just critically important."

"Okay, this actually is important," he says, nodding solemnly. "I need a second opinion. If you were sorting Abby into one of the Hogwarts houses, where would she go?"

"Obviously Gryffindor."

"YES. Oh my God. Thank you."

Abby shakes her head. "Yeah, so this one and his boyfriend just spent two hours arguing about whether I'm a Gryffindor or a Hufflelump."

"*Hufflelump*?" Simon covers his face. "I can't. Jesus Christ. Abby, you're embarrassing yourself. Anyway," he says, sliding his hands away, and giving me a thumbs-up, "Molly, you're awesome."

"Yup. She's awesome. You're awesome. Go gloat to your boyfriend," Abby says, shooing him out.

As soon as he's gone, her whole expression changes. "Hey. You okay?" Her brow furrows.

I nod slowly. I don't know how Abby does this. Either she's really perceptive, or I'm way more of an open book than I think I am. I've never quite been able to figure that out.

"Yeah, that's not the nod of someone who's okay." She squints at me. "What's up? Did you talk to your moms?"

"About . . ."

"About the booze."

"Oh. No. This is . . ." I pause—and the silence just hangs there. The thing about Skype is that you can actually watch an awkward silence play out in real time. There's Abby's face, eyebrows knit, pressing her lips together slightly. And in a tiny rectangle in the corner: me, eyes cast downward. Probably because I'm watching myself and not the webcam. I'm sure there's some kind of metaphor buried in that.

"Molly?"

"Hmm?"

"You're in a daze."

I blink. "I am? I am. I'm sorry." I rub the bridge of my nose.

"Is it Cassie?"

"What?"

"Is she still pissed about orgasm-gate?" Abby stretches and leans back, and I catch a glimpse of her bedroom walls—pale pink, plastered with collages of Taylor Swift, *The Fault in Our Stars*, and the rest of her favorites. It's just like her room in Takoma Park, but bigger—Abby's world, expanded. "Because that's dumb. Want me to yell at her for you?"

I laugh weakly. "Thanks."

"Seriously, have you guys talked about this?"

"No." I scoot back, leaning against the wall.

"You need to talk about it."

"I know, but the wedding's in ten days, and, just, you know. I don't want everything to be weird."

"You don't want it to be weird? I think that ship has sailed." She raises her eyebrows. "Seriously, just talk to her. You'll feel better."

"I know."

"Good."

We're both quiet. I watch her draw a nervous breath.

"Okay, listen," she says finally. "I don't want to overwhelm you, but, uh." She looks me in the eye. "Can we talk about this guy Reid?"

The breath whooshes out of me.

"What about him?"

"Well, Olivia called me."

I feel this wave of panic. I touch my cheeks, and they're burning. "What?"

"So." She lifts her shoulders. "Who is he? What's going on with you guys?"

"She said something was going on?"

"I'm just speculating."

"With her and Reid?"

"Molly." Abby rubs her eyelids. "No. Okay. That is not what Olivia said."

My heart pounds. "What did she say?"

"Let's start with this. Do you like this guy?" She twists her mouth sideways. It's the Abby version of the Molly Face. It's the patented Abby Suso *don't bullshit me* face.

"I feel like we've been talking a lot about me. How are you? How's Nick?"

"Oh, we're great. Our relationship is great. You know what helped a lot with that?" She stares me down. "Admitting I liked him."

She knows, and I know she knows, and she knows I know she knows, and onward to infinity. But I can't make myself say it. Twenty-seven crushes, and the first time it actually counts, I can't seem to make the words come. Honestly, there must be something wrong with my wiring. Because girls are supposed to tell each other everything. It's the fundamental law of friendship.

I like Reid. I have a crush on Reid. I want to make out with Reid. I'm half in love with Reid. More than half. Way past half.

"See, you tricked me," Abby says, wagging a finger. "I thought you liked Hipster Will."

"I don't."

"But you hung out with him."

"Olivia told you that?"

She nods. "But you're not interested in Will."

I bite my lip. "No." *Nor is he interested in me.*

"Then why'd you hang out with him?"

"I don't know."

"You totally know." She's smiling faintly. "Come on. I think you need to say this. Like, own it. It's okay."

"Yeah." I nod. "I'm . . ."

There's this pause.

She looks at me. "Wow. Like, you can't. You actually can't admit it."

I cover my face.

"This is so sad and adorable."

"I'm twelve years old. I know."

"You seriously are." She laughs. "Which is okay! But you're gonna have to turn thirteen."

I shrug.

"All right. I'm going to draw this out of you. First question.

If you're not into Will, why did you hang out with him?"

"Okay, I'm not—"

"Answer the question."

I take a deep breath. "Because Reid was hanging out with Olivia."

"Yeah, you *might* have misinterpreted that." She grins. "But let's keep going. So, Reid was hanging out with Olivia, and then you called Will . . ."

"No, I texted him."

"Whatever. You got in touch with Will because you wanted . . ." She trails off.

"I wanted to make Reid jealous."

"Because you like him."

"I like him."

"There you go."

"Yeah." And I'm blushing so hard, and it's stupid, because I'm not in middle school. I'm not twelve. I'm not this much of a mess.

"You like him!" Abby says.

"But it's not anything. We haven't even kissed."

"Yet." She's beaming.

"Stop being smug."

"You don't even know smug. Wait till you kiss him. Come find me then."

"I'm not going to find you."

She bursts out laughing. "Yeah, okay. Do you know what you didn't just say?"

My whole body is blushing. Because I know she knows, and probably everyone in the entire world knows.

I didn't say I wouldn't kiss him.

Maybe I actually will.

23

HI. I KNOW I PROBABLY shouldn't be texting you this late

But I need to tell you some stuff, and I don't want to talk myself out of it. So, yeah.

First of all, I'm really sorry.

Reid, I am so sorry. I was an asshole to you. You probably don't want to talk to me right now.

I totally get it.

It's not fair of me to be a jerk about you hanging out with Olivia

Especially when I was hanging out with Will

That sucked. And I'm sorry.

But here's the thing

Actually, here's a lot of things

There are some things we've never talked about that we

probably should talk about.

Like how I'm not interested in Will. And he's not interested in me.

And how everything's just a little off-kilter right now, like with Cassie and Mina.

Which has nothing to do with Olivia!

And is obviously not a good reason to keep you from making out with her.

Except

Please don't make out with Olivia.

Because that's the other thing.

I don't think you should make out with Olivia.

Because

I can't believe I'm about to say this

24

THREE DOTS.

25

HE'S TYPING SOMETHING.

My hands are shaking so hard, I can barely hold my phone.

My stomach aches, and the area below my stomach aches, and the area below that aches. There is a good deal of lustful aching occurring.

Hey. I'm here, he writes.

Hey. Hi.

Three dots.

Hi! Okay. So, I guess we should talk?

Yes

But maybe we should do it in person

My heart beats extra fast. Yes. Okay. Where are you?

Home. Where are you?

Home!

I can be there in five, he says.

Here's the thing they don't tell you about time: there are spaces in between seconds. And sixty seconds is actually a pretty huge number. Three hundred seconds might as well be infinity seconds.

I slip outside and settle onto the porch swing to wait for him.

And then he's here.

He's wearing new sneakers. It's the first thing I notice. Brownish-gray with white laces, vaguely vintage looking.

"Hey."

"Hey." I smile up at him. "Want to sit?"

"Yes. Okay." He nods firmly—and he looks so sweetly intense that I have to giggle. He sinks down beside me, close enough that our legs touch. I am very aware that our legs are touching. I think my brain must have been built for this kind of awareness.

"I like your shoes," I say.

"Oh, thanks." He runs a hand through his hair. He seems jittery and unsettled. "That was Olivia's idea."

"Yeah."

He turns to face me. "So, let's talk about Olivia."

I need to breathe. I need to be cool. If Reid tells me he kissed her, I have to be happy for him. For them.

I nod, and he's quiet. We swing back and forth gently.

"Are you guys together?" I ask finally.

"What? No. I told you that."

"But you like her."

"No! Not like that. I want to introduce her to Douglas." He pauses, and I can see him swallow. "I've been talking to her about you."

His eyes flick toward me, his fingers trailing along the armrest of the swing. I can barely catch my breath.

It's the middle of the night.

I'm on the porch swing.

Next to Reid.

Reid, with a needlessly detailed map of Middle Earth on his shirt. Reid, with his hazel-gold eyes and wire-rimmed glasses and the starlight in his hair and his very soft mouth. Not that I'd know. But I highly suspect his mouth is soft.

I stare at my knees.

"So, do you want to talk about the thing?" he asks, after a moment.

"The thing?"

"The thing you were about to tell me."

"Oh yeah. The Thing." I smile slightly.

"The Not Supposed to Make Out with Olivia Thing."

"Yes. That is a Thing."

"And there's a reason for this Thing."

"Yes."

"Beyond the fact that she's not the person I'm in love with."

"In love?"

"I don't know." He smiles. And then he picks up my hand and threads our fingers together.

Oh.

My heart's in my throat.

"I'm going to kiss you," I say, and I hear my voice shaking.

"That's a good idea."

He wraps his arms around me, and the swing creaks faintly. I think my brain has become unglued. I lean forward. Somehow, my body knows how to do this.

And I do this.

His mouth is softer than I even thought.

I sneak him up to my bedroom. I'm actually sneaking a boy up to my bedroom. And for a minute, we just stand there grinning at each other.

Did I mention Reid is in my bedroom?

He steps closer. "Yeah, I'm just going to—" And almost before I can process it, his lips are on mine.

I don't think. For once. And I'm not even slightly careful. My eyes slide shut, and my hands slip over his shoulders, and I kiss him back. I kiss him like it was my idea. I don't know what I'm doing, but maybe it doesn't matter, because we're kissing. Again. Finally. Finally. His hands find my waist, and he pulls me even closer. So close I can feel his heartbeat. And then I feel him smile against my lips, and I open my eyes. "What?" My lips tug upward.

"No, I'm just . . ." He hugs me tightly. "This is actually happening."

"Yeah." I smile.

"Right." He kisses me again, softly. "I'm just so . . ."

"I know." I tuck my head into his shoulder and sigh.

We're quiet for a moment. And then we both speak at once.

"I'm really glad—"

"Do you want to—"

He laughs. "You go first."

I swallow. "Do you want to go over there?" And I'm blushing. God. I don't know how to do this part. I don't know how to say this in a movie way.

Hey, so my bed's over there.

Hey, we could try this horizontally.

Anyway, he gets it. He nudges his shoes off and climbs onto my bed, stretching his arms out toward me. I take his hands, and he tugs me closer.

"I don't want to crush you."

"You won't." His eyes are bright behind his glasses.

"Okay, but . . ."

"Here." He pulls me gently onto the bed and wraps his arms around me. "This okay?"

"Yeah." Every part of my body is pressed against part of his. "You're sure I'm not—"

"You're not crushing me." He smiles.

"And my hair's in your face."

"I like it. Is that weird?"

"I don't know." I laugh, but the sound falls away as soon as our lips meet.

And it's different, lying down. I don't know how to explain it. But there's this prickle below my abdomen, and it makes me want to kiss him even more. Kiss him everywhere. I tilt my face sideways and press my lips against the line of his jaw. Into the crook of his neck. I slide down and kiss him gently on the collarbone.

"Oh," he says, more breath than sound. And there's this sudden, soft pressure against my jeans. I think he's hard.

God.

My heart is pounding.

"I'm just—" he says. I thread my hands into his hair and kiss him harder. His eyes drift closed again. And I think I might understand. Almost. I think I know why this is such a big deal. To some people.

To me.

But he pauses, breathing heavily. "Molly, I don't want . . ."

"Oh. God. Sorry, I didn't mean . . ." I pull myself up clumsily.

"No, no. I mean, I want to. But not." He exhales. "Maybe not yet."

"Me either. I'm so sorry."

He sits up, sliding his legs out, and he grabs my hand. "But seriously," he says. "I want to."

"Okay."

"Like, a lot." I look at him sideways, and his dimple flickers.

God. I can't stop staring at our hands. Reid threads our fingers together and softly traces his thumb along the length of my index finger. And something below my stomach squeezes taut. Maybe it's actually possible to combust with joy. Maybe that's actually a thing.

"So, did you even check your mailbox?" he asks, completely out of nowhere.

"What?"

He leans back and smiles up at me, still breathing hard.

"Wait, you sent me something?"

"Nope." He grins.

"I'm so confused." I lean back next to him, and he tilts his head toward mine.

"I didn't send you anything," he says. "I just think someone else might have."

"Good to know," I say, and I bury my face in his chest.

It's funny. I didn't know I could feel like myself in this kind of moment.

But I do. I feel extremely me.

26

BUT WOW. NO ONE WARNS you how tender your mouth feels after making out.

Making out. That was me.

I press my lips gently with my fingertips and immediately tap into my phone's selfie camera to examine them. They look bee-stung and swollen. I look like a different Molly. Now I'm wondering how people kiss without the whole world knowing. Maybe it's like flossing. Maybe if you keep kissing, your lips get used to it. I think I could do that. I could make kissing a habit.

Missed texts from Reid, sent at four fifteen this morning.

It's official

That was the best thing that has ever happened to my mouth.

That includes Cadbury Mini Eggs

And egg-free cookie dough (no offense!)

I giggle, scrunching my legs up. None taken!

He writes back immediately. Whew! Three dots. Also, hi.

Hi. Beaming-smile emoji.

I am entirely made of butterflies.

Last night, he writes, actually happened. Right?

I THINK so?

I hope so.

Me too.

This is weird, he writes. But good weird.

So good weird. I smile while typing. And I never thought I'd make out with a guy wearing a map of Middle Earth on his shirt.

Three dots.

Oh, Molly. Okay. We better talk.

I sit up in my bed, feeling suddenly nervous. He's typing something else.

So, you're not WRONG, per se, but you should probably know that Tolkien actually hyphenates "Middle-earth." Smiley emoji with a single nervous tear.

This is what Reid wants to talk about the morning after we kiss. I grin while I type: Hey, you're kind of adorable.

Hey. So are you.

There's a soft knock on my door.

One sex! Someone's here.

OMG, YOU PERVY IPHONE. Sec. Not sex.

TOO LATE! he writes. Three dots. Does this count as sexting?

I think so?

Another knock, and the door cracks open, revealing Patty. "Sweetie, are you up?"

Oh God.

"I'm up."

"Oh, great." She steps into my room, shutting the door behind her. My mind races. She knew about the alcohol. Now she knows about Reid. I can tell from her face. How do moms always know?

I try to play it cool. I scoot up the bed, leaving room on the end. "You can sit."

She does, scooting backward against the wall, and I realize she's holding an envelope. "So, this was in the mail for you."

She hands it to me, and now I can't stop blushing. It's the size of a birthday card, and all it says on the front is *Molly.* No address.

So, it's hand-delivered.

So maybe *that's* why Reid walked Olivia to my house.

And now I'm desperate to open it. Which means Patty needs to leave. I give her the *okay, Mom, we're good, thanks for stopping by now* stare.

Which never works.

"So, sweetie, we really need to talk about what happened on Monday."

Oh.

My heart sinks.

She leans back on her hand. "I'm really glad you and your sister have made some new friends. I know it's been hard with Abby gone."

I nod.

"And they all seem like really cool people."

"I'm sorry about Will and the alcohol," I blurt. "I know that was dumb of us. You can ground me. Seriously."

"Sweetie, you're not dumb. Please don't say that."

"Sorry."

"And you're not grounded. We obviously don't condone you and your sister drinking." She pauses, lips quirking upward. "But from what I understand, you didn't actually drink anything."

"Cassie told you that?" My mouth falls open.

"Did she misremember?"

"No, it's just . . ." It's just the fact that I was an utter asshole to Cassie, and she still covered for me. "Is Cassie grounded?"

"She got off with a warning. Anyway." Patty tucks her knees up and wraps her arms around them. "I wanted to check in with you about something."

"Okay."

"I know we've talked a little about birth control . . ."

My face grows warm. "Oh, I don't want to talk about this."

"I know." She smiles. "But this is important. Especially

since it seems like things . . . might be happening."

Oh God.

"Things," I repeat.

"Well, I know your friend Reid stopped by last night."

I mean, they ALWAYS know.

"We're not having sex," I say quickly.

"I know, sweetie. But you might." She scoots closer to me. "We should think about starting you on the pill. Sometimes I forget you're seventeen, you know?"

I squeeze my eyes shut. This conversation. I cannot. Hypothetical sex talk: sure. Patty probing into my sex life in particular? Holy. Fuck. No.

She laughs. "Stop looking so traumatized."

"I'm not having sex," I say again.

"Good. Look, I'm in no hurry for you to have sex. Believe me. I'm just saying, we should acknowledge that it's a possibility."

"So . . . you think I should be on the pill."

"I think it's worth considering," Patty says. "You know, I went on it in high school. Senior year and all through college, right up until I met your mom."

It's hard to imagine that time before my moms got together. I guess they could have dated other people. Patty might have even dated guys. I've honestly never asked.

There's something about exes. I've never had an ex-anything. The whole idea of it seems intolerable. Falling out of love.

Becoming strangers. The thought of that happening with Reid makes me want to cry. And I'm not even in love with Reid yet. I don't think.

I don't know.

It's funny—if you take away the kissing, you basically have Nadine and Aunt Karen. Their ruined intimacy. Their faded closeness.

Ex-sisters. Which sounds exactly like *existers.* And I guess it fits, because that's exactly how things fall apart. That's all it takes. Just the fact that you're two different people. Just the fact that you exist outside each other. I get this ache in my chest when I think about it. I try to shake the feeling away.

Patty's smiling. "So, are you going to tell me about him?"

I cover my face. "Nope."

"Are you official? Is he your boyfriend? Check yes or no."

"Mom."

"Okay. But are you happy?"

I nod, smiling through the cracks between my fingers.

She squeezes my shoulders. "Kind of funny watching you and your sister go through this at the exact same time. You guys are cute."

"Hmph."

"Does Cassie know?"

"About Reid?"

Even saying his name makes me self-conscious. I slide my hands off my face, but my heart sort of skips.

"I don't think so." I bite my lip. "I don't know. Were we really loud last night, or something?"

Patty's eyebrows shoot up.

"No. Oh God. I did *not* mean it like that." I grin into my elbow. "I meant, like, on the stairs. His footsteps. Not anything else. I'm going to stop talking."

She pats me on the shoulder. "That's probably a good idea."

I open the envelope as soon as she leaves. And it's Reid's favorite card. The most badass of all greeting cards, with the most amazing Queen Elizabeth *don't fuck with me* expression. *I observe and remain silent.*

On the inside, he's written this: *I'm watching your every move, and I choose not to say anything . . . yet.* And he's signed it *Love, Elizabeth.*

Oh my God. He's such a goof. He is the actual weirdest. I can't stop smiling.

And maybe I'm freaking out just a little bit.

Because we're working the afternoon shift together today. And because, technically, the last time I saw Reid, I was making out with his face.

Which is good. Better than good. Better than best.

But now I don't know what to wear. And my hair is kind of a catastrophe. And I can't stop pacing around my room. Back and forth, from my closet to my mirror. Like, I just want to wear something normal. But I want it to be *cute* normal. I want

Reid to think I'm cute. Pretty. Gorgeous. I don't want him to think yesterday was a mistake. Not that he would think that. I just need to get this right.

Unfortunately, nothing—*nothing*—in my entire closet looks okay on me today.

I need to collect my shit and take my Zoloft and calm the fuck down.

I think I'll wear a skirt. I have this dark yellow skirt, a tiny bit shorter than what I usually wear, but I think it's okay, because I'll wear it over tights. I pair it with this navy ruffled shirt with tiny flowers. But it looks dumb, so I take it off and try another. And another. And six more shirts after that. But then I finally go back to the navy one, which is fine, as long as I wear a cardigan, too.

A perfect fall outfit. In July. It's just going to have to fucking be this way.

I step outside, and it's one of those sun-kissed summer days. The air just has this softness. I'm running early, so I take the long way through town, past the purple house, past the shops. It's quiet here on weekday mornings. Everything's calm and hazy, except the commotion in my stomach. Which turns into fireworks and marching bands and atomic bombs as soon as I reach the entrance of Bissel.

Because of *Reid*.

There's this thing Patty told me about, where your stomach pretty much functions like a second brain. They call it the enteric nervous system, and it lives in your gut, and when it thinks there's an enemy nearby, you get this surge of hormones. It's sort of a fight-or-flight response. And I guess it applies to crushes, too. Or boyfriends.

Not that Reid's my *boyfriend.*

But my stomach thinks Reid is an enemy. I consider this scientific proof that I've stepped into something terrifying. Falling in love is terrifying.

Not that I'm falling in love. But maybe I'm a little bit lovesick.

When I see him, I smile. I honestly can't help it. He's working the register, alone behind the counter. Which looms between us like the Great Wall of China.

And then there's Deborah. "Yay, you're here," she says. "We just got a new shipment of teacups. Want to unpack everything and get the price stickers on them?"

"Sure," I say, eyes flicking up to Reid.

"I could help," Reid says.

His mom looks surprised. "I thought you loved the register."

"But I really love teacups."

"Noted," she says. Then she sends us to the storage room. I shut the door behind me, and for a moment, we just look at each other. I may not be capable of words.

He's wearing a shirt that's sort of different from his usual T-shirts—white, with blue baseball sleeves. His hair is kind of messy, and his eyes look almost gold.

I am utterly, enterically nervous.

"I don't know how this is supposed to work," I say finally.

He laughs. "Me neither."

I settle onto the floor against the wall, tugging my skirt down over my legs. He slides down the wall, next to me.

"I got your card," I say.

"*My* card?" He raises his eyebrows.

"Oh, I'm sorry. I got *Elizabeth's* card."

He nods solemnly. "That was nice of her."

"Yeah. Except also kind of . . . threatening?"

"Hmm." His dimple flickers. "Maybe she's jealous."

"Maybe."

And there's this tiny, hanging pause.

I bite my lip. "So, I guess we should talk?"

"Or we could not talk," he says.

"Not talking is good," I say softly.

His hand finds mine. Our fingers lace together.

"I really wish that door would lock," I add.

"I wish my mom wasn't on the other side." He squeezes my hand. "I want to kiss you."

He says it so quietly, it's almost a sigh.

I laugh. "I'm so relieved to hear that."

"Seriously?"

I nod, burying my face in his shoulder. I breathe in deeply. "You smell good."

"Like deodorant?" he suggests.

I grin. "Like you."

"I think that's my deodorant."

"Well, I'm glad you wear deodorant."

He kisses my head. "Let's go back to you being relieved I want to kiss you. Did I somehow not make that clear last night?"

I shrug.

"Or this morning?" He pulls out his phone, scrolling up through his messages. "Let's see. Here's the part where I said kissing you was the best thing that ever happened to my mouth. Here's where I said you were better than Mini Eggs. Better than *Mini Eggs*, Molly."

"I know."

"How do you go from *better than Mini Eggs* to thinking I don't want to kiss you again?"

"I don't know." I smile. "I just didn't want to make any assumptions. . . ."

"Well." He glances quickly at the storage room door, as if expecting his mom to burst through it. Then he draws in a breath and cups my cheeks gently.

And he kisses me.

"Oh."

"You can make assumptions with me," he says. "You can assume anything."

"You mean—" I begin.

He cuts me off. "Yes."

I laugh. "You don't even know what I was going to ask."

"Doesn't matter." He kisses me again. "Do I want to kiss

you? Yes. Do I want to do more than kiss you? Yes. But am I willing to take it slow? Yes. And do I want to be your boyfriend?" His voice cracks slightly, but the word comes out emphatically. "Yes."

"Okay."

"Okay to what?" He actually looks nervous.

"To all of it." My heart is in my throat. "Except taking it slow. I don't want to take it slow."

"Then let's not." He laughs.

"Good."

So, I think that means I have a boyfriend. I'm Molly with a boyfriend. Reid Jerome Wertheim is my boyfriend.

I don't even know if my brain can process those two words as a unified phrase. "My" and "boyfriend."

As in: *My boyfriend is an excellent kisser. My boyfriend has five cats. My boyfriend stayed over until four in the morning. My boyfriend is the reason I am very, very tired right now.*

But it's a good kind of tired—a sun-dappled, floating kind of tired. It is the most hazily lit movie dream of my entire dreaming career. I want to put this on pause. I want to stretch out this moment. I want to just exist inside of it.

And now I feel a little bad for Elizabeth, because I totally just stole her boyfriend. And I'm really, really sorry about it, and I know she's a queen, but the thing is, she's dead. And I'm alive.

I feel very, very alive.

27

SO, NOW MY BRAIN IS a two-color pie graph: one part Reid, one part wedding fever. NOT that I'm fevering over the thought of marrying Reid. I am most decidedly not visualizing myself in wedding dresses. I've given literally no thought to the viability of covering a wedding cake in Cadbury Mini Eggs. All obsessive wedding fantasies are wholly dedicated to the wedding that's happening in my backyard. In a week.

I swear to God, it's like a switch got flipped. Everything had been relatively calm—until it suddenly wasn't. I'm pretty sure there's an anxiety lever somewhere, and someone cranked it to UTTER PANIC FREAKOUT MODE.

That someone is Patty.

Patty, who has her laptop at the breakfast table, open to the ten-day forecast. "They're saying scattered showers. We should get a tent, right? Just in case? Do you think we need one with full siding? It looks like that's an option, but we'd probably need to rent fans."

Nadine boops Xavier on the nose and hands him a sippy cup. "You don't want to just move everything inside if it rains?"

"You think we can fit thirty-five people in this house?"

Cassie and I eat our cereal in silence. This is strangely like watching reality TV. I can almost picture Patty as a talking head, overlaid with an animated wedding veil and sound effects.

"And Cass, you need to get a dress or pants. You can't wear shorts to this."

"Who said I was wearing shorts?" Cassie looks confused.

Nadine shakes her head and shoots Cassie a tiny smile.

"Well, good. Don't do it." Patty exhales. "Great. Okay. I just need to call the tent company. And Deenie, you talked to the caterers?"

"Yup. We're scheduled for Thursday."

"Okay, we've got Olivia on photography—and I'd really like to pay her, by the way."

Cassie shrugs. "Yeah, she's not gonna let you."

"Hey," pipes Nadine, "don't let her bring that Schulmeister kid. They're still broken up, right? Because I do not need my doorstep darkened by that little shitwiper on my wedding day. Nope to the nope."

Cassie covers her mouth, giggling.

"Anyway, maybe just talk to her about payment, if you

don't mind. And Molly, you've got all the decorations under control, right?"

"Right."

She rubs her temple. "I know I'm forgetting something." She looks at Nadine. "What am I forgetting?" Then she proceeds to sit down where there isn't a chair.

"Mama," says Xav. "Uh-oh!"

Cassie and I exchange wide-eyed *holy shit* expressions.

"Okay. I'm taking over," Nadine says. "You." She points to Cassie. "Deal with Olivia. And you." She turns to me. "Centerpieces. And one of you needs to be ready to wrangle your grandmother. I don't need Betty stirring shit up."

"Oh my God," Cassie says. "Nadine, you're a stone-cold 'zilla."

"Damn straight."

"Oh," Patty says. "Molly, are you bringing the boy?"

"Wait, what?" Cassie asks. She turns to me, eyes glinting.

"Um."

"You can bring him," she says, rubbing her forehead. "That's totally fine. I just need to know by Friday."

Cassie jabs me with her elbow. "The *boy*?"

I bite back a smile.

"The fuck, Molly?"

"I love these heartwarming family moments," Nadine says. "Anyway." She turns to Patty. "You're done. Go take a nap."

Patty nods dazedly and heads for the stairs.

. . .

Nadine and Xavier head out to storytime, leaving Cassie and me alone in the dining room. For a minute, neither of us speaks.

Then Cassie looks at me. "There's a boy?" she asks. And there's something in her voice. Maybe wonder, maybe anger. I don't know.

I shrug. I feel myself blushing.

"How could you not tell me?"

"I don't know."

"*You don't know.* Jesus. I'm your twin fucking sister."

I meet her eyes finally. "Well, I didn't think we were on speaking terms."

"Well, we weren't."

I laugh nervously. "Well, okay."

"But I'm over it, okay? We're talking. Tell me about the boy." She slides her elbows forward, cupping her chin in her hands.

"Um. What do you want to know?"

Cassie smiles and rolls her eyes. "Uh, let's start with this: Who is he?"

I blush. "Reid."

She laughs.

"What?"

"No, it's just the least surprising thing ever."

"Oh."

"So what's the deal? You guys kissed? He's your boyfriend? What?"

"Yes." I grin into my sleeve.

"What?" She swipes my arm. "Wait, which one?"

"Both."

Her mouth falls open.

I swipe her back. "Stop looking so surprised."

"I'm not. I'm just excited. This is a huge deal, Mo." She scoots closer to me and hooks an arm around my shoulders. "Holy shit. You have a boyfriend."

"And you have a girlfriend."

"I know. It's weird." Then she rests her head on my shoulder and sighs.

And for a moment, we just sit there.

"God, I feel like we have so much to talk about," I say. I squeeze my eyes shut.

"Definitely," she says.

Then she lifts her head off my shoulder. When I open my eyes, she's staring down at the table, lips pressed together.

"Okay, I want to say something to you," she says after a moment. She slides her arm off my shoulders and wrings her hands together. "So, I don't know how to say this without pissing you off or hurting your feelings, but I need you to hear me out. I'm just going to put it all out there, okay?"

My shoulder muscles tighten—I feel myself getting defensive. But I try to shake it off. "Okay."

She bites her lip and nods. "So, I feel like things have been kind of off between us since I started dating Mina."

I nod.

"Right? I'm not imagining it?"

I swallow. "No."

"And, like, I have to admit, it really pissed me off at first. Because I could not understand why you couldn't just be happy for me."

"I am, though! I'm so happy for you."

"I know, but it's also like you think Mina's replacing you."

"No, that's not . . ." I look up at her. "I don't think that."

"But you said that," Cassie insists. "At the party. You said I was ditching you for Mina."

"Yeah." I exhale. "I'm sorry."

She shakes her head. "I'm not trying to make you apologize. I'm just saying, I think we should talk about this. I don't think this is just going to go away, you know? Maybe it will be better now that Reid's in the picture, but . . ."

I shut my eyes. "I don't know."

"Honestly, it's getting to the point where every thing I do, I'm worrying about how you're going to take it. Like, I don't want to be that person who gets into a relationship and ignores everyone else. We hate that person."

"You're not—"

"And I'm trying really hard, you know? I feel like you don't give me any credit for that. I invite you to everything. The sleepover, the party, the fucking pottery place. Everything."

I feel nauseated, and I don't know why. "You don't have to do that."

"I know!" She throws her hands up. "I know I don't. But I want to."

"I don't want to be a person you have to tiptoe and walk on eggshells around."

"No, Molly, you're not." She shakes her head. "You're not. It's just I'm having trouble balancing this. I'm not used to having another person be this important to me."

She's staring at her knees, tears pooling in her eyes.

"And I don't want to lose us, you know?"

I feel my eyes prickle, too. Everything's a little blurry. I can't seem to focus. I press my fist into my chin.

"I'm scared it's inevitable," I say finally.

"What do you mean?"

"Growing apart. Look at Nadine and Aunt Karen."

"Don't you think that's a little different? Aunt Karen is a homophobe."

"No, I know. But still." I swallow. "How many sisters do you know who are as close as adults as they were growing up?"

"Well, I don't know many adult sisters . . . ," Cassie says, smiling faintly.

"You know what I mean, though. It's like, we used to tell each other all of this stuff. Who we liked, or hooked up with, or whatever. But then there's this shift. It's like our loyalties switch over, and the relationship becomes the main thing."

"Okay, we haven't *switched over* our loyalties—"

"But we will." I take a deep breath. "Even if it's not with Mina and Reid. Eventually. It's the normal thing that happens. You don't marry your siblings."

"Yeah, that would be a smidge incestuous," Cassie says.

"Just a smidge."

She laughs, and then sniffs.

"I mean, obviously, you're right," Cassie says finally. "And I guess that's kind of why I wanted the Will thing to happen. Like, maybe if we dated best friends, it wouldn't be like that for us."

"Right."

"But . . . Will's a no-go, huh?"

I shake my head, smiling.

"So, what do we do?" Cassie asks.

"I don't know."

She sniffs again. I look over at her, and there are tears streaking down her cheeks. "Shut up. This is sad," she says, smiling wetly.

"I know."

"Change is fucking hard. It's fucking tragic."

"Change can go fuck itself," I say, and I like how it sounds on my tongue. *Fuck itself.* It catches Cassie off guard. She laughs so hard, she can barely catch her breath.

And all of a sudden, I can't help but wonder: are the

ancestors tuned in to this moment? And do they get it?

I bet they do.

Because that's the thing about change. It's so painfully normal. It's the most basic of all tragedies. Sisters in the Paleolithic period probably felt shitty about this stuff.

And it's weird how I can *know* this, but it doesn't make it hurt less.

28

REID COMES OVER ON WEDNESDAY to help me test my cake recipe.

And I guess I can't really put it off any longer: I have to ask him to be my date this Sunday. But in a totally no-pressure kind of way. Because this doesn't have to be a Thing. It's just a date. To a wedding. In which the brides are my parents. ALL RIGHT? NO BIG DEAL.

"Okay, it's ten thirty now." He leans back against the fridge. "And I'm supposed to be at work by noon. So, don't let me—oof."

I kiss him so hard, it sets off the ice machine.

"Oh," I say, and he laughs, hands catching me around the waist. This is still the strangest thing. Strange that I'm doing this. Strange that I survived not doing this. I don't know how I ever went five minutes without kissing, much less thirty-two thousand minutes.

But I like the way Reid kisses with his glasses on. I like the way my brain feels hazy. We probably shouldn't be doing this in the kitchen, especially because Cassie's home. She could walk in at any minute. Which is horrifying. Because I suddenly understand why Cassie got so mysterious about Mina. I can't explain it, but I get it.

I kiss Reid again. Maybe if we keep kissing, I won't have to ask him to the wedding. He'll just know. He's probably expecting it anyway. Unless he's not. Unless he's thinking: *whoa, I hooked up with this girl last week, and now she wants to bring me to her parents' wedding.*

HEY, LIFE: STOP BEING SO AWKWARD.

Reid pauses. "What was that beep?"

"Oh! The oven's done preheating." I exhale. I make myself step back.

I am baking. I am baking a tiny cake and a bunch of cupcakes, and I should probably think about mixing the batter. At some point. Eventually.

He kisses me again, softly.

"Molly?"

And oh.

It's Olivia, wide-eyed in the doorway.

I whirl around, brightly. "Hi!" My hand slides back, and an entire collection of dry measuring cups clatters to the ground.

It is a very loud clatter.

Because it is very silent in here.

"Oh," she says. "I don't mean to interrupt."

"You're not interrupting!" I grin. I'm totally grinning. If I grin hard enough, I'll probably look super casual and she'll know there's nothing suspicious going on here. She didn't *actually* see anything. She probably just imagined it, because I am SO CHILL AND CASUAL RIGHT NOW.

She stares at the ground. "Okay, well, Cass and I are going through some of your family photos to put on display. Just in case you wanted to, you know . . . but I guess you're busy."

"Oh, yeah. We're baking!"

"I can see that."

My entire face is burning. I didn't even know Olivia was here, much less in the doorway.

"So, uh. If you guys want to do photos, we'll just be in the dining room," she adds.

"Okay, great," I say quickly.

Her eyes flick up to Reid and back down to me.

"Great, well . . ."

She's gone before I even say good-bye.

I feel entirely unsettled. I head to the dining room as soon as Reid leaves, but all I find are a bunch of photographs. Cassie and Olivia are nowhere.

I don't want to freak out about this, but here's the thing: even if Reid isn't into Olivia, I have no idea how Olivia feels about Reid. I guess I'm feeling very tender toward her all of a sudden. Even though a week ago I was dreaming about throwing things at her face.

A-week-ago Molly was kind of a shitty person.

I have to make this right. I take a deep breath and text her.

Hey, are you still here?

Nothing. Nothing.

And then three dots.

Hey! In Xav's room with C. You guys should come up here.

God, she thinks Reid is with me. That I would do that. That I would flaunt him like that. *Heeeeeyyy, Olivia, guess what. HE'S MINE HE'S MINE HE'S MINE.*

The thought alone makes me wince. I don't think I'm a HE'S MINE kind of girl.

I take the stairs slowly, my heart in my throat.

Xavier's room is the size of a walk-in closet. Seriously, my moms got him one of those train track area rugs from Ikea, and it covers his entire floor. When I open the door, Olivia and Xavier are building a tower out of blocks. Except that's entirely inaccurate. *Olivia* is building a tower. Xavier is destroying a tower.

"Hey," I say, scooping him into my lap. He wriggles out of my arms immediately. "I'm really sorry I missed the photos."

"It's cool. I hear you were busy." Cassie waggles her eyebrows, and Olivia snickers. They are the worst. Both of them.

I grin into my fist and settle in next to Cassie, our backs against the crib.

She leans toward me. "So, Reid's coming to the wedding, right?"

"Um. Hopefully? I haven't asked him yet."

I glance at Olivia, who looks as serene as ever.

"Well, you better fucking get on that," Cassie says. "And tell him I have to talk to him."

I narrow my eyes. "About what?"

"About how if he breaks your heart, I'll castrate him. Just your basic protective sister shit." She stands up, stretching. "Hold that thought. I've got to pee."

She shuts the door behind her. Olivia smiles up at me. "Molly, you have a boyfriend."

I need to not smile. This is not a moment for smiling. This is a moment for being as little of an asshole as humanly possible. This girl just got dumped by the likes of Evan Schulmeister. And now the guy she maybe likes is my boyfriend. I nod, carefully, staring at my knees.

"I so called that."

"You did?" I look up at her tentatively. "Are you mad?"

"Why would I be mad?"

"Oh. God. I thought maybe you liked him."

There's a sudden crash as Xavier topples a block tower. He looks from me to Olivia and back to me, lip trembling.

"Buddy, you're the one who knocked it down," I remind him. Sometimes you can trick Xav into not having a meltdown. But he collapses into Olivia's arms.

"Oh, I don't," Olivia says. "I mean, I like him as a friend, definitely, and I think he's cute. Like, he's really cute."

"That is true." I bite back a smile.

"Definitely cuter than Will, in my opinion." She blushes.

Oh God. She likes him.

"I'm really sorry," I say quietly.

"You shouldn't be! Please don't be sorry. Anyway, I already knew he was in love with you."

"What?" I stop short.

"Every time I've hung out with him, all he did was talk about you."

I grin into the sleeve of my cardigan. "Oh."

"Yeah." She smiles. "Seriously, I don't want to get in the way of that." She squeezes Xavier's foot. "I really want this for you, Molly."

I think my brain has shut down. I can't think of a single thing to say. All I know is this: Olivia is definitely a better person than me.

"Yeah, but I want you to be happy, too," I say finally.

She shrugs. "I am."

"But I want you to be in love. With someone better than Evan."

"Anyone's better than Evan," she says.

"Good point."

And now I'm furiously matchmaking in my head. Obviously, Will's off the table, since Olivia doesn't even see his cuteness. And Max is kind of an asshole. But I'm curious about Douglas. Reid swears he exists. Olivia and the elusive Douglas. I know Reid ships it.

"Have you—" I start to say, but Olivia cuts me off.

"I know what you're thinking." Olivia rests her chin on Xavier's head. "But I don't actually want a boyfriend right now."

"Really?"

"Not even a little." She smiles.

I turn it over in my head. I can't decide if this is funny or sad, but I've spent so much time wanting a boyfriend that I can't imagine not wanting one. I can imagine *saying* I don't want one. But I can't imagine it being true.

And maybe that's just me, a little broken after twenty-six rounds of unrequited love. Maybe this is a side effect.

29

FRIDAY NIGHT. DEEP BREATH.

So, I've been trying to ask you something for a couple of days now

But I can't seem to get the words out.

So I guess I'm doing this over text, because I'm the actual worst

Any chance you're free on Sunday? As in, the day after tomorrow?

Because there's this wedding I'm going to, and I kind of need a date . . .

30

BUTT-EARLY, SATURDAY. THE BOYFRIEND REPLIES:

Okay, I have an idea

Like a WEDDING idea.

So, you know those pennant things that look like shark teeth?

People make cake toppers like that!

They're held up by chopsticks. I didn't make this up. I found it on Pinterest.

WHY AM I LOOKING AT PINTEREST, MOLLY? What is this madness?

I think I must miss you.

Or maybe Pinterest is actually an adorable disease transmitted only through your saliva?

Your *adorable* saliva.

The Adorable Saliva of Molly Peskin-Suso.

That should be the title of your autobiography!

Anyway, I know you're at the alterations place getting altered.

(But hopefully not too altered.)

(I really like you unaltered.)

So, just know that.

Also, I really think you should do this cake topper.

(In case this isn't clear, this is me saying yes. I am down for this wedding and anything else you want to bring me to, ever, especially if cake is involved.)

31

UNALTERED? I WRITE. LIKE AN un-spayed cat?

Oh. Oh no. I mean, YES. Please don't get spayed.

I have a boyfriend who sends texts asking me not to get spayed. I don't think I'll ever get tired of Reid's weird mind. Ever.

I'll try not to! I write. And then: I'm really glad you're coming.

So, I'm not getting altered. I'm not even getting my dress altered. We're just here for my moms, here being the bridal boutique alterations department. Cassie and I are on a velvet couch outside the changing room, surrounded by mirrors. I'm trying not to stare at myself.

Patty steps out of the changing room and sighs. "Oh God. See, now I don't know about the strapless."

Cassie raises her eyebrows. "Isn't it a little late in the game for that?"

"You look perfect," Nadine says, smiling.

"I don't look like a pale, boobless forty-eight-year-old?"

"You do." Nadine kisses her. "And I like it."

Cassie sinks into the couch cushions and covers her eyes. "Stooooooooooopppp. Get a room."

"Get used to it, Kitty Cat," Nadine says. She looks in the mirror, grins, and unbuttons her top button. "What do you think?"

"Perfect," I say. And they really are perfect. Nadine's wearing light gray pants and a white button-down from the grooms' section. I actually watched her tell a consultant that her priority was "boob accessibility." Patty's boobs, on the other hand, are trapped behind epic amounts of Alençon lace. They're both so totally beautiful. I know it's weird to think that about your parents, but it's true. I can't believe they're getting married tomorrow.

Nadine turns to me suddenly, eyes glinting. "So, Molly, are you bringing Reid to this thing?"

Cassie turns to me and beams. "Your boyfriend," she adds. "Just reminding you."

Boyfriend. Still not used to it. I grin into my fist.

Through the mirror, I catch a glimpse of Patty and Nadine watching us. They look especially twinkly-eyed, and I can tell Patty's gearing up to say something. She's got that look. But she's intercepted by the bridal consultant for some last-minute stitching.

Okay, this should be a thing. Like a service you can order. Someone to sweep your mom away at the exact moment she's about to say something awkward.

Unfortunately, Nadine decides to carry the baton. "I want to hear more about this rad boyfriend."

Cassie giggles.

I roll my eyes. "Oh, he's rad."

"I mean, I didn't even know this was in the pipeline," she adds. "Momo, you've been holding out on us. Didn't even know you liked anyone."

"I knew," Cassie says smugly.

I feel warm all over. "Do we have to talk about this?"

"Aww, baby. I'm just happy for you." She squeezes onto the couch between Cassie and me, and hooks an arm around each of us.

"She's wanted a boyfriend for so long. Soooooo long," Cassie says.

I wrinkle my nose. "Okay, that just makes me sound pathetic."

"What? No!"

"Aww, Momo, why do you think that?"

Because. I don't want to be that girl. I want to be the other kind of girl. The Olivia kind. Totally cool with being single. Not even interested in a relationship right now.

"Because I don't want to be a girl who needs a boyfriend," I say.

"Well, of course you don't need one," Nadine says. "But it's okay to want one."

I shrug.

"Momo, I'm serious. You get to want whatever you want." She tugs the end of my hair. "And you know what? Love is worth wanting."

"Agreed." Cassie grins.

"I just didn't think it would ever happen." I blush. "I guess I'm just a late bloomer."

Nadine bursts out laughing. I feel the corners of my mouth twisting upward. "What?"

"Late bloomer? Mo, you're seventeen."

"Exactly."

"In what universe does that make you a late bloomer?" She squeezes my shoulder. "There's no schedule for this stuff. I didn't have a girlfriend until the end of senior year. And your mom never dated in high school."

"Really?"

"Really."

I pause. "I don't know. Yeah. It just felt like I was waiting forever."

"Oh, I know, baby. I don't mean to discount your feelings here." She disentangles her arms and clasps them in her lap. "Yeah, the waiting sucks. Especially when you start feeling like it's never going to happen."

"Exactly!"

She smiles. "Have I ever talked to y'all about when I was trying to get pregnant?"

"I don't think so," Cassie says.

I shake my head.

"Yeah. It was a long-ass journey. I mean, we tried on and off for ten years. All kinds of doctors. Nobody knew what was up."

"Are you serious?" Cassie asks.

And I'm stunned. Maybe I shouldn't be. I don't know. I guess it makes sense that my moms didn't randomly decide to have another baby sixteen years after the first two. But I never realized Nadine was actively trying. For ten years. I can't wrap my head around it.

"And then it just worked, you know? And I was forty-two. Nobody thought there was a chance in hell at this point, but there you go."

"Wow. I did not know that," I say.

Nadine smiles. "I know. I guess it's weird to talk about, because I never want you guys to feel like you belong to me any less than your brother. You know that's not the case, right?"

"I know," I say quickly.

"But your mom and I always wanted three kids. That was our plan. And we thought we were so ahead of the game popping two out at once. Little did we know . . ."

"Xav was fashionably late," Cassie says.

"Something like that. But you know, there's an upside here. Because when you spend so much time just intensely wanting something, and then you actually get the thing? It's magic."

All of a sudden, I feel like crying. In a good way. In the best way. Because I know exactly what she means. It's butterflies and haziness and heart eyes, but underneath all that, there's this bass line of *I can't believe this. I can't believe this is me.*

I can't quite articulate the sweetness of that feeling.

It's finding out the door you were banging on is finally unlocked. Maybe it was unlocked the whole time.

32

THERE'S NO REHEARSAL DINNER. THERE'S no rehearsal anything. But all the out-of-town people get here on Saturday night, and it's actually starting to feel real.

Grandma Betty is at the Marriott, and my Suso grandparents are staying at the bed and breakfast up the road. I think my moms' college friends are getting in tomorrow morning.

But Abby's coming tonight. With Nick. And she's staying at our house.

I set up the air mattress in my room, and Cassie moves her stuff in. I don't even care that we'll basically have to sleep on top of each other. It's the first Suso slumber party in over a year.

The doorbell rings just as we're putting dinner dishes away, and I catapult into the foyer. I move so quickly, I actually skid across the hardwood.

"Oh my God." Abby's in the doorway, jumping up and down.

"You're here!"

"I'm here! You're here!" She inhales deeply. "Ahh! You smell like Molly."

"Wait, is that—"

"It's a good thing!"

Which makes me think of Reid. And his deodorant. I shouldn't blush.

"I can't believe you're actually here."

"I'm here. And look who I brought!" She beams, stepping back. "Molly, this is Nick. Nick, Molly."

It's funny the way some people look just like their pictures. Like Simon. But Nick is actually cuter in person. Way, way cuter. He has these magnetic brown eyes that don't entirely translate in photos.

"Hey." He stands awkwardly in the foyer with a big canvas duffel bag. "Thanks for letting me come to this."

"Are you kidding? Of course!"

Outside, I hear the beep of the car locking. Moments later, Isaac appears, dragging two suitcases. "Hey, Mo," he says, practically kneeling to hug me. Isaac is six foot four. No joke. He makes Reid look short.

It occurs to me that he's a nice height for Olivia.

But no. Nope. She doesn't want that. Banish the thought.

Nick and Isaac take the bunk beds in Cassie's room. It's

actually funny, having Abby and Isaac here without their parents. Uncle Albert and Aunt Wanda are staying in Isaac's studio apartment on U Street—which is honestly a half step up from a frat house.

"What'd your mom think of your flip cup table?" Cassie asks him.

Isaac grins. "Tablecloth and vase of flowers."

"Genius."

As soon as Abby shuts my bedroom door, Cassie bursts out with it. "Molly has a—drumroll please—boyfriend."

"What?" Abby gasps. "Oh my God. You kissed him. Really? Oh my God!"

"I KNOW," Cassie says. "And she didn't even tell me." She flops backward on the air mattress.

"I didn't tell anyone," I say.

"Except our moms."

"I didn't tell them! They found out."

"Oh, I'd like to know this story," Abby says.

"There's not really a story. Patty heard us."

Abby and Cassie burst out laughing.

"What?" I ask. I feel myself smiling.

"Heard you doing *what*?" Abby asks.

THIS AGAIN.

"Not that. God. Talking. Just talking."

"Sure."

"Maybe kissing."

"There you go," Cassie says. She picks up a pillow, throws it at me, misses, *picks it up again*, and smacks me.

"Pillow fight!" Abby yells, making her voice super high. "This is the fantasy, right? Should I tell Nick this is happening?"

Cassie nods. "Tell him we're pouring honey on our boobs."

Abby laughs, pulling out her phone.

"Wait, seriously? Are you texting him that?" Cassie clambers toward Abby, who smoothly twists away from her. "Wait, let me see."

"Nope." Abby grins. "This is confidential."

"My ass is confidential."

"Let's hope so."

And it's funny, watching them bicker. It's like falling backward through time. I feel perfectly content. I don't even want to talk. I just like being here.

I text Reid. I think you're going to have to dance with me tomorrow.

Three dots.

Ohhhh no. I don't dance.

AND YET.

You have NO IDEA how clumsy I am, Molly.

I laugh. *I have some idea . . .*

My dance moves have actually killed people.

"Look at this one giggling into her phone," Abby says.

I look up, smiling guiltily—and I catch a sudden glimpse of myself in the mirror across the room.

It's the weirdest thing. My hair is unbrushed. I'm wearing what may actually be one of Nadine's maternity shirts. And pajama pants. And there's a spot of toothpaste in the corner of my mouth.

But for the first time in maybe ever, I feel really beautiful.

33

I'M TOO EXCITED TO SLEEP. I keep thinking about the wedding and Reid and the centerpieces and my outfit.

I'm in love with my dress. The design is so simple: soft and blue green, with short sleeves, and a layer of tulle under the skirt. That's it. But it fits me in exactly the right way. It doesn't make me look skinny. I think it makes me look fat on purpose.

I keep touching the fabric. I can't wait to get dressed.

There's something in the air. I feel this buzz of anticipation. Outside my window, I see my moms lining two long tables with chairs. There's definitely no tent. Maybe Nadine talked Patty out of it. But it's sunny and warm. I almost sigh with relief.

My whole morning is devoted to decorations. I think I've finally nailed it: vintage Coke crates for height, painted mason jars at different levels, and flowers—mostly baby's breath, but some hydrangeas. I'll stagger Olivia's painted animal figurines all around, plus family photos, framed in painted wood. Then I'll drape the fabric garland over the ceremony space, kind of like a scraggly chuppah, and Isaac says he'll help me hang twinkle lights from the trees.

And I actually think I might cut up my bead string. Because I'm suddenly obsessed with the idea of magazine bead napkin holders.

Seriously, I could do this for a living. Maybe one day I will.

Though these stone-cold bridezillas can be a little challenging. I'm fielding texts from both my moms every few minutes.

Sweetie, can you remind Isaac to tip the rentals guys?

Momo, I need you to find the laptop charger

Mission abort! CHARGER HAS BEEN LOCATED.

The caterers just arrived. Maybe you could get them set up in the kitchen? Thanks!!!

I mean, I'm still in pajama pants, but I guess that's almost like pants. I run down the stairs and almost bump directly into one of the caterers. "Oh God. I'm sorry." I look up. And my whole face goes warm. "Julian?"

"Oh, no way! You're Elena's friend. Molly, right?"

My eleventh crush. Julian Portillo of the Experimental Breakfasts. And now he's a caterer. Go figure.

"So your moms are getting hitched," he says.

"Yup." This is surreal. "Wow. How are you? How's Elena?"

"Aww, she's good. I'm good. I'm at Georgetown. Just

finished my sophomore year, and I'm catering this summer. I love it."

"That's so great."

He smiles, and hey: there are those dimples. Maybe I have a thing for dimples.

"Oh, and I should introduce you. This is Carter Addison," Julian says, touching my arm lightly.

As if on cue, this lanky, curly-haired white guy sets down a covered tinfoil pan and ambles over. "Hey," he says, smiling. And he's sort of cute, too. He has this big, open smile. "I'm the sous chef," he says.

"And the boyfriend." Julian grins. "Carter, this is Molly. She's the daughter of the brides."

Boyfriend. I did not see that coming.

"Really nice to meet you," I say.

"You too. And mazel tov!"

I walk them through our kitchen and show them the appliances and my cupcakes and everything I can think of. "I don't know if this is helpful."

"It definitely is," Julian says. "This is great."

"Good." I nod. And for a minute, we all sort of stand there, smiling awkwardly. I've never really been good at forming words in the vicinity of Julian Portillo.

"So, I don't want to rush you or anything," Julian says, finally, "but maybe you should get dressed? Don't get me wrong, I dig the plaid pants . . ."

"Oh, crap," I say.

"Oh, she's blushing!" He hugs me. Julian Portillo hugs me. "Man, you're the cutest." I catch him winking at Carter. "You know, if I'd ever liked girls, you'd have been the one, Molly."

I don't think there are words to explain how I feel.

Okay, you know the emoji that's laughing and crying all at once?

It's that. I am that.

I get dressed quickly and run back downstairs, just as Mina and Olivia are arriving. They're pretty early—I actually think they carpooled. Olivia hugs me as soon as she sees me. "Congratulations!"

Cassie wanders over to meet us. "So, I just had the best conversation with Grandma."

"Really?"

She grimaces, and I laugh.

"Grandma has just informed me that when a bisexual woman marries another woman, she becomes a lesbian."

"Oh no," Olivia says.

"And I'm like . . . Grandma, just no. No. Infinite side-eye."

Mina laughs. "She's very well-intentioned, though."

"And she's not even drunk yet," says Cassie. Her eyes drift sideways, and she nudges me, grinning. "Hey. Your boyfriend's here."

I blush. It's just weird. Maybe it's the fact that everyone

knows. I mean, it is never-ending, this weirdness. I'll never have a handle on this.

Reid is standing near the back steps, wearing a button-down shirt. So, now I know: Reid is ridiculously cute in a button-down shirt. He smiles at me, and I smile back, and it's like someone put the world on pause. Just for a moment.

I think I like not having a handle on this.

It feels like six o'clock will never come, but it does—and all of a sudden, we're lined up beneath the garland chuppah. Cassie, Abby, and me, plus Isaac, holding Xavier. Xavier, who is wearing a tiny gray suit.

He is perfect.

"Welcome, all," greets my aunt Liz.

She isn't technically my aunt. She's not technically a minister either, but she got certified online. "Patty and Nadine have asked me to keep this short and sweet and relatively PG-13, which . . . we'll see."

Everyone laughs.

"Anyway, I'm Liz, and I was Nadine's roommate at Maryland, roughly, I don't know, a billion years ago." Nadine snorts. "So, true story: freshman year, we get our class schedules, and Deenie is pissed. Because they've put her in Biology 101—which she'd *already taken* in high school, and this was *fucking bullshit*—"

There's this burst of laughter from the tables, because

you can totally picture Nadine saying that. I sneak a glance at Abby's parents—Uncle Albert looks stern, and Aunt Wanda is smiling brightly with raised eyebrows. Abby glances at me sideways and grins.

"Anyway, she huffs off to class, muttering and raging under her breath. And then she comes back around lunchtime, and I ask, 'Okay, so, are they going to let you transfer out? Are they going to accept your credits?' And Nadine is like, 'Ohhhhh. Yeah. I like that class now.'"

Nadine covers her face, laughing.

"And I'm like, *what*?" Liz continues, eyes glinting. "So, this morning, you were ready to chain yourself to the door of the dean's office over this, and now you're like, 'Oh, this class is the best.' And I'm just totally baffled by it." Liz pauses for dramatic effect. "Until a few weeks later, Nadine introduces me to Patty Peskin. Her TA."

There's clapping and whooping from the tables, and Nadine and Patty are looking at each other and giggling. There's something weird about seeing your parents so openly adoring each other. I'm not saying it's bad. Just weird.

For the millionth time today, my eyes find Reid.

He smiles.

And I smile.

"So, do you, Nadine, take this woman, Patty, to be your wife, to have and to hold, to honor and cherish, in sickness and in health, as long as you both shall live?"

"I do," Nadine says. I've never seen her smile so widely.

"And do you, Patty, take this woman, Nadine, to be your wife, to have and to hold, to honor and cherish, in sickness and in health, as long as you both shall live?"

Patty sniffs. "I do."

Warm fingers thread through mine—Abby. I squeeze her hand tightly.

"Should we put a ring on it?" asks Liz.

I laugh. Everyone's laughing. And Patty's sobbing, which isn't surprising, but even Nadine is crying a little. That's kind of a big deal. I've only ever seen her cry once, and she was literally giving birth at the time.

"So, by the power vested in me by the state of Maryland, I now pronounce you legally and awesomely married."

Then they break the glass, and everyone giggles and yells mazel tov, and a few people whistle.

And then. Well.

There's a single moment in the life of parents when they get to make out in front of their kids. This is that moment. It can't be stopped.

I wouldn't stop it if I could.

Reid finds me straightaway and hugs me. "That was really awesome."

"Thanks!" I lean into his chest, breathing in his deodorant. "Did you cry?"

"NEVER." His dimple flickers. "A little."

"Aww." I grin up at him. He takes both my hands.

And for a minute, we just stand there like that, looking at each other.

He shakes his head. "Molly, you're killing me."

"What?"

He pauses. His cheeks are pink. "You just look really, really pretty."

His voice is so soft. I feel my breath hitch. Because in all my years of watching movies, I've seen this look on a lot of boys' faces. But I've never seen someone look that way at me.

"So do you," I say quickly.

He laughs. "Why, thank you."

Julian and Carter have set all the food out on a picnic table—brisket and corn bread and rolls and grilled vegetables. There's the kosher stuff and vegan stuff and gluten-free stuff, all meticulously labeled. And there are stacks of those fake china plastic plates. It's definitely a self-serve kind of wedding.

It's still light out, but a few people are dancing by Xavier's swing set. There's a slow song playing, and I can't quite place the artist. It's definitely a famous British guy. Maybe Sam Smith.

"Are you hungry?" Reid tugs on my hand.

"I guess so?"

"Or do you want to find Abby?"

"That works, too."

"You are so easy to please today." He grins at me.

"I know!"

I just feel so achingly happy. Like the happiness is bubbling over. I could do anything right now, and it would be the exact right thing. This is invincible joy. I can't ruin it. I can't even put a dent in it.

We sit at the end of one of the tables, next to Abby and Nick. "Look at how cute your moms are right now," Abby says.

They're sitting on the back steps, holding hands and talking. Totally removed from everyone, for a moment. I see Olivia sneaking closer with her camera. They don't even notice her pointing, focusing, and clicking like a paparazzo.

Then, she walks over to Cassie and Mina on the grass, smiling as she taps through her viewer window to show them.

Cassie's beaming.

"For someone who thinks of herself as such a cynic," I murmur.

"I know. Cassie's actually the biggest mush of all of us. Pure goopy-hearted grossness." Abby laughs. "Hey, before I forget, look who's here."

She lifts her chin slightly, gesturing to a point behind my back.

I turn my head, and my mouth falls open.

"Oh my God."

Abby grins. "I know!"

"Did you know she'd be here?"

She shakes her head. "Should we go say hi? Can we leave you two dudes alone for a sec?"

Nick and Reid look at each other. "Um, sure."

Our boyfriends.

I stand, smoothing my dress down. Abby takes my hand, and we walk across the lawn.

Aunt Karen's sitting alone at a table, hands folded across her chest. She looks stiff and uncomfortable and, honestly, sort of miserable.

But she's here.

Holy shit.

She lights up when she sees us. "Hey, babies!" she says. "Oh my goodness. Look at you two. You look beautiful. So grown-up."

She hugs us both, and we settle into seats on either side of her.

"The backyard looks different. Was it landscaped?"

"Um, yeah. Like, two years ago," I say.

Aunt Karen nods.

"So. Um. How are the dogs?"

She brightens a bit. "Oh, they're good. They're real good. They're staying with my friend Madge, and her husband's grilling steaks tonight. New York strips."

"Um. For the dogs?" Abby asks.

"Mmmhmm. They love steak."

"That is really special," Abby says, cutting her eyes toward me.

Aunt Karen smiles. "They're really special dogs. Abby, I

was just telling your mom about my shepherd mix, Daisy, and she said—"

"Aunt Karen, I thought you weren't coming," I blurt.

There's this beat of silence.

And then finally, she says, "Well, I guess I couldn't miss it."

"Does Nadine know you're here?"

She purses her lips. "I assume so."

"Do you . . . want me to go get her?"

"Oh no," Aunt Karen says quickly. "It'll just be . . . you know. This is her night. And Patty's night," she adds awkwardly.

As soon as she says it, I realize she's never mentioned Patty by name before, ever.

"And I'm not here to complicate things," she continues. "Deenie and I have a lot to talk about, obviously, and I owe her . . ." She trails off, shaking her head. "But not tonight. Tonight, I just wanted to be here."

"Well, thanks for coming, I guess."

"Is that you, mamaleh?"

I swivel to find Grandma Betty, holding one of the picture frame centerpieces—which she sets facedown on the table as she settles into the chair beside me.

Oh my goodness. Family overload.

"Hi, Grandma."

I find I'm sucking in my stomach. I guess I feel self-conscious around her sometimes. For just a split second, I wish I'd worn Spanx.

"Have you met Aunt Karen?" I ask quickly. "I know you know Abby."

"Of course. Lovely to see both of you again."

I tap the edge of Grandma's frame. "What picture is that?"

"It's a very unflattering photograph of me. I want to know who picked this to be a centerpiece." She shakes her head and smiles. "I'm lodging a formal complaint."

That kind of throws me. I didn't know old people still got self-conscious about that stuff. Now I totally want to see the picture, of course—and Abby must be thinking the exact same thing. "Betty, you have to show us! We won't tell anyone."

"If you show us, I'll hide it for you," I add.

Grandma grimaces but turns the frame over in her hands.

Abby gasps. "Oh my God, that's a stunning picture."

And it is. Holy shit. This photo. It's black and white, and Patty's just a baby, so it must be from the late sixties. But Grandma's the one I can't take my eyes off of. She's in her twenties, smiling gently. Balancing Patty on her hip and looking straight at the camera.

She looks exactly like me, except old-timey and beautiful.

And she's fat.

When I look up, she's gazing at me with an expression I can't quite read. "I'm hard on you, aren't I?"

I blush. "I don't know."

"I hated being overweight. I gained seventy pounds when

I was pregnant with your mother. I felt like I was living in a different person's body."

I pause. *Inhale.* "I get that." *Exhale.* "But I don't feel like that, you know?"

"I know, and that's a good thing. I'm so sorry, mamaleh. I shouldn't turn my issues into your issues." She takes my hand and squeezes it. "You are absolutely beautiful."

I feel my cheeks burn. Here's the thing: I'm used to being told I have a pretty face. Or pretty hair, or pretty eyes. But it's different, being called *beautiful.* Just beautiful, without conditions. And for some reason, it's even stranger hearing it from Grandma Betty than from Reid.

It makes my eyes prickle.

Grandma clears her throat. "Anyway, wasn't that just the loveliest ceremony?"

"It was," Abby says.

Aunt Karen shrugs. "It was nice," she says softly.

That shrug. The particular set of Aunt Karen's shoulders. It's as if that shrug contains forty years of secrets and fighting and road trips and bunk beds.

The thing is, it's exactly how Nadine shrugs.

And suddenly, I can picture it: Cassie and me, twenty years from now. Married. To Mina. To Reid. Or not. Maybe we'll marry people we haven't even met yet. Maybe we'll never marry at all. We might see each other every day. We might see each other once a year. Maybe it will ebb and flow and change with the decades. Maybe we'll never pin it down.

I think every relationship is actually a million relationships.

I can't decide if that's a bad thing.

It's better when the sun sets. I think it's the twinkle lights. There's something magical about twinkle lights on tree branches. A few people have gone home, but even more people are dancing, and Abby and Nick are right in the middle of it. I haven't talked Reid into dancing yet. Right now, he's primarily focused on being smug about the paper pennant cake topper.

Which, admittedly, was his idea.

Which, admittedly, turned out adorably.

But now we're back at the table, and Reid's holding my hand while talking to Olivia, and Xavier's passed out in Cassie's arms. Mina's eating a cupcake, wiping her hands on a napkin between bites. But despite the movement all around us, there's this stillness in the air.

"I could never actually be a wedding photographer," says Olivia.

"Why not?"

"Too many perfect moments. I can't keep up with them."

I feel suddenly choked up. "Yeah."

Reid squeezes my hand.

The song changes to something loud and fast, and I catch a glimpse of Isaac on the makeshift dance floor, spinning one of my moms' friends in circles. I think he's wearing a bunch of my magazine bead napkin holders as bracelets. Aunt Liz is perched on Xav's tire swing, gesturing emphatically, making my moms laugh. And Abby's parents are defiantly slow-dancing, despite the music. It's actually kind of sweet.

"I think I'm going to snap a few more pictures," Olivia says.

"Okay," Cassie and I say in unison, with perfectly matching intonation.

Olivia narrows her eyes, pointing a finger at each of us. "It's like you two are twins or something." As she walks away, she pantomimes an explosion from her head. *Mind. Blown.*

Mina giggles, and she and Cassie exchange these smiley, soft-eyed glances. I look away quickly. Not because I'm an eleven-year-old boy.

Just—you know. So they can have their moment.

I think this is me letting go. Bit by bit. I think these are our tiny steps away from each other. Making not-quite-identical footprints in not-quite-opposite directions.

And it's the end of the world and the beginning of the world and we're seventeen.

It's an awesome thing.

Acknowledgments

Hi, reader! My book is in your hands. I've been anticipating this moment like Molly anticipated her first kiss. There were moments when I was certain this story would never come together.

Somehow it did. Because I have some really awesome wingmen, wingwomen, and wingpeople who made this book happen.

Warmest thanks to:

Brooks Sherman, best of dudes and best of agents. You are wise and weird and wonderful, and I am so lucky to have you in my corner.

Donna Bray, who made this book come alive. You believed in Molly when I didn't, and you helped me find this story's heart. All my bee ladies are for you.

My extraordinary teams at Harper, the Bent Agency, and New Leaf. I'm so grateful for Alessandra Balzer, Viana Siniscalchi, Caroline Sun, Nellie Kurtzman, Patty Rosati, Molly Motch, Bess Braswell, Eric Svenson, Margot Wood, Kate Morgan Jackson, Suman Seewat, Veronica Ambrose, Bethany Reis, Chris Bilheimer, Sarah Creech, Alison Donalty, Barbara Fitzsimmons, Suzanne Murphy, Molly Ker Hawn, Victoria Lowes, Charlee Hoffman, Jenny Bent, Pouya Shahbazian, Chris McEwan, and so many others kicking ass behind the scenes.

My amazing publishing teams abroad, including Penguin/Puffin in the UK, Australia, and New Zealand, Blossom Books in the Netherlands, Hachette Romans in France, and Intrinseca in Brazil. Extra Mini Eggs for Anthea Townsend, Ben Horslen, Clare Kelly, Vicky Photiou, Myrthe Spiteri, Lotte Dijkstra, and Mathilde Tamae Bouhon.

Kimberly Ito, my CP and agent sister, who has kept me sane for years. Molly and Cassie couldn't pick a better person to share their birthday with.

Beckminavidera, which is basically a marriage at this point. Adam Silvera, I'm pretty sure you own half my brain. David Arnold, you inspire me to write honestly and spell Middle-earth as Tolkien intended. Jasmine Warga, you are the Balzer to my Bray. (Plus my main hetsie and honorary Beckminavidera member, Luis Rivera.)

Team Double Stuf: Nic Stone, Angela Thomas, and Stefani Sloma. Your texts are magic, and you're even awesomer in person. I'm so grateful to know you.

Team Erratica: Emily Carpenter, Manda Pullen, Chris Negron, and George Weinstein. I'll see you at Rojo!

The BTeam—my beautiful agent siblings—with extra hugs for Heidi Schulz (insert underutilized emoji here), Kimberly Ito, Angela Thomas, Adam Silvera, Lianne Oelke, Sarah Cannon, Mercy Brown, Jessica Cluess, and Rita Meade.

My extraordinary sensitivity readers, who brought Molly's community to life: Angela Thomas, Nic Stone, Wesaun Palmer, Alex Davison, Dahlia Adler, Tehlor Kinney, Tristina Wright, Nita Tyndall, Ashley Herring Blake, Brian Gould, and Ellen Oh. Your support, feedback, and generosity have meant everything to me.

The countless friends in this community who have held my hand and kept me going. I'll never be able to name you all, but here's a start: Jen Gaska, Aisha Saeed, I. W. Gregorio, Katherine Locke, Marieke Nijkamp, James Sie, Jeff Zentner, Kayla Whaley, Corinne Duyvis, Alex London, Tim Federle, Nicola Yoon, Marcy Beller Paul, Diane Capriola, Lance Rubin, Jennifer Niven, Greg Changnon, Denisa Patron, Julie Murphy, Rachel Simon, Michael Waters, Camryn Garrett, Emma Trevayne, Rockstar Kevin Savoie, Gaby Salpeter, Cody Roecker, J. C. Lillis, Summer Heacock, Eline Berkhout, Johanna Mehner, Tom-Erik Fure, Shelumiel Delos Santos, Laura Silverman, Bieke Paesen, Rachel Strolle, Maddie Wolf, Wulfie, Jasmine Pearl Raymundo, the Not So YA Book Club, Little Shop of Stories,

Foxtale Book Shoppe, and so many others. I love you all.

The friends who saved me, made me laugh, and made me a little less careful: Diane Blumenfeld, Jaime Hensel, Jaime Semensohn, Lauren Starks, Amy Rothman, Emily Townsend, Mike Goodman, Rachael Zilboorg, Jenny Mariaschin, Josh Siegel, Betsy Ballard, David Binswanger, Molly Mercer, Evan Diamond (so much cooler than Evan Schulmeister!), Sarah Beth Brown, Raquel Dominguez, and lots and lots of others. Also, Takoma Mamas—can you tell how much I miss you?

The librarians, booksellers, bloggers, and publishing pros who have made miracles happen for my books.

The fat kids. You're beautiful.

Caroline Goldstein: this book is obviously a love song to you; Sam Goldstein, my personal Xavor Xav; Jim Goldstein, king of all dads; Eileen Thomas, who knows my brain.

My family: Adele, Gini, Curt, Jim, Cyris, Lulu, Steve, Gael, Dan, Allison, Peter, Jeff, Janet, Larry, Jenny, Joe, Josh, Sarah, Jay, Eliza, Zachary, Milton, Pat, Leigh, Adam, Gayatri, Candy, William, Cameron, Gail, Kevin, Linda, Bill, and the whole Overholts gang. You guys are so wonderful.

Owen and Henry, the lights of my life.

Brian, my Reid (but with cooler shoes). I love you.

And to Grandma Molly. I never knew just how much I could miss a person. I lost you while drafting this. I thought of you every time I typed your name. What would I give to hear you call me mamaleh one more time?

Turn the page for a sneak peek at

LEAH ON THE OFFBEAT

1

I DON'T MEAN TO BE dramatic, but God save me from Morgan picking our set list. That girl is a suburban dad's midlife crisis in a high school senior's body.

Case in point: she's kneeling on the floor, using the keyboard stool as a desk, and every title on her list is a mediocre classic rock song. I'm a very tolerant person, but as an American, a musician, and a self-respecting human being, it is both my duty and my privilege to blanket veto that shit.

I lean forward on my stool to peer over her shoulder. "No Bon Jovi. No Journey."

"Wait, seriously?" says Morgan. "People love 'Don't Stop Believin'.'"

"People love meth. Should we start doing meth?"

Anna raises her eyebrows. "Leah, did you just—"

"Did I just compare 'Don't Stop Believin'' to meth?" I shrug. "Why, yes. Yes I did."

Anna and Morgan exchange a capital-L Look. It's a Look that says *here we go, she's about to dig her heels in.*

"I'm just saying. The song is a mess. The lyrics are bullshit." I give a little tap on the snare for emphasis.

"I like the lyrics," Anna says. "They're hopeful."

"It's not about whether they're hopeful. It's about the gross implausibility of a midnight train going, quote unquote, *anywhere.*"

They exchange another Look, this time with tiny shrugs. Translation: *she has a point.*

Translation of the translation: *Leah Catherine Burke is an actual genius, and we should never ever doubt her music taste.*

"I guess we shouldn't add anything new until Taylor and Nora are back," Morgan concedes. And she's right. School musical rehearsals have kept Taylor and Nora out of commission since January. And even though the rest of us have been meeting a few times a week, it sucks rehearsing without your singer and lead guitarist.

"Okay," Anna says. "Then I guess we're done here?"

"Done with rehearsal?"

Welp. I guess I should have shut up about Journey. Like, I get it. I'm white. I'm supposed to love shitty classic rock. But I kind of thought we were all enjoying this lively debate about music and meth. Maybe it went off the rails somewhere, though, because now Morgan's putting the keyboard away and Anna's texting her mom to pick her up. I guess that's game over.

My mom won't be here for another twenty minutes, so I hang around the music room even after they leave. I don't really mind. It's kind of nice to drum alone. I let my sticks take the lead, from the bass to the snare and again and again. Some fills on the toms. Some chhh chhh chhh on the hi-hat, and then the crash.

Crash.

Crash.

And another.

I don't even hear my phone buzzing until it pings with a voice mail. It's obviously my mom. She always calls, only texts as a last resort. You'd think she was fifty or a million years old, but she's thirty-five. I'm eighteen. Go ahead and do the math. I'm basically your resident fat Slytherin Rory Gilmore.

I don't listen to the voice mail, because Mom always texts me after—and sure enough, a moment later: So sorry to do this, sweetie. I'm swamped here—can you catch the bus today?

Sure, I write back.

You're the best. Kissy emoji.

Mom's boss is an unstoppable robot workaholic lawyer, so this happens kind of a lot. It's either that, or she's on a date. It's not even funny, having a mom who gets more action than I do. Right now, she's seeing some guy named Wells. Like the plural of *well.* He's bald and rich, with tiny little ears, and I think he's almost fifty. I met him once for thirty minutes, and he made six puns and said "oh, fudge" twice.

Anyway, I used to have a car, so it didn't matter as much—if I beat Mom home, I'd just let myself in through the garage. But Mom's car died last summer, so my car became her car, which means I get to ride home with thirty-five freshmen. Not that I'm bitter.

We're supposed to clear out of the music room by five, so I take apart the kit and carry it into the storage closet, drum by drum. I'm the only one who uses the school kit. Everyone else who plays has their own set in the finished basements of their personal mansions. My friend Nick has a customizable Yamaha DTX450K e-kit, and he *doesn't even drum*. I could never afford that in a billion years. But that's Shady Creek.

The late bus doesn't leave for another half hour, so I guess I'll be a theater groupie. No one ever cares if I wander into rehearsal, even though the show opens on Friday. Honestly, I crash rehearsal so often, I think people forget I'm not in the play. Most of my friends are—even Nick, who'd never auditioned for anything in his life until this. I'm pretty sure he only did it to spend time with his sickeningly adorable girlfriend. But since he's a true legend, he managed to snag the lead role.

I take the side hallway that leads directly backstage, and slip through the door. Naturally, the first person I see is the peanut himself, my number one bro, demolisher of Oreos: Simon Spier.

"Leah!" He's standing in the wings, half in costume, surrounded by dudes. No clue how Ms. Albright talked so many guys into auditioning this year. Simon shrugs away from them. "You're just in time for my song."

"I planned that."

"You did?"

"No."

"I hate you." He elbows me and then hugs me. "No, I love you."

"I don't blame you."

"I can't believe you're about to hear me sing."

I grin. "The hype is real."

Then there's a whispered command I can't quite hear, and the boys line up in the wings, amped and ready. Honestly, I can't even look at them without laughing. The play is *Joseph and the Amazing Technicolor Dreamcoat*, and all of Joseph's brothers are wearing these fluffy fake beards. I don't know, maybe it's in the costume notes of the Bible or something.

"Don't wish me luck," Simon says. "Tell me to break a leg."

"Simon, you should probably get out there."

"Okay, but listen, don't take the bus. We're going to Waffle House after this."

"Noted."

The boys shuffle onstage, and I step deeper into the wings. Now that the flock has cleared, I can see Cal Price, the stage manager, stationed at a desk between the curtains. "Hey, Red."

That's what he calls me, even though I'm barely a redhead. It's fine—Cal's a cinnamon roll—but every time he does it, there's this hiccup in my chest.

My dad used to call me Red. Back when he used to call me.

"Have you seen this one?" Cal asks, and I shake my head. He nudges his chin toward the stage, smiling, so I take a few steps forward.

The boys are lurching. I don't know any other way to describe it. The choir teacher bangs out some French-sounding song on the piano, and Simon steps forward, hand on his heart.

"Do you remember the good years in Canaan . . ."

His voice is shaking, just a little, and his French accent's a disaster. But he's funny as hell up there—sinking to his knees, grasping his head, moaning—and I don't want to oversell it or anything, but this just may be the most iconic performance of all time.

Nora sidles up to me. "Guess how many times I've heard him sing this in his bedroom."

"Please tell me he has no idea you can hear him."

"He has no idea I can hear him."

Sorry, Simon, but you're too precious. If you weren't gay and taken, I'd totally marry you. And let's be honest, marrying Simon would be amazing—and not just because I had a sad, secret crush on him for most of middle school. It's more than that. For one thing, I'm totally up for being a Spier, because that family is literally perfect. I'd get Nora as my sister-in-law, plus an awesome older sister in college. And the Spiers live in this huge, gorgeous house that doesn't have clothes and clutter on every surface. I even love their dog.

The song ends, and I slip out and around to the back row of the auditorium, known among the theater kids—aspirationally—as Makeout Alley. But I'm all alone back here, and only halfway participating. Surveying the action from across the room. I've never been in a play, even though Mom's always trying to get me to audition. But here's the thing. You can spend years drawing shitty fanart in sketchpads, and no one has to see it. You can drum alone in the music room until you're decent enough for live shows. But with acting, you don't really get to spend years stumbling along in private. You have an audience even before there's an audience.

A swell of music. Abby Suso steps forward, wearing a giant beaded collar and an Elvis wig. And she's singing.

She's amazing, of course. She doesn't have one of those limitless voices like Nick or Taylor, but she can carry a tune, and she's funny. That's the thing. She's a straight-up goofball onstage. At one point, Ms. Albright actually guffaws. Which is saying something—not just because who knew guffawing was an actual thing people did, but because you know Ms. Albright has seen this thing a thousand times already. Abby's just that good. Even I can't take my eyes off her.

When the show ends, Ms. Albright herds the cast onstage

for notes. Everyone drapes themselves all over the platforms, but Simon and Nick scoot to the end of the stage, next to Abby. Of course.

Nick slides his arm around her shoulders, and she tucks up closer to him. Also of course.

There's no Wi-Fi in here, so I'm stuck listening to Ms. Albright's notes, followed by an unsolicited ten-minute monologue from Taylor Metternich about *losing yourself* and *becoming your character.* I have a theory that Taylor literally gets off on the sound of her own voice. I'm pretty sure she's having tiny secret orgasms right before our eyes.

Ms. Albright finally shuts it down, and everyone streams out of the auditorium, grabbing backpacks on the way—but Simon, Nick, and Abby wait in a cluster near the orchestra pit. I stand and stretch and head down the aisle to meet them. And a part of me wants to spew praise all over them, but something stops me. Maybe it's just too painfully sincere, a little too fifth-grade Leah. Not to mention that the thought of fangirling over Abby Suso makes me want to vomit.

I high-five Simon. "You killed it."

"I didn't even know you were here," Abby says.

Hard to know what she means by that. Maybe it's a secret diss. Like, *why are you even here, Leah?* Or maybe: *I didn't even notice you, you're so irrelevant.* But maybe I'm overthinking this. I've been known to do that when it comes to Abby.

I nod. "I heard you guys were going to Waffle House?"

"Yeah, I think we're just waiting for Nora."

Martin Addison walks by. "Hey, Simeon," he says.

"Hey, Reuben," says Simon, looking up from his phone. Those are their characters' names. And yes, Simon plays a guy named Simeon, because I guess Ms. Albright couldn't resist. Reuben and Simeon are two of Joseph's brothers, and I'm sure this would all be adorable if it didn't involve Martin Addison.

Martin keeps walking, and Abby's eyes flash. Honestly, it's pretty hard to piss Abby off, but Martin does it just by existing. And by going out of his way to talk to Simon, like last year didn't happen. It's so fucking audacious. Simon doesn't even talk to Martin that much, but I hate that he does at all. Not that I get to dictate who Simon talks to. But I know—I can just tell—that it bugs Abby as much as it bugs me.

Simon turns back to his phone, clearly texting Bram. They've been dating for a little over a year, and they're one of those vomitously happy couples. I don't mean that in the PDA-sense. They actually barely touch each other in school, probably because people are prehistoric dickwads about gay stuff. But Simon and Bram text and eyefuck all day long, like they can't even go five minutes without contact. To be totally honest, it's hard not to be jealous. It's not even just about the true-love-heart-eyes-get-a-room-dudes fairy-tale magic. It's the fact that they went for it. They had the balls to say *fuck this, fuck Georgia, fuck all of you homophobic assholes.*

"Are Bram and Garrett meeting us there?" Abby asks.

"Yup. They just got out of soccer." Simon smiles.

I end up in Simon's passenger seat, with Nora in the back, digging through her backpack. She's wearing rolled-up jeans, covered in paint, and her curls are tied back in a messy knot. One ear is pierced all the way to the top, and she has a tiny blue nose stud she got last summer. That girl is honestly too adorable. I love how much she looks like Simon, and I love that they both look like their older sister. They're a total copy-paste family.

Finally, Nora's hand emerges from her backpack, holding a giant, unopened bag of M&M's. "I'm starving."

"We're literally driving to Waffle House. Right now," Simon says, but he stretches his hand back to take some. I take a handful, and they're perfectly melted—which is to say, they're not quite melted. Just a little soft on the inside.

"So, it wasn't too much of a shitshow, right?" Simon asks.

"The play?"

He nods.

"Not at all. It was awesome."

"Yeah, but people are still messing up their lines, and we open on Friday. And freaking Potiphar screwed up a whole song today. God, I need a waffle."

I pull out my phone and check Snapchat. Abby's posted this epically long story from rehearsal, and it's like a montage from a rom-com. A snap of Nick and Taylor singing onstage. A mega close-up selfie of Abby and Simon. An even closer one of

Simon's face where his nostrils look so big, Abby stuck a panda graphic inside one of them. And Abby and Nick, over and over.

I stick my phone back in my pocket. Simon turns onto Mount Vernon Highway. I feel antsy and strange—like I'm bothered by something, but I can't remember what. It's like a tiny pinprick in the back of my mind.

"I can't figure out what song you're doing," Nora says.

It takes me a moment to realize she's talking to me, and a moment after that to realize I've been drumming on the glove compartment.

"Huh. I have no idea."

"It's like this," Nora says, tapping a straight one-two beat on the back of my seat. *Boom-tap-boom-tap.* All eighth notes, quick and even. My mind fills in the rest of it immediately.

It's "Don't Stop Believin'." My brain is an asshole.

Fall in love with these books from

Becky Albertalli!

And don't miss *Leah on the Offbeat*,
the heart-fluttering sequel to
SIMON vs. THE HOMO SAPIENS AGENDA,
when it hits shelves April 24, 2018!